PENGUIN METRO READS
THE GIRL OF MY DREAMS

Durjoy Datta was born in New Delhi, India, and completed a degree in engineering and business management before embarking on a writing career. His first book—*Of Course I Love You!*—was published when he was twenty-one years old and was an instant bestseller. His successive novels—*Now That You're Rich!*; *She Broke Up, I Didn't!*; *Ohh Yes, I Am Single!*; *You Were My Crush*; *If It's Not Forever*; *Till the Last Breath*; *Someone Like You*; *Hold My Hand*; *When Only Love Remains*; *World's Best Boyfriend*; *Our Impossible Love*—have also found prominence on various bestseller lists, making him one of the highest-selling authors in India.

Durjoy also has to his credit nine television shows and has written over a thousand episodes for television.

Durjoy lives in Mumbai, loves dogs and is an active CrossFitter. For more updates, you can follow him on Facebook (www.facebook.com/durjoydatta1) or Twitter (@durjoydatta).

The Girl of my Dreams

DURJOY DATTA

Penguin
metro reads

An imprint of Penguin Random House

PENGUIN METRO READS

USA | Canada | UK | Ireland | Australia
New Zealand | India | South Africa | China

Penguin Metro Reads is part of the Penguin Random House group of companies
whose addresses can be found at global.penguinrandomhouse.com

Published by Penguin Random House India Pvt. Ltd
7th Floor, Infinity Tower C, DLF Cyber City,
Gurgaon 122 002, Haryana, India

First published in Penguin Metro Reads by Penguin Random House India 2016

ISBN 9780143424628

Typeset in Bembo STD by Manipal Digital Systems, Manipal
Printed at Thomson Press India Ltd, New Delhi

www.penguin.co.in

The Girl of my Dreams

1

It happens in an instant and yet everything seems to stretch out interminably.

One moment I'm gazing at her, that pale white face half covered with hair as black as night itself is smiling at me, and the next I'm urging her to look at the road. The smiles on our faces die out. It's too late. A taxi is rushing towards us, driving on the wrong side. She swerves the car to the right to avoid collision and heads towards the divider railing. The taxi too swerves to its right. She corrects course, but it's too late. She slams on the brakes and the car makes a dying screech. Something breaks. She is thrown forward. There's no seat belt to slow her down as her face smashes against the steering wheel and bends like a half-formed clay mask. Her face scrunches, her jawline contorts, her teeth are knocked out. Her eyes protrude inhumanly . Blood spurts. It feels like I can reach out and hold her face but my hands move slowly through the air. I hear my own ribs snap like dry twigs against the impact of the seat belt. A shooting pain rises in my chest when the seat belt pushes me back. The world spins outside the windshield. Once. Twice. She is still smiling at me, her face turned at an awkward angle from the neck, her lips cut and bloody. Suddenly, the car flips over the railing and slams into a truck on the opposite side of road. A deathly silence descends. Time freezes. Pieces of glass and tissue and teeth stay suspended mid-air, unmoving. Through the pain, I'm looking at her once-beautiful face, the face I fell in love with, now a chaos of blood, distended tissue, and shards of bone and broken teeth. I reach out for her face. It takes forever. And then a disquieting crunch fills the air. Metal against metal, bone against bone, bone against flesh, flesh against metal. I'm thrown backward and forward. My legs twist and tangle. Ligaments snap, bones break. A jagged piece of the metal enters my thigh and comes out from the other side where I can't see it. Glass shatters and fragments lodge deep in my face. My skin singes from the *heat. The burning smell of rubber engulfs us. Orange-red flames lick everything up. I try opening my eyes, now flooded with blood from my forehead. She's being thrown like a rag doll inside the roll cage of the car. Her eyes are open and she's looking at me. I look for signs of her but can only see my own gory reflection staring back. There's no trace of life in those eyes. But she has a smile on her face. A cold, frozen, dead smile. A stray piece of metal pierces through my shoulder blade like a hot axe through butter and pins me to the seat. The car flips again and she's thrown out of the windshield. I give her my battered hand but she's out of sight. The car slams to the ground again. I snap out of the seat belt and slam against the roof of the car. I start to lose consciousness. I shout her name but only a whimper escapes my lips. Shreyasi . . .*

Daman woke up with a start. He had wet his bed again. Urine and sweat clung to his body and stank up the room. He shivered. His shoulders and thighs throbbed with pain. He ran his fingers over the deep gorge on his right shoulder; a pink scar had replaced where once was flesh. The alarm clock screeched in the background. With trembling fingers he switched it off. He rummaged the bedside drawer for his pills and swallowed them dry. Eighteen months had passed since the night of the accident but the nightmares hadn't abated. The pills helped but only to an extent. He got up and washed himself. He changed the bedspread and threw the soiled one into the washing machine before his mother could notice. Out of habit, he punched 'Shreyasi' into the search engine of his phone. Many faces showed up but none of them seemed like the girl from his dreams. He closed the tabs. At least in today's nightmare the girl was behind the wheel; she was dead because she was driving, not because of him. At the breakfast table, his mother noticed Daman's discomfort. She asked, '*Shopno dekhli abaar?* (Saw that dream again?)'

Daman nodded. 'She drove. She died. I lived. Still can't remember her face clearly,' he said.

'Are you taking your pills on time, Dada?' asked Puchku, Daman's younger sister.

'Yes, Puchku . . .'

'Don't call me Puchku! My name's Ritu, call me that.'

'You're Puchku, no matter how hard you try.'

'*Kintu oi me taa jeebit acche*. That girl is still alive. You know that, right? I don't know why you keep seeing these dreams,' his mother said, her voice laced with bitterness.

'I know.'

'Morning dreams indicate exactly the opposite of reality. *Tor or shonge gaadite choda hi bhulhoyechhe*. You shouldn't have taken a lift from a girl you didn't know. That was a mistake,' said his mother, her voice quivering in anger, like it was only yesterday that Daman had taken a lift from a stranger who nearly drove him to death.

'Maa, leave it now,' said Puchku.

'Yes, of course, I will leave it. But you don't know what we went through because of that girl,' grumbled Maa.

Daman's parents had spent the subsequent six months anxiously waiting for him to wake up after the accident; another three when he was treated for debilitating post-traumatic stress disorder (PTSD). If it were up to his mother, the girl would have been long dead, just like in Daman's nightmares. But the girl had escaped unscathed and had left the country since. Daman had never met her before (or after) the bloody night of the accident. He didn't know where she was from, what she did, or how he came to be in her car or what they talked about during that short, fateful drive. He hadn't even managed to edge out the fuzzy remembrance of her face. The paleness of her skin, that haunting smile, those dead eyes were all he remembered of her—the rest of the details always mutated between two nightmares. Everything apart from her name had been wiped clean off his memories. Post his accident, he had been diagnosed with dissociative amnesia (though he preferred the name psychogenic amnesia because it was much cooler) which totally wipes out the memories of traumatic incidents leaving memories before or after the incident intact; it's the brain's coping mechanism. The condition had buried his memories of incidents leading to the traumatic accident in his subconscious. There was a blank where a sepia-coloured reel of his trip to Goa should have been. Only a name remained. It seemed like a cruel joke. He remembered making plans with his college friends, getting on that flight, checking into the hotel but everything else . . . poof . . . the next thing he remembered was being woken up and ushered into physical therapy. 'It wasn't a mistake,' said Daman.

He looked at his watch. He was late. Avni, his girlfriend, had already left three texts on his phone. She wondered if he was okay because he hadn't texted her since morning. Despite seeing her for the last eight months, Daman hadn't told her about Shreyasi or the nightmares. *What's the point?* he always thought, *it's not like I know her, she's only a shadow.* He finished his breakfast hurriedly and left. On the way out, he saw a few envelopes jutting out from their apartment's letter box. As he flipped through the credit card bills, telephone bill, amongst others, he noticed that all of them had been carefully slit open, their contents read and then put back in, as is. He put all the envelopes back inside the box except the one with the logo of Bookhound Publishers India emblazoned on it. On his way out, he lodged a complaint with the watchman of the society knowing full well that just like before, no action would be taken against his pesky, nosy neighbours. In the cab, he opened the envelope. Inside it was a letter welcoming Daman Roy to Bookhound Publishers' line-up of authors. He smiled, read it twice and slipped it back inside the envelope.

And that's when he noticed a deep red lipstick mark on the envelope.

Like someone had kissed it.

2

Not for the first time, an argument had broken out in a coffee shop in South Extension, Delhi. Daman leant back in his chair and shook his head in disappointment. Their coffees had turned cold. There were only a few people around, most of them were languorous with sleep. The grumbling voices of Daman and Avni didn't reach their ears while they waited for their takeaway cappuccino and latte.

'Can't you see my point?' asked Avni.

'There's nothing to argue about. I am quitting. I need to concentrate on my writing,' answered Daman. He lit a cigarette and puffed on it hungrily.

'But you—'

'No, I can't. It drives me crazy when I want to write and instead I'm staring at blueprints of a power plant. I can't do it any more.'

Avni had the words and arguments ready before she agreed to meet today but they crumbled in the wake of Daman's all-consuming obsession of seeing his name on a novel. She had spent nights losing sleep over Daman's maddening decision to leave a promising job to pursue a career in writing but now she sensed it was a lost battle. She leant forward and held Daman's hand.

'If that's what you want to do, I will be with you,' she said. 'In happiness and in madness, I will be with you.'

A hint of a smile crept up on Daman's face and he clasped Avni's hand. 'I knew you will come around,' he said. His eyes glimmered with hope and foolish dreams as he talked breathlessly there on. 'I will sign the contract in a couple of days. Jayanti Raghunath is going to be my editor. She's a bit of a bitch but she's phenomenal, the best in the business.

She's the one behind all the bestselling books you see in the market.'

Avni nodded dutifully. She knew nothing of writers and writing till she met Daman eight months ago and had fallen witlessly in love with him. Having grown up in a family of chartered accountants and bankers and moneylenders, both money and keeping an account of money was what her life centred on. Sports, arts and other creative pursuits were for the deranged, synonyms for gambling, signs of the weak and the delusional. What were the odds of a writer succeeding? Or a painter becoming famous and appreciated? With numbers, you're certain.

Her parents knew of Daman as a mechanical engineer from Delhi Technological University working in Siemens Power and Engineering Limited as a design engineer, not as a wannabe writer who had a book contract waiting for him. Even the words felt strange as she would roll them over her tongue: 'My boyfriend is a writer. Yes, that's what he does full time. No, it's not a hobby. That's all he does. He writes stories for a living.' The only writers with careers were journalists who wrote for newspapers, not novelists with foolhardy dreams of churning out bestsellers.

'What is the book going to be about?' asked Avni.

He took a long drag of his cigarette. 'Shreyasi.'

Avni's brows knitted. 'Why do you keep using that name?' she asked, her voice bitter.

'I just like the name,' answered Daman.

Avni forced a smile on her face. *I hate that name.* 'And the guy's name in the book? You will use yours?' she asked.

'Jayanti says I should use mine. Right now it sounds a little narcissistic.' He paused before continuing, 'But there's no running away from it. That's why they signed me on, isn't it? Jayanti says I should stitch the posts on my social media accounts, including my blog, into a coherent story. I already have a readership, so it will help the book sell when it hits the bookshops.'

'If you use your name with Shreyasi's, readers will think Shreyasi is a real person,' argued Avni.

'How does that matter? The book will have a fiction disclaimer,' answered Daman.

Avni had not met Jayanti Raghunath but she loathed how much trust Daman placed in her. It was she who filled Daman's head with notions of having his name on the spine of a book, being on the bestsellers' lists, signing copies by the dozen, and being shortlisted for literary prizes with cash components that wouldn't even pay for a month's groceries. A few weeks back Daman had come back dizzy with excitement after his meeting with Jayanti Raghunath, 32, Executive Editor, Bookhound Publishers, the biggest English-language publisher in India. She had called him to an opulent five-star property and had blown him away with technical jargon, marketing terms and the sophistication of her publishing team. They made him feel big, important, talented, wanted.

Daman was but an amateur scribbler when Jayanti had spotted him on the Internet. He used to write short stories about an eponymously named boy Daman and a girl named Shreyasi on Facebook, Tumblr, Wattpad, his blog and wherever he could find readers.

Avni had stumbled on these short pieces of fiction when she followed Daman's social media profiles on the Internet after their first long conversation. She must have fallen in love with him because she felt envy pierce her heart like a rusted dagger and lodge itself there. The stories felt real. She thought Shreyasi was a real person, an ex-girlfriend, a crush, or worse still, a current girlfriend. She had stopped talking to him for a few days till he clarified.

'She's fictional, she exists only in my head. I use my name because it helps me visualize things better,' he had said.

'So there's no Shreyasi?'

'No, of course not. Not in my life at least,' he had assured her. 'I just like the name.'

'Are you sure? Writers are liars, my friends always say. They make up stories for a living,' she had said with a smile.

Daman had laughed it away.

But as they started seeing each other more often she had hoped Daman would start using her name and not Shreyasi. But it didn't happen. The imaginary mistress, Shreyasi, stayed in his stories. She never uttered a word though. What could she have said? Shreyasi was fiction, made-up, while she was real. It was her hand Daman held, it was her body that Daman embraced, and it was she who he said he was in love with. *I'm the ONE, not Shreyasi*, she would convince herself.

Some of his online readers knew Shreyasi was fictional, while others thought it was more of a memoir, real incidents and stories with a smattering of fiction. Avni and Daman had cut a pastry to celebrate the first time one of Daman's stories went viral and was shared over a thousand times. Avni had suffered that day. Daman had noticed it, because a few days later he'd written a story with the female lead's name as Avni. She had been ecstatic but her happiness soon turned to ashes in her mouth. The comments were harsh. No one wanted to read about this new character, Avni. They wanted Shreyasi back. They had rejected Avni.

Why? Why? Why Shreyasi and not me? She's not real! I'm real! Avni had thought bitterly.

Though Daman deleted the comments, she often lay in bed recalling the words, WE WANT SHREYASI, and cried herself to sleep. In time Avni learnt to live with it.

'So what do you think?'

Avni broke out of her reverie. She hadn't been listening. 'Umm. It's terrific. I'm so happy. So when are you going to tell your parents?'

Daman frowned. 'Never if I can help it. You know how my dad gets. He wants me to suffer at a job I hate for the next thirty years.'

'Have you decided on a title yet?'

Daman grinned widely. He flicked his cigarette away and leant into her. '*The Girl of My Dreams*,' he said. 'That's the name of the first book in the series.'

'There will be more than one?'

'Jayanti thinks it will be good to capitalize on the characters I have already created. She wants to change a few things but I don't think I will let her. Moreover, Shreyasi as a character is perfect.'

No, she's not! thought Avni hotly. *She's your mistress, that's what she is.* But she said nothing to him.

A little later, Daman excused himself to go to the washroom. Her eyes followed him. Just as he went in, Avni noticed a girl at the far end of the coffee shop staring at the closed door of the men's washroom. A few seconds passed but the girl was still unblinkingly staring at the door. An eerie feeling gripped Avni's heart. The girl was looking at the door and mumbling something, as if she talking to it. 'Daman,' Avni heard the name escape the girl's lips. Avni wasn't sure at first. 'Daman,' the girl whispered again. Most of her face was hidden behind her thick, dark cascading hair that fell down to her waist. With a jerk the girl turned her eyes to look at Avni. Her face was pale as a corpse and her thick black hair melted into darkness. She held Avni's gaze. Her eyes were eerily opaque. She was beautiful but there was something terrifying in her beauty, something cold and sinister and hypnotic. The girl smiled at Avni. Avni's heart thumped. She looked away. Her arms were covered in goose pimples. Avni pretended to text to pass the time. She could still feel the strange girl's onyx-like eyes on her. Her relentless stare made Avni feel like a spider had crawled inside her clothes. *What is taking Daman so much time?* Time passed slowly. She could still faintly hear the girl's mumblings but couldn't make out a word except one. 'Bitch. Bitch. Bitch. Bitch. Bitch.'

'Hey?'

'Huh?'

'Where are you lost?'

Avni noticed she was sweating. Daman took his seat and blocked the girl out of her view. She breathed easy.

'I was thinking we should go out and celebrate in the evening,' said Avni.

Daman flashed a thumbs up. 'Sure. I will call you. Aren't you late?'

Avni nodded and he asked for the bill. Before long, the waiter placed the bill on their table. After he collected the money and left, Avni noticed a stray piece of paper on the tray. She picked it up.

'What's that?' asked Daman and took the paper from her.

On the paper written in a beautiful handwriting was a message.

Daman read it out: *Best of luck for the book. I know it will be beautiful.*

—*Only yours, Shreyasi, The Girl of Your Dreams*

A bell clanged loudly in the background. Avni turned towards the noise and saw the girl walk out of the door. The bell was attached to the door. When she turned back, she found Daman laughing. He thought it was Avni's idea of a practical joke. Avni smiled weakly and then stared at the lipstick impression on the piece of paper.

A deep, dark, ominous red.

3

Daman checked his reflection in the dirty, speckled mirror. His white shirt was new, bought just for today, but it looked pale under the weary tube light. He had been meaning to change the tube for the past couple of months but hadn't got around to it. He wouldn't have had to care about the tube light or the faulty stove or the leaking tap if he still lived with his parents but . . . He popped the pills he'd kept on the shelf under the mirror and chewed on them. He hoped the bitter aftertaste would be a reminder to not drink. In any case, the pills didn't make for happy companions with alcohol. He always felt as if the combination made his brain devour itself.

He shaved twice, cut himself in three places, and dabbed the aftershave balm he had bought the day before. There was plenty of time before he had to leave. He paced around nervously in his apartment. He smoked to calm his nerves. Jayanti had told him these parties seldom started on time. It wasn't as much a party as a get-together with everyone who had worked on his book, *The Girl of My Dreams*. After toiling tirelessly for six months, quitting his job and moving to a one-room-kitchen of his own, draining gallons of coffee, spending hours arguing with Jayanti over specifics, which stopped just short of them verbally abusing each other, the book was due to hit the stands in two weeks and today he would have the first copies in his hands.

Traffic was sparse but he drove slowly, steering away from the faster lanes and the SUVs. His car was practically new. It had cost him most of his advance from the book. He felt rich as he grasped the stitched premium leather on the steering wheel. His father hadn't been impressed with his extravagance and had called him stupid and rash like

he always did. He drove past Rajouri Garden and Naraina
Vihar. He had just taken the serpentine flyover at Dhaula
Kuan when it started to rain. A drizzle and then a downpour.
He slowed down even further and switched on the blinkers.
He had barely driven for a kilometre when a speeding
motorcycle overtook him from his left and grazed his car
ever so slightly. His lips turned into a snarl. Daman stepped
on the gas. The engine responded with a groan and a roar.
Daman's blood tingled with anger, his scars throbbed. Water
splashed all around him. Within seconds he was driving next
to the motorcycle. Daman rolled down the window. The
motorcyclist noticed him gesticulating. He weaved away from
Daman, accelerated and whipped into more traffic. Daman
didn't let up. He chased him down ten kilometres away from
the skirmish to the motorcyclist's destination. Parking right in
front of the motorcycle, he jumped out of the car, his hands
clenching and unclenching. The motorcyclist had scarcely
taken off his helmet when Daman swung wildly, getting the
man square on his jaw. His knuckles rang with pain. Before
the man could recover, Daman landed three more blows,
each one catching the man's face. The man stumbled and
fell. Daman walked away from him, his heart continuing to
pump urgently.

It felt good.

He put the key into the ignition and drove away from the
scrambling man. 'I can do with some duelling with Jayanti too
today, for tampering with and destroying my book.' He stared
at the rear-view mirror. He tried to smile. 'It's not destroyed.
She knows what she's doing.' He drove. 'Calm down. Calm
down.' Jayanti and he had come a long way since they'd signed
the contract and the path had been thorny.

*

Daman bided his time in his car, in the parking lot of Olive Bar & Kitchen. It had been half an hour since he had battered the man but he was still antsy. At a distance he saw Jayanti step down from her Audi Q5 and hand over the keys to the valet. Dressed in a shimmery silver dress, she looked resplendent, almost royal. Tall and tight like a whip, she strode towards Olive's entrance, her thick thighs straining against her dress. In her hands she carried a little brown bag.

'*The Girl of My Dreams*. Author copies. My copies. My book!' His name would be on a book for all of eternity. It would be his legacy. And yet happiness eluded him. He stepped down from the car, checked his hair and his smile in the side mirror. He missed Avni. Things would have been much easier had she been there. She would have calmed him down.

Daman sauntered towards the entrance, practising his smiles.

Hands went up, wine glasses in the air, and everyone shouted his name in unison as Daman walked in. Jayanti Raghunath stepped ahead, smiled widely, hugged him and thrust a glass of wine in his hands. Daman's refusal withered when it met with shouts of 'Drink! Drink!' from the others. *Just one drink*, he thought.

She introduced him to everyone. Most of their faces were flushed and they were inordinately happy with the book. They were also a little drunk. Ritwik, a smallish, fat, jovial guy, had designed the cover. Shraboni, a beautiful dusky girl with a strong voice, had worked on the final edits. Farhad, a tall, fair, handsome man with a little paunch, was the fiction marketing head. There was also a bunch of guys from the production and sales team whose names Daman had forgotten as soon as he heard them. The waiter refilled his drink. The wine was expensive and delicious, better than

'This is not me,' he hears the girl say.

'But . . . but, you left me,' says Daman.

'The book, the fucking book!' the girl mumbles and brings down the spanner in a deadly arc . . .

*

He woke up with a jerk. He tried to feel his face; he wasn't hurt but he was bleeding from a small cut on his lip. He was in the driver's seat of his car. It was parked outside his apartment building. He stumbled out of the door on all fours and promptly vomited. He belched and retched and vomited till there was nothing but air inside him. He slumped against the front tyre. Sitting there he drifted in and out of sleep, sweating under the beating sun. It wasn't until noon that he was wide awake. He found himself inside the car with the air conditioner on full blast. He shivered. He turned the AC down. Sitting inside the car, he cursed himself for having drunk so much and strained to think what happened the night before. The motorcyclist. The party. Jayanti. The book. The waiter. The dream. The girl? Another fucking dream. He rummaged through the glovebox for his phone. There were twenty missed calls from Avni and a few from his parents. He called Avni first. 'Hey?'

'What the hell is happening, Daman? I have been calling you since forever. I was so scared!'

'I . . . I just got drunk last night,' he said. 'I only just got home.'

'I called Olive and you had left when they closed. Where were you?'

'Yes, yes. I drove back home and passed out in the car. I just woke up,' he said. He pressed his hand against his head which was bursting with pain. He needed a Crocin.

4

When he opens his eyes next he sees a girl in the driver's seat smiling at him. 'Hi,' says the girl.

'Are you for real?' he asks, or is this again a dream? 'Show me your face,' he slurs. He sees the girl smile. 'I will remember your face,' he says. 'I hope you do,' he hears the girl say. He mumbles a few words, smiles stupidly and drifts off. He wakes up and finds himself in the back seat. 'Where are we going?' he asks. 'Are you Shreyasi?'

No one answers.

His head swims. The world spins violently around him. In the driver's seat he sees the girl again. Dark hair, white skin, deep dark eyes, violently red lips, as if she has stepped out of his book, *The Girl of My Dreams*. She's Shreyasi. He's sure of it. He smiles in a drunken stupor. 'Are you Shreyasi?' he mumbles and giggles. 'No, I am dreaming, Jayanti killed you,' he says in disbelief. 'She destroyed you,' he continues. 'I am dreaming, it's the pills and the alcohol,' he says to himself. 'I shouldn't have had the last bottle . . .'

'Sleep, you're drunk, baby,' he hears the girl say.

And like a child, he sleeps again. He wakes up. The car is parked in a deserted area. There's silence. He tries to help himself up but loses balance. Falling forward he cuts his lower lip and bleeds. The girl is reading his book, *The Girl of My Dreams*. She turns towards him. The kindness has drained out of her face. She is glowering. 'Why?' she asks. She pulls out a spanner and keeps it on the passenger seat. Then she takes out a lipstick and darkens her lips in the rear-view mirror. Putting the lipstick back in, she raises the spanner as if to smash his face with it . . .

'Why?' shouts Daman.

'This is what will work. This is what sells. Write this, DAMAN! I KNOW MY JOB! LISTEN TO ME! THE BOOK WILL TANK OTHERWISE,' she had said every time Daman got into a shouting match with her.

After numerous delays and skipped deadlines, Daman had given in.

Daman drank through the rest of the evening. Slowly everyone left. Jayanti was the last to leave. She told Daman he could stay if he wanted to. After she left, Daman sunk back into the couch and ordered for numerous refills. Things became muddy thereafter. He started to read the book. The sentences Jayanti had written floated outside the book, coiled around his neck and squeezed it. His chest tightened. Before long he tossed it away. He ordered another drink. He passed out soon after and dreamt of angry readers burning his books in large piles.

EVERYONE WILL HATE SHREYASI.

He woke up to a waiter staring at his face and asking him to leave. He stumbled out of Olive with an unfinished bottle of champagne and walked to his car. He put the bottle to his lips. He sat in the car and closed his eyes. He fumbled for his phone to call himself a cab but couldn't find it. He imagined ripping Jayanti's throat out. He passed out.

'SHREYASI! SHE IS AWESOME!' shouted Shraboni, closing her eyes and raising her glass in the air. 'WOOOHOOOO!'

Daman pulled a face and sulked. *This is not my FUCKING SHREYASI. It's JAYANTI'S SHREYASI.* Daman said, 'You need to congratulate Jayanti for that. My Shreyasi was different.'

'Don't say that,' interjected Jayanti.

'What the fuck am I supposed to say then?'

'SHREYASI! WOOOOO!' shouted Shraboni.

The people at the other tables looked at them strangely. Jayanti asked Ritwik to take Shraboni away. She turned to Daman after she left. 'See? I told you. Let the book come out. Everyone will love the new Shreyasi. You can mope all you want if she doesn't work. It will be on me.'

The waiter asked Daman if he needed a refill. He knew he shouldn't drink; blackouts were common with him. But he needed to forget. He nodded. The waiter filled his glass to the brim. There was no point in pursuing the Shreyasi conversation any more. What's done was done. Jayanti had bulldozed her way into the book and wrecked the Shreyasi Daman had thought of. The Shreyasi in the book was a far cry from the cracked, lunatic, lovely, peculiar girl he had painstakingly created. His pale-faced Shreyasi was a mathematics major, a gold medallist no less, working with a start-up that made algorithms for search engines. She filled her time reading thick books on organic chemistry and ancient history and dead religions. She liked museums, caffeine, fire, multiple orgasms, Daman (the character), occasional BDSM and knock-knock jokes. The new Shreyasi—the one Jayanti created and forced down Daman's throat—was a cow, a girl from a Mills & Boon book. Coy and polite, she was an English major, an intern at an online news portal. She was all parts boring and bullshit.

anything he had had before. *It's my day*, he reminded himself. *I will call a cab.*

A little later, a cake was cut and Daman was handed over the first copies of *The Girl of My Dreams*, a 350-page-long book with a red and black minimalist cover, amidst frenzied claps and long hugs. They left him alone to enjoy the copies. Daman held a copy in his hands, smelt it, flipped through the pages, and ran his hands over the cover. He wasn't as joyful as he had imagined he would be all those months back when he'd signed the contract. Jayanti turned up next to him and put an arm around him. Her breath smelt of wine.

'Like it?'

No. Daman nodded.

'I told you, didn't I? It will all be okay when the book comes out. You stress about the little things.'

'Little things? Shreyasi was not a little thing.'

Jayanti scowled. 'Now don't start that again. Those changes were important. That's dead and buried. This is your day! Enjoy the moment, Daman. This will be the start of something amazing.'

Daman skimmed through the book as Jayanti droned on about how excited everyone was. The more he read the more he was filled with revulsion. Between his words, Jayanti's words protruded like ugly, jagged rocks. This book was as much Jayanti's as it was his; she hadn't just edited it, she had written large parts herself. He wanted to scream. Instead he drank.

'Hmmm.'

'Okay, wait. I will dispel your fears,' said Jayanti and waved Shraboni down. Shraboni was already hammered. She stumbled twice before she placed herself in front of Jayanti and Daman. 'She's read the book. Twice,' said Jayanti. 'Who's your best character, Shraboni?'

'You drove back home drunk? What is wrong with you, Daman?' she snapped. 'And what was that text you sent me?'

'What? What text? I didn't send you anything . . .' he said. '. . . that I remember.'

Avni read out the text. 'Bitch. You don't deserve him.'

'I didn't send that,' he said. He added after a pause. 'I must have been trying to send it to Jayanti.'

'Why her?'

'The book, Avni. I got the author copies and it's . . . it's not what I expected. I will talk to you in the evening. I feel like I'm dying right now—'

'Do you want me to come over?'

'No, I will manage. See you in the evening? Okay? I will talk to you in a bit,' he said and disconnected the call.

He found the text he had sent Avni in the Sent folder. He was glad he didn't end up sending it to Jayanti. But he wondered why he referred to himself in the third person. 'I should stop drinking.' He looked around for the books in the car. He checked the glove compartment, the boot of the car, even below the seats. He couldn't find them. He figured he must have left them at the restaurant. Disappointed, he stepped out of the car to call Jayanti and ask for more copies. He had just dialled her number when he noticed what he thought was the burnt jacket of his book a couple of yards away from the car. He disconnected the call. *Is it the book?* He walked closer to inspect. He bent over the smouldering heap of ashes. All that was left of the five author copies of *The Girl of My Dreams* was blackened paper and ash. He picked out one half-burnt jacket which had miraculously escaped the flames. *When did I do this?*

He texted Jayanti asking her to courier him more copies of the books. Daman trudged back to his apartment thinking of the book. The opening line that described Shreyasi written by Jayanti came rushing to his head—*Born in 1988, fair-skinned Shreyasi was every boy's dream; nice and soft-spoken, she was a bundle of joy and kindness,* Daman's stomach churned.

Jayanti's words ran in Daman's head.

'Everyone will love the new Shreyasi.'

Fuck.

5

'Daman Roy, the author of *The Girl of My Dreams*, reached for Jayanti Raghunath's neck and crushed her throat. He grabbed her by the hair and rammed her head repeatedly against the glass walls of her cabin till the cracked glass dribbled with blood and brains. Her body slumped to the ground, her fingers twitching, her legs trembling. Daman stomped on her smashed skull till she was unrecognizable. A fitting punishment for changing his book to a hunk of shit.'

He snapped out of his reverie. He was staring at the cracked glass walls of Jayanti's cabin. Jayanti sat smiling in her chair, waiting for Daman to speak.

'Why does this room smell like shit?' asked Daman.

'Can we come to the point? You—' answered Jayanti.

'You said everyone will love this new Shreyasi. They fucking hate her,' grumbled Daman.

'You have no idea what you're talking about, Daman. Stop pacing around first and sit down. You're freaking me out,' said Jayanti leaning forward in her chair, hands crossed over the proofs of the book that was due for printing. Three cups of black coffee lay empty on her table. Hundreds of paperback and hardback books lay stacked in teetering towers around her table. Millions of words by authors known and unknown were scattered all around her. Jayanti looked at Avni. 'Ask him to calm down a little, will you?'

Avni tugged at Daman's arm. Daman sat down. He spoke, 'Are you kidding me, Jayanti? People don't like my book. Go, check the reviews online. They hate the Shreyasi in the book, the Shreyasi you created, the Shreyasi you wrote out. She's just someone whom the protagonist loves and fucks. She needed to be more than that. And I'm goddam tired of answering the question if the main guy in the book is me. I told you we should have given the guy a different name than mine.'

'We are NOT having this conversation again. Because we used your name, people think it's a true story and readers lap up true stories like anything. You should know that, right? Even movies do that all the time. Do you really think those movies are based on true events? Bullshit!'

Daman had feebly protested about the edits and rewrites till the day before the book went into print but there was no winning against the cunning of Jayanti who predicted doomsday for the book if they didn't do that.

'I will just read the reviews out. Wait,' said Jayanti Raghunath, searching the Internet for reviews of *The Girl of My Dreams*. 'Here.' She read them out. '"The book is a classic romance." "Loved the ending." "In love with Shreyasi" "I cried so much in the book. Heart emoji. Crying emoji. Heart emoji." "I totally heart emoji heart emoji the story." What are you talking about? Most of the reviews are good.' She turned her MacBook around.

Daman rolled his eyes.

Avni pulled the laptop close and perused the reviews. They were overwhelmingly positive. But these weren't the only reviews online. For the past few days, Daman had been mailing Avni every bad/average review of the book. Especially those where Shreyasi had been called a spineless, stereotypical, weak damsel in distress, and the ones where Daman had been called a failure of a writer, his story old wine in a new well-marketed bottle. The most scathing reviews were from people who had read Daman's short pieces of fiction on Facebook before he had signed the deal and had come to fall in love with the old Shreyasi. They called him a 'sell-out'. He blamed it all on Jayanti's overbearing editing. If only Daman had known that behind that beautifully elongated body, those kind, tired eyes of Jayanti, there was a manipulative, control-freak shrew . . . Avni had borne most of the brunt of Daman's anger, being the only one who could keep him from self-destruction.

Jayanti continued, 'Look, Daman I don't know what kind of acceptance you're looking for but selling 15,000 copies of a debut book in the first three weeks constitutes a resounding success. You need to stop thinking what a few people think about your lead girl character. Look at the bigger picture. The book is a hit! It's even on the Bharatstan Times Bestseller list.'

'Why don't you tape it to your head and strut around then?' snapped Daman.

'I don't know what you're complaining about, Daman. Other debut authors would kill to be in your position right now.'

'She has a point,' said Avni.

Daman threw Avni a murderous look. He said, 'Should I clap for you, Jayanti?' He mocked her. 'People out there are calling me another Karthik Iyer, the lowest fucking denominator.'

'Listen, Daman. You were writing notes on Facebook when I spotted you and gave you this book deal. Dare you make it sound like I wrecked your career! I gave you a career if you look at it closely.'

'You spotted me, remember? You came to me. You offered me a book deal because you thought the book would work. It wasn't charity. You knew I had an audience online that would buy the book. You knew my book had potential.'

Jayanti laughed throatily. 'Audience? Online? Like really? Followers on Twitter and Facebook don't mean anything, Daman. It doesn't cost money to like or share something. It takes a good relatable book, a marketing plan, a smart editor, a smart publicist to sell a book. People share videos of poor people dying all day with sad smileys and complain about how wretched the world is but won't part with a rupee for them. How would you have made them spend on you?'

'They already did. Data isn't free, Jayanti.'

'Haha. Big joke, Daman. You're so funny. Why don't you put that in your next book, haan?'

Avni looked at the two of them volleying verbal insults like a spectator at a tennis match. Avni had been in this cabin once before. It was the day Daman had signed the contract for his book which was supposed to change his life. That day she had noticed the massive cloth board behind Jayanti Raghunath's heavily cushioned chair. It had been covered with jackets of all the bestsellers Jayanti had edited in her decade-long career. Some thirty-odd books in ten years. The probability of success had made Avni nauseated. *What if Daman's book doesn't go up there?* But today the board was covered completely with a white chart paper. 'I'm getting something done here,' Jayanti had offered as an explanation. It wasn't the only thing that had changed in the cabin. The desk looked new. Even the printer and the laptop and carpet looked largely unused. The glass wall was cracked and splintered. And the room smelt strange. Like it was heavily perfumed to cover up a rotting corpse.

Avni stole glances at her watch as they continued to argue. Her meeting at Avalon Consulting would start in another half an hour. If she were to get stuck in traffic there was no way she would make it on time.

'Daman?' she said. 'I want to stay but I have to get to work.' She wanted to say, 'For your and for my sake. Look around you, Daman. So many authors. And only a few names have made it to that board of hers. The money from your advance is already running out. If only you hadn't bought the car . . . if only you hadn't left your job . . . I have to work so you can write.'

Jayanti and Daman both looked at her. She pointed at her watch. Daman nodded knowingly. Avni got up and hugged him. She whispered in his ear, 'Stay calm,' and took his leave.

Jayanti said after Avni left, 'You are good writer, no doubt about it, but you still have a lot to learn. Do you know why you finally agreed to all my changes, Daman? It was because you were scared. You were scared the book wouldn't work. That's why you fought with me, but didn't fight enough, that's why you dissented, but not enough. Because in those moments of doubt you trusted your editor who has been in this industry for far longer than you have.'

'Yes, it was wrong to trust you. You fleeced me. I left my job and moved out of my parent's house because of your deal. And what did you offer me? A shitty royalty percentage and an editor like you?'

'No one forced you to sign the deal. You could have fought harder for Shreyasi. But you didn't. And you got enough money and a bestselling book if I may add. Maybe you wouldn't be so angry if you hadn't spent all the money buying that car of yours.'

'Oh, so now you're my financial advisor? What next? You will dictate what I should eat?' ridiculed Daman.

'Enough, Daman. I don't take nonsense from my authors, especially first-time authors, and you would be off my roster if you weren't talented—'

Daman ignored her aggressive tone and interrupted her. 'Whatever, Jayanti. The fact of the matter is that there will be a book with my name on it with a character that's as shitty as Shreyasi. Nothing you say will ever change that.'

Jayanti shrugged. 'You know what won't change? That you can be a writer. That you can sell books for a long time if you let me tweak a few things. You won't have to go back to your engineering job any more. And that would mean a lot to a whole lot of people,' said Jayanti. 'You know how many authors in India can claim to earn a living out of just writing? A handful! Karthik Iyer, Anuj Bhagat, Karan Talwar, Gurpreet Kaur . . . and I can put you in that league. If you can't be grateful I think you're being short-sighted. Listen I have been doing this a long time. Fixing books, that's what I do and I do it well.'

Just then, the door was knocked on by the office boy and Jayanti was summoned for a meeting. She looked at Daman and spoke, 'I need to go now. When you go back home, think about what this book can do for you. Also when you realize I am talking for your own good, start writing your second book and we can proceed with signing the deal for it.'

Daman scoffed. 'No way.'

'We all need to earn, Daman. I know you have burnt through the advance money from the first book.'

'You did this to me—'

'Let me finish. You're refusing to do any book launches for *The Girl of My Dreams*. How long do you think the book can sustain without any publicity? So think rationally and stop acting like a brat. Do a couple of book launches for this book and then start work on the next one. We make a great team, Daman. Never forget that. We are all working for you. You stand to gain the most out of it.'

'. . .'

'I like you, Daman. You have passion and I like that but you need to take things easy. I got to go now,' she said and got up. 'I will wait for your decision.' She stretched out her hand to shake his. Without another word Daman strode out of the room, leaving Jayanti's hand hanging mid-air. Jayanti watched him go. The reason why she liked Daman was also the one why she hated him. He was passionate, almost a little mad, teetering on the edge of insanity, and she could see that in his neurotic and chaotic writing. Of course, it was her responsibility to tone down the madness of his book. She remembered Daman's raging eyes the day she gave him the author copies of *The Girl of My Dreams*. She was terrified for a second; it felt like he would smash the wine bottle against her face. Thankfully he hadn't and the evening had run smoothly.

It was only that coy little girlfriend of his who could keep him grounded. Jayanti hoped she would knock some sense into him.

She looked around and sighed. Someone had broken into her cabin a week ago. Her desk, her laptop, the printer were amongst the many things the intruder had vandalized and spray-painted on. The intruder had even tried to throw her chair through the glass wall. She had to get it changed. But the most disgusting thing had been the smell. The floor was smeared with human faeces and water from the sprinklers. They had to shut the entire office down for two days because of the debilitating stench. Despite the perfume, Jayanti could still feel the ungodly smell lurking. Whoever had broken in hadn't even spared the books. A few of them were burnt, and amongst them were Jayanti's copies of *The Girl of My Dreams*. Luckily, the water sprinklers had taken care of the fire before it could spread. The CCTV cameras at the Bookhound office had long been defunct so they didn't record who did it or how it happened. A couple of years back, a crazed fan had broken in and stolen a few advance copies of Karthik Iyer's book. Screwball fans had always been a part of this industry, but even Jayanti admitted that this was the farthest anyone had gone.

She picked up her laptop and closed the pages with the reviews. As she turned to leave, her eyes fell on the bare white chart paper she had covered the cloth board with. Behind the chart paper was the most telling review of Daman's book, spray-painted in bold red letters over the jackets of the bestselling books Jayanti had edited over the years.

LEAVE DAMAN ALONE, YOU STUPID WHORE. EAT SHIT.

6

Daman was early to reach Summerhouse Café. A tall glass of cold coffee sweated on his table, untouched. He had successfully resisted the temptation to order a beer. It wouldn't be the first time if he were to have one drink too many and run amok at this pub. He smiled thinking of the time he had sneaked behind the bartender, filched a new bottle of Jack Daniels, and replaced it with his urine-filled beer bottle. This had taken place only three years ago but now it seemed like another lifetime.

'Oh, the celebrity is already here!'

'Screw you, Bhaiya,' said Daman stepping down from his high stool. He gave Sumit a one-handed hug.

'You seem to be in a foul mood,' said Sumit and ordered two beers. He noticed the glass of cold coffee and cancelled Daman's. 'Wise choice,' he said. 'Remind me to go easy as well. I have a date later tonight.'

'You?' joked Daman placing his gaze on Sumit's paunch.

'Tinder date. I got a match as I climbed up the damn stairs,' said Sumit. Sumit always complained about the stairs of Summerhouse Café. They were tall and misshapen and a horror to climb down when drunk. 'She's coming here.'

'Here?'

'I told her I would be at Summerhouse and she told me it's exactly where she and her friends are hanging out tonight. This has to be my quickest conversion from a conversation to a date. I think my game is getting better.'

'Show me her picture,' asked Daman, still incredulous.

Sumit fished out his phone and showed him the photograph. Daman smirked. 'That's just a pair of lips.'

'The sexiest lips in the universe you mean. Just look at them,' said Sumit, turning the close-up picture of the girl's blood-red lips towards him again.

'Best of luck,' said Daman. 'I hope she's a not a guy. Or a serial killer.'

'We should meet more often. You might be my lucky charm,' said Sumit poking Daman's shoulder.

Daman sniggered. Although Sumit was Daman's senior in college, Sumit and he had struck up an unlikely friendship which had strengthened over the last six years. Unlike Daman, Sumit hadn't dreamt up a fantasy for a career and put his fate in the hands of a wench like Jayanti. He had been biding his time at Alstom Engineering. Sooner or later he would immigrate to the Middle East, get a resident visa, buy a Japanese-made SUV and never look back. Sumit awkwardly climbed up on the high stool.

'So? Did you read it? What did you think?' asked Daman.

Sumit took a long, big gulp of his beer. 'I am with Jayanti Raghunath on this. I never thought I would like anything you wrote. She did a good job of making the book readable.'

'You can't be serious. Did you really like the Shreyasi she wrote? C'mon!' spat Daman.

'I did. She was way better than the strange Shreyasi you wrote about in those Facebook posts.'

'She wasn't strange,' protested Daman.

'No, she wasn't strange. Strange doesn't even cut it. In one of your stories on Facebook, she burns the guy's phone just to prove a point. In another, she shears off her hair in protest against the guy's behaviour. Who the fuck does that? That's not strange, that's complete madness!'

'That's love. Well, not the usual garden-variety love, but still. Moreover, she had reasons to do those things in the incidents preceding her actions. She was doing everything to protect her relationship. I would have done the same thing,' he argued.

'You're twisted, Daman.' Sumit laughed. Then he continued, irritably, 'Whatever, man. The new Shreyasi's believable and she's nice. Jayanti knows what she's doing. But I wish she'd made you change the name as well. Shreyasi isn't even a nice name.'

Daman rolled his eyes. 'Bhaiya, you're still stuck there?'

'Yeah, right! You're the one who never tires of writing posts using her name and now you have written a book using that name and it's me who's stuck there. Brilliant. Just fucking brilliant,' snapped Sumit.

'It's just a name I use. You know that.'

'Hmmm. Are you still getting those nightmares?'

'Yes.'

'Does she still die in those nightmares?'

'More or less. Sometimes she doesn't.'

'Do you remember anything else?'

'No, nothing. It's just those few seconds before the drive, different versions of the same dream,' said Daman.

'You're taking the pills?'

Daman nodded. Sumit sighed and said, 'The next time you think of her name, just remember the girl who holds that name nearly drove you to your death.'

'You're never going to forget that, are you?'

'Of course I am never going to forget that. It was us who suffered for six months in that hospital. Not that girl. She ran after the accident. I hate her and I hate her name. I would have really liked it if you hadn't used that bitch's name. You could have used Avni's name instead,' said Sumit.

Sumit along with Daman's father had spent months running from one doctor to another to take second opinions and then third. Later, once he had woken up, they had driven him to physiotherapy and psychotherapy sessions. The coma had wiped out certain memories but Daman had responded rather favourably to both therapies. When he had first regained consciousness, he had even forgotten how to walk or use the toilet or to hold a pen.

'The girl in the car has nothing to do with the girl in the book. I don't even know what she was like. It's just a name I picked for a character.'

'Just a name? Then why does the Shreyasi in the book look exactly like the Shreyasi from the car wreck? The pale face? Long black hair?'

Daman didn't have an answer for that. He said, 'Fuck it. Can we talk about something else?'

'If I were Avni I would have strangled you before you used any other girl's name in the book. I don't know how she tolerates you. You shouldn't have happened to a girl as nice as she is. Tell me, have you told her about the nightmares?'

'There's no need. She already worries about me a lot. And again, can we talk about something else?'

'But promise me you will come to me if the nightmares get worse? We can put you back in therapy. PTSD is not to be taken lightly. The relapse of PTSD—'

'Of course, Bhaiya. I will tell you.'

Sumit took another big gulp of his beer. He said, 'And stop being so sullen about the book. It's not good for your mental health. It's selling well you told me. So just enjoy your success.'

'I don't want to be another Karthik Iyer.'

'Now who the hell is that?' said Sumit, asking the waiter for a repeat.

'He's a writer who writes these stupid love stories. He must have written some twenty of those and it's the same thing over and over again. Loser boy, beautiful, cheesy girl, they fall in love, a couple of funny scenes, a few intimate conversations, a tragedy and all is well that ends well. He keeps writing about his girlfriend, Varnika. They are supposed to be the perfect couple to base your relationship goals on.'

'I would love to read him. It's exactly what's missing in the world. Love. You should write a cute love story.'

Daman threw his hands up in protest. 'Fuck me. It's like the *Matrix*. Everyone is fucking Agent Smith. Are you sure you're not Jayanti Raghunath in drag?'

'Of course!' said Sumit and cupped his man boobs and pretended to lick them.

Daman told him it was gross and inappropriate. An hour later, Daman asked for Sumit's leave. Avni was free from office early, what was now a rare occurrence, and they were going for the new Marvel movie. Daman left and Sumit waited for his date, the girl with blood-red lips.

7

Sumit passed the time by checking out the other women in the pub. Before long, a girl Sumit had thrown stolen glances most evening broke away from the rest of her group and walked towards him, a smile writ large on her face. In a little yellow summer dress and flats, she stood out in the dark pub. All this while she had been reciprocating his gazes with ones that lasted unusually long. If she had picked Sumit out from a crowd this would be a first. Without a word, she climbed on to the stool Daman had sat on earlier and thrust her hand out towards Sumit.

'Hi,' she said. Her thick, long hair streaked in bright brown and shocking red colours, was tied in a tight, high pony. There was an eerie twinkle in her deep, dark eyes. A dark shade of red lipstick glowed under the dim lights of the bar.

'Hi!' And just as he looked at her closely, it dawned on him. 'Are you?' The girl nodded. 'So you're not a boy? And you're not a serial killer?'

'I'm definitely not a boy. You can't really say about the latter, can you? But if it came to it, I think I will enjoy a good murder,' said the girl with a smile. 'I'm Shreya.'

'Sumit.'

'I like your tie.'

'I like your hair,' said Sumit.

'I just got it dyed yesterday. The red is a little splotchy and uneven. I am hoping it will get better. I was getting bored of the black.'

'It looks perfect,' he said. 'Since when have you been here? I saw you—'

'I came before you. I was with my friends.' She pointed to her motley group of friends, all of whom were dressed in office formals and were drinking. 'I saw you walk in minutes after we were matched on the app. Tinder isn't really my thing. I'm more of a long-term commitment girl but I felt a little risqué tonight,' said the girl, smiling and fluttering her eyelashes at him.

Risqué indeed! thought Sumit. 'So you were already here when we got matched. Why didn't you come say hi?'

'I didn't want to interrupt you . . . Ummm . . . okay, I have to admit, I liked watching you and your friend talk. But I don't want you to think of me as a crazy stalker who follows people and tries to know everything about them before she meets them. I'm totally not that person,' she said and placed her hand on Sumit's and smiled.

'Of course not, why would I? And even if you were a stalker, I wouldn't mind it,' said Sumit winking.

'Are you flirting with me?' She giggled. 'Yeah, you're right though. Aren't we all stalkers beneath our righteous selves? What are we if not curious?'

Sumit smiled.

She continued, 'Was the person with you that writer whose book just came out?' asked the girl, her eyes glinting like obsidian gemstones. 'Daman Roy?'

'You recognized him? You should have introduced yourself. He would have been so stoked! Have you read his book? Or the posts he puts up on the Internet? Oh. I totally forgot to ask if you want to drink something?'

The girl smiled sweetly and ordered a Bloody Mary. Sumit asked for the same.

She continued, 'I might have eavesdropped on your conversation. It's an old habit, I can't help it. My ears pricked when I heard my name. So I thought you were talking about your date this evening.'

'Your name? Oh! Shreya and Shreyasi. No, no, we were talking about someone else entirely!'

The drinks arrived. Sumit reached out to pass a glass to Shreya but she slapped his hand away. 'Ow!' said Sumit.

'Just precautionary,' said the girl. Sumit looked at her, puzzled.

'Rohypnol?' she said. 'Date rape drug? You would be surprised to know how easy it is to get your hands on it. You look like a decent guy but I make it a point to not let others touch my drinks. I wouldn't want to feel dizzy and nauseated and wake up in your bed twelve hours later, naked and raped.'

Sumit nodded and let her slide the drink towards herself instead. 'So what were you and your friend talking about?' asked the girl. 'You seemed to be fighting about something.'

'Oh. You wouldn't want to know. It was noth—'

'I would want to know. Tell me. Oh. Don't be surprised. I'm an Aquarian. We are an inquisitive bunch, especially when drunk.'

'Ah. It's nothing, really. He's obsessed about a girl he shouldn't be. It's not even a girl. He's obsessed about a name. He used her name in the book and he shouldn't have. She . . . she nearly killed him.'

The girl gasped. 'Did she? How?' she asked, her voice took on a throaty, seductive tone.

'Oh. It's nothing.'

'You can't throw that statement at me and not tell me the entire story.'

Sumit told her how on the last day of their trip to Goa a couple of years ago, Daman had taken a lift from a girl on his way back from the liquor shop. He told her about the accident, of how they found Daman in the mangled wreckage of the car, and of the time Daman had spent in the hospital fighting for his life.

'What happened to her?'

Sumit didn't answer. After a long pause, he said, 'She can burn in hell for all I care.'

'You are angry, but I don't understand why,' said the girl. 'Shouldn't you be happy for your friend? It seems like you can't respect that he still loves her. For someone on Tinder, you should know how hard it is to find love. Isn't that why we resort to these hook-up apps? To find intimacy because we can't find love? Swiping right at smeared-on lips, and professions, and About Me sections one can't verify but hope to be true. I think he's lucky to be obsessed about someone. You should support him, not berate him.'

'What? What are you even saying?' asked Sumit. He would have walked off had the girl not been so . . . sexy. 'She nearly killed him. And yet he romanticizes that bitch.'

'I think you should be more respectful towards women. And how do you know the girl was be blame? Maybe Daman was driving the car? Either way, you have no right to call her a bitch.'

'Let's drop this.'

'Why? This is interesting. I do love a good love story. I told you, I'm a long-term girl,' said the girl, clutching Sumit's hand tighter. Sumit looked at her. She was way out of his league and it was becoming clear that it was she who would dictate the course of this date.

The girl continued, 'In your opinion, keeping aside your bias against this girl, you think he's still in love with her, right?'

'Of course not. The girl in the car is not the one he writes about. He just uses her name. The girl in his posts is a figment of his imagination, he has constructed her out of nothing. He remembers nothing about the girl in the accident. So it's impossible for him to be in love with someone who doesn't exist.'

'What if she does exist? What if she's exactly how he had described her in his posts on Facebook?'

Sumit laughed. 'Then I will ask Daman to be careful! The girl he created for those Facebook posts was horrendous. The one in the book Jayanti, his editor, created was still okay. That's also what we were fighting about. Just in case you wanted to know,' Sumit said frowning. 'Are you sure you want to continue this date? Because I'm not the writer. I could give you his email ID if you want.'

'Of course, I want to continue this date, baby. I matched you on Tinder, didn't I?' said the girl. Sumit didn't know if she was being sexy or sarcastic. She continued, 'So, from what I understand, Jayanti butchered the character Daman had created in the 860 posts he wrote after that accident or whatever. But then Daman let her do so. That's not very encouraging, is it? Letting someone trample over your love story like that? But you wouldn't understand and neither would Jayanti. What would you know of love and writing?'

'Are you like a fan or something?' asked Sumit.

She was no longer holding his hand, he noticed.

'He still loves Shreyasi, I know. He just needs to be reminded. How do you think Daman would react if Shreyasi, the girl in the car, comes back to his life?'

'She wouldn't.'

'What if she does?' she asked, eyes glinting.

'I will send her back to where she would have come from,' he snapped.

'Would he dump his current girlfriend? Avni, right? I read his tweets and updates. He doesn't mention her much. I'm sure he will dump her if Shreyasi would want him to. He doesn't love her.'

'What—'

The girl said, 'I need to go to the washroom real quick if you don't mind. I will be back before you know it. I really like you. I see us meeting a lot more often, baby.' She ran her fingers over his face.

Before Sumit could say anything she had left, striding away from him into the crowd. *She's crazy!* thought Sumit. Good sense told him he should bolt. *But she's hot,* his heart said. So he stayed put and ordered another cocktail instead. *Maybe more alcohol would make her more tolerable.* He had one and then another and she hadn't come back. He paid the bill and searched for her in the washroom. Her friends had left. He checked all the floors, jostled through the crowds calling out her name but couldn't find her anywhere. Tired and angry, he decided to call it a night. He had just stepped out of the main door of Summerhouse Café when suddenly the world around him dimmed. His knees buckled and he had to grab hold of the railing to keep himself from tumbling down the jagged stairs of Summerhouse Café. He pried his eyes open but sleep came over them like waves. He tried fighting it but it was too strong. A numbness took over. His eyes closed. His hand came off the railing and he stumbled down the stairs like a dead man.

He woke up bruised and bloodied on the pavement twelve hours later.

His wallet was missing and so was his phone. He had a terrible hangover.

Not from the alcohol but from Rohypnol, a popular date rape drug.

8

Jayanti Raghunath put everything together in a week—posters for social media, media interviews, the banners at the venue, and little ads in the newspapers. Daman closed his burning eyes and lay down on his bed. He had stayed up the entire night and a good part of the morning mailing personalized invites for his book launch to every subscriber. Earlier that week, goaded by Avni, he had agreed to do one book launch for the *The Girl of My Dreams* at the Oxford Bookstore in Delhi. 'You should do it,' Avni had said. 'People love the book and you. It's only a handful who liked the earlier version of Shreyasi. Jayanti was saying that book launches will help the sales. And you know that—' Avni had stopped short of mentioning his money trouble and instead rubbed her soft lips against his neck and kissed him. 'I will be there to smother anyone who says the book was bad, okay? But right now I need to smother you.' She had slipped her hands inside his jeans and there was nothing else to be said that night.

He slept for a few good hours. When he woke up, Avni had already left for work and he had three missed calls from his mother. They were supposed to have lunch together. He got up, washed himself quickly, put on a fresh T-shirt and left for his parents' house. 'Parents' house . . .' The words sat uncomfortably on his tongue. Only six months back it had been his house as well. Before long he stood outside the door, the house barely a ten-minute walk from his own. His mother got the door. He could smell the food and his father's dissent as soon as he stepped in.

'*Ei to, eshe gaeche!* (Look, he's here),' said his mother and kissed him on his cheek. 'You haven't eaten anything since morning, have you?'

His mother called for Puchku, Daman's thirteen-year-old sister, who came running to Daman, hugged him, told him she missed him, and then chided him for not replying to her texts.

'I was writing, Puchku.'

'Oh please, Dada. You mean to say J.K. Rowling or G.R.R. Martin don't look at their phones for days?'

'Fine, I'm sorry.' He pulled at her cheeks and she slapped his hands away. She wasn't six any more though Daman still treated her as a toddler. 'Did you read my book?'

Puchku shook her head. 'You asked me not to. A couple of my friends did. They said it was nice. They even sent you messages on Facebook and tweeted you. You haven't replied to them yet.'

'I haven't yet got the time.'

'Oh. My brother is a big shot now. Do you have stalkers too?'

'Very funny. No.'

His mother told them to sit around the dining table. The food was getting cold. Daman's father got up from the couch and settled at the table, still staring into the newspaper. Puchku and Daman joined him. Lunch was served. They ate in silence for the next ten minutes.

'There's a book launch this weekend. I want all of you to come.'

'I know!' shrieked Puchku. She looked at her mother. 'Can I go, please? Please? Please? Please? Please?'

'Of course you can. It will be fun. Get your friends along too,' said Daman.

His father kept the newspaper on the table. 'There's no need to encourage him. And Puchku, you have your exams on Tuesday. You're not going to miss your tuitions.'

'It's only one day, Baba!' she protested.

Daman's father glared at Puchku and then at Daman. 'She's not going.'

'Fine, whatever.'

'*Shunchho*. Look at how he talks. Is this how you talk to your father? After all we have gone through for you?'

His mother's shoulders drooped. Resigned, she looked into her plate, waiting for the conversation to run its course.

'It's just one day. You're being unreasonable and you know that,' said Daman.

'I'm being unreasonable? You're saying this? Look what your son is saying. You left your job for this nonsense. And then bought that car you didn't need, and now you want to drag your sister into this and you call me unreasonable? I will not let you influence her. *Kichhu tei naa.*'

'What's with you and my car?' retorted Daman.

Daman had heard how Baba had left the house with a tyre rod from his WagonR to wreck Daman's new car the day it was delivered. It had taken both his mother and Puchku to restrain him. The accident hadn't brought the father and son closer. It had torn them apart. His father thought that Daman should live his second chance at life conservatively, while the latter did not want to waste this new life that had been gifted to him. After the accident and the endless therapies, his father had a few nightmares of his own.

'My book is a hit, Baba. It's all over the newspapers. It would help if you read that too along with all the other nonsense you keep reading.'

'So? So what? It's there today, it will be gone tomorrow. Then wave the newspaper in the banks and ask them to give you money, okay? You know what the problem with you is, you got everything easy in your life. ACs in your room, there's always food to eat and nice clothes to wear. That's why you take everything for granted. You're taking your life for granted!'

Daman rolled his eyes.

'Look.' He pointed at Daman's mother. 'This is what he does. After all that we have done for him, this is what he does.'

Daman shoved fistfuls of rice inside his mouth. 'Maybe I should have just died in that accident,' he muttered under his breath.

Daman's father banged the table. Before Daman's mother could intervene, he rushed to Daman's side and smacked his face. Daman tasted blood in his mouth as he staggered and fell out of his chair. He rubbed his palm over his singed face and clenched his fist. Hot tears flooded his eyes, his ears burned red. His father kept staring at him. Daman relented and, picking himself up, walked out of the living room. It was the only way he could have kept himself from taking a swing at his father. He slumped on the bed in his old room and wiped tears and snot off his face. *I shouldn't have cried. He wins if I cry. Why the fuck did I cry?* The last time Baba had hit him was when he told him he had quit to be a writer. Baba had threatened to disown him then. Daman had retorted saying there wasn't much to be disowned from anyway. Baba had asked him to leave the house if wanted to pursue his unwise dreams. He had moved out the next weekend. It was more out of defiance that he bought the car than anything else. That was the last straw in their perennially turbulent relationship, a pig-headed father and a, very often needlessly, mad, rebel son.

'You shouldn't have said that to Baba. Why do you have to be so mean to him?'

He turned to see Puchku standing in the doorway. She walked in and closed the door behind her.

'I'm fuck—'

'Language.'

'He's like a broken record, Puchku. Why can't he just stop? How difficult is it for him to understand I didn't want to do that job? You know what I should do? I should just go back and join my job, write a suicide letter saying that the stress and the unhappiness is driving me to death, and then ram my car into a pole and make sure I don't walk out of it alive this time. Maybe that will teach him a lesson.'

'Please don't say that ever again.'

'I—'.

'And you weren't driving the car the first time around.' Daman dismissed her with a wave. She frowned. 'Always remember that,' she said, this time more seriously.

'I know that, don't I? I was in the car.'

'Yes, you were.'

'And had I been driving it, I wouldn't have crashed it, would I? Anyway, can't you cut your tuitions and I will drive you to the book launch? Baba doesn't have to know.'

'Baba will skin me alive if he finds out. He's turned his house into Fort Knox after you left. You just can't see the chains around my ankles. He would be especially mad if he found out I got into that car of yours.'

'It's as if I drove the fucking car.'

'Language, Dada.'

'Fine. Fine. I'm sorry. I will get you videos of the event, okay?'

She smiled. 'You will send me videos? You don't even text me, Dada. Now I will have to take an appointment to meet my bestseller author dada.'

'Please.'

'Seriously, Dada. My friends are so psyched that I'm your sister! I even bumped into a fan of yours in the metro. And she was so pretty, but then I remembered you're already dating Avni and didn't take her number. She was so smitten by you!

Why are you looking at me like that? I'm not lying! I told Maa also.'

'Did you spot her with a book?'

'No. She spotted me. I was with my friends and she came and talked to me. She told me she recognized me from the picture you had posted of us. Imagine! My friends were all so impressed. She was really nice too. I already told you that, right? Look at you grinning.'

'Why shouldn't I! Go tell this to Baba. What did she say about the book?'

'Err . . .'

'What? Don't tell me you're lying now. I thought—'

'I'm not. It's just that . . . she didn't . . . like . . . the book.'

Daman frowned. 'So what was she a fan of? Oh. The posts I used to write? Okay. Fine.'

'Don't be disheartened, Dada. She was still a gigantic fan. She couldn't stop talking about you. She walked me to our house as well. She even asked me to tell you she is prepared to forgive you about the book.'

'What? Who's she to forgive me about anything? Not my fault if she bought it and didn't like it!' snapped Daman.

Puchku found it amusing so see Daman take it to heart. She came and sat near him. Daman instinctively hugged her. It was then he realized how much he missed being around his quarrelsome, unbearable, precocious sister.

'Did she give a name?'

'Ummm. I didn't ask. But she told me she knows you.'

'Knows me? How?'

'She told me you had met her in Goa,' mumbled Puchku, wary of talking about Goa.

In Daman's house that episode was always talked about in hushed tones. Daman frowned. Daman's memories from that trip to Goa were hazy at best. 'Goa?'

'Yes, that's what she said.'

'I don't remember meeting any girl there,' said Daman.

Puchku wrested free of his embrace. 'You did meet someone,' grumbled Puchku.

'Apart from Shreyasi.'

'We don't take her name in this household.'

'Oh, c'mon. Not you as well!' protested Daman. 'Okay, whatever. I won't take her name. But there's something I need to tell you, Puchku. Do you remember what Baba, Maa and I used to tell you just before you left for school every day? Don't take sweets from strangers. Don't believe if anyone tells you they have been sent by your parents. Don't let them take you anywhere. Don't look them in the eye. Don't even talk to them. I know you're thirteen but I want you to remember that. If anyone comes and talks to you like this girl, don't respond beyond a sentence or two. Say thank you and just walk away. Do you hear me?'

'I'm not a kid—'

'Of course you're not. But you still walked with someone alone for a really long time. You are aware of the stretch from the metro station to here, where anyone can—what I am trying to say is, don't interact with strangers.'

'And despite your paranoia you took a lift from one?'

Daman rolled his eyes. 'Then learn from me and don't do what I did.'

Just then, there was a knock on the door and their mother walked in. She told Puchku to go finish her lunch and ask her father if he needed anything. Puchku nodded and left. Daman stared at his feet while his mother came and sat next to him.

'When will you stop arguing with your baba, Daman?'

'It was—'

'I don't want to know whose fault it was. Can't I have one peaceful day in this house?'

'I'm sorry.'

Her mother nodded, she blew her nose into the end of her saree and wiped away her tears. Lovingly, she cradled Daman's face and kissed him on the forehead. She smiled and asked, 'How's Avni? How's her job?'

'She's good.'

'Won't you ever make us meet her? If you and her . . . you know, I will be less tense about you.'

'I will. When the right time comes. She keeps busy with her job.'

'You have been with her for over a year now and the right time hasn't come? *Ei ki baba.*'

'Maa.'

'Okay, okay, you know best.'

'Fine, I will make her meet you soon, okay?'

His mother nodded. 'Daman?'

'Yes, Maa?'

'There's no way you can write and still do your old job? Your baba—'

Daman stared hard at his mother and his mother took back her words. Daman spent the rest of the afternoon playing Uno with Puchku and munching on begun bhajas his mother served in seemingly endless quantities. In the evening he dropped Puchku to her tuition class and promised to send the video of the book launch. He had boarded a rickshaw back home when his phone beeped.

Number withheld.

He picked it up.

'Hello?'

There was no answer. He disconnected the call after ten seconds. His phone beeped again.

'Hello?'

Someone breathed heavily on the other side. Click. The phone disconnected. Daman muttered curses under his breath. It happened again. Daman put the phone on silent this time as he put the phone back in his pocket. When out of boredom Daman fished out the phone again he found it glowing. Number withheld. He received the call with a mind to blast the caller.

'Hello, whoever this—'

'Hello, Daman.'

'Hello?'

'It's nice to hear your voice again.'

'Who's this?'

'Thank you for the invitation for the book launch. I would have imagined getting a separate invite, not a bulk email, but I guess we are past that, aren't we?'

'Excuse me?'

'The graphics in your mail invite were a little shabby but design was never one of your strong points, was it? You were always the one with the words,' said a girl's raspy voice from the other side. Her accent and diction were crisp, the tone authoritative.

'Excuse me? Who's this?'

'You know me.'

'Actually I don't know you at all.'

'Now aren't those the magical words every lover wants to hear,' said the girl, her voice prickly like shards of glass on a soft carpet.

'Whose lover?'

'Yours, Daman. The only lover you have ever had. The only lover you will ever have.'

'What is this?'

'I am your fan and your lover, Daman.'

'I am disconnecting the call right now.'

'Are you sure about that?'

'Yes. Stop wasting my time and don't call on this number again. I hope this is enough of a warning,' Daman said.

'Oh. I note a haughty sting in your voice. Has the release of the book changed you, Daman? Your sister insists it hasn't. But then she's naive. We had a good time that day. She has quite a mouth on her, that one. She's an intelligent girl though. Why do you send her to those tuitions? She doesn't need them. I'm sure she's brighter than her teacher. She's beautiful too, just like you, baby. Both of you take after your mother.'

Daman gaped. 'What? What are you talking about? When did you? How?'

'You sound scared, Daman.'

'Oh please—'

'You know what it reminds me of?'

'I'm disconnecting—'

'It reminds of me of the first time you were inside me. You mewed like a cat. You were worse than a virgin, trembling, scared, and so turned on. There's something about us and cars, don't you think?' she said, her voice a low hum now. Almost a soft whisper.

'How did you? You met my sister?'

'You were scared you would come within the first few thrusts. I took you out of me and wrapped my lips around your cock. You quite liked it. I remember how your head jerked back and you closed your eyes,' whispered the girl.

'What? What are you talking about?' asked Daman.

'You want to know why I called?' Before Daman could say anything the girl continued, her voice now vulnerable. 'It's a cry for help, Daman. A request. A complain. From a lover's sad heart. If you care to listen.'

'Avni? Is this a joke—'

'DARE YOU CALL ME BY THAT WHORE'S NAME!'

A second passed before Daman recovered from her booming outburst. 'I'm going to hang up now. This is not funny. And if you ever hang around my sister—'

The girl giggled and then laughed throatily. Before long the laugh turned into a soft sob. Daman's fingers hovered over END CALL but he couldn't bring himself to do it.

'You're right about that at least. It's not funny. Nothing of it is funny, Daman. Are your nightmares funny, Daman? The ones in which I die?'

'Who are you? Who the fuck is this?'

'Do I need to tell you who I am . . .'

Her voice trailed off. The girl was crying on the other end. Daman was sure of it.

'I need to cut the call right now,' said Daman.

'You shouldn't do the book launch. Every time I see a mention of that vile book, it pierces my heart. I don't know if I can ever forgive you for this. How could you allow yourself to do this?'

'Hey—'

'You insulted your own love story. WHY? It's the last thing I would have expected from you. But why do I still love you? Why do I still think of our time together? Why do I still think of our last ride all the time?'

'Our last ride?'

'I do share your nightmares, Daman.'

'I have no idea what you're talking about,' snapped Daman.

'The nightmares I die in. I wish I did.'

'Listen, enough!' shouted Daman.

'I will see you at the book launch,' she said. 'If you still decide to do it. I love you so much.'

Click. He stared at the phone, bewildered. With trembling fingers he called Avni. She picked up after the third ring. 'Hey? Where are you?'

'In a meeting,' Avni whispered into the phone. 'Can I call you back in an hour?'

'Hmm,' said Daman and cut the call.

Who is it if it's not Avni?

Has she come back?

10

Daman had written most of his first book at the British Council, a library in the outer circle of Connaught Place where he now sat and tapped mindlessly through blogs and browsed through the new releases in the fiction section of an online retailer. On weekdays the British Council Library would be deathly quiet and he could pick any corner of the library and get some writing done or read a book. It helped that the Wi-Fi was blindingly fast. It had been an hour and he had had the extra sweet coffee from the dispenser, a soggy chicken burger which he washed down with Coke and yet he didn't feel like writing. Time and again, he would think of the inexplicable phone call he had received. It couldn't be her. There wasn't a snowflake's chance in hell it was her. She wanted to have nothing to do with me. What the girl said on the phone was nonsense. Nothing happened between them. *Lips wrapped around my cock? Bullshit. I would have remembered.* He went to the old string of emails exchanged between him and Shreyasi, the girl everyone hated and asked him to stay away from. And yet . . .

From: damanroy111@gmail.com
To: shreyasibose07@gmail.com

Hi.
I am fine. Thank you for not asking. Is this a rude beginning to a start of a correspondence? But you should know I am mailing you despite my friends and my good senses asking me not to. Queer thing I talk about senses. It's only recently I got back

to them. That car ride with you left me
sleeping for six months and in therapy for
another few. It broke my body and my mind.
I just thought I will update you on this.

How did I get your mail ID? It was almost
as hard as the therapies, mind you.

P.S. How badly were you hurt in the
accident? I am told you walked away from the
hospital with minor fractures? Seems like I
got the wrong end of the stick here.

Daman

From: shreyasibose07@gmail.com
To: damanroy111@gmail.com

Hey. m sorry bout what happened. i was okay
after the accident. thanks

From: damanroy111@gmail.com
To: shreyasibose07@gmail.com

You drove me off the road and nearly killed
me. And that is your reply?

Daman

From: shreyasibose07@gmail.com
To: damanroy111@gmail.com

i didn't. the taxi came from the wrong side.
read the accident report

From: damanroy111@gmail.com
To: shreyasibose07@gmail.com

Do you think I didn't read them? I did. But
we were drunk, weren't we? I remember making
us drinks in ragged memories I have of the
night. Anyway I didn't mail you to blame
you. The taxi guy was to blame. But he's
quite dead.
    Daman

From: shreyasibose07@gmail.com
To: damanroy111@gmail.com

a sip of vodka doesn't make anyone drunk.
whats the point of this.

From: damanroy111@gmail.com
To: shreyasibose07@gmail.com

I thought we will catch up.
    Daman

From: shreyasibose07@gmail.com
To: damanroy111@gmail.com

why.

From: damanroy111@gmail.com
To: shreyasibose07@gmail.com

It might sound a little bizarre to you but I
dream of you sometimes. They are not always
dreams. Sometimes they are nightmares,
flashes of the accident. Do you get them as
well? I have PTSD and mild memory loss. I am

quite all right though. If I keep taking my
pills, that is.
    Daman

From: shreyasibose07@gmail.com
To: damanroy111@gmail.com

No

From: damanroy111@gmail.com
To: shreyasibose07@gmail.com

The funny bit is I don't even remember your
face correctly. It's all faint outlines.
I remember your long, thick hair and your
sunburnt skin but the face changes a little
in every dream. Even the colour of your eyes
changes. I searched all over the net for
pictures of yours but I am guessing you are
not a fan of social media.
    Daman

From: shreyasibose07@gmail.com
To: damanroy111@gmail.com

no

From: damanroy111@gmail.com
To: shreyasibose07@gmail.com

You're still working in that start-up you
told me about?
    Daman

From: shreyasibose07@gmail.com
To: damanroy111@gmail.com

i never worked in any start-up.

From: damanroy111@gmail.com
To: shreyasibose07@gmail.com

Oh.
    Daman

From: damanroy111@gmail.com
To: shreyasibose07@gmail.com

Are you still reading books on the Roman
Empire? Or is the Aztecs?.
    Daman

From: damanroy111@gmail.com
To: shreyasibose07@gmail.com

?
    Daman

From: damanroy111@gmail.com
To: shreyasibose07@gmail.com

Least you can do is reply?
    Daman

From: shreyasibose07@gmail.com
To: damanroy111@gmail.com

i am not into history. you are imagining
things

From: damanroy111@gmail.com
To: shreyasibose07@gmail.com

Okay. My bad. My memories of that night
are at best vague. Must be someone else
then. Everything gets mixed up in my head.
Watched *Black Hawk Down* a few days earlier
and voila . . . in the next dream, you
were telling me you're an amateur pilot.
My bad.
    Daman

From: damanroy111@gmail.com
To: shreyasibose07@gmail.com

If you wouldn't mind, could you share a
picture of yours if you have one? I faintly
remember (though I could be dreaming wrong)
clicking one with my camera in the car but
it got smashed.
    Daman

From: shreyasibose07@gmail.com
To: damanroy111@gmail.com

listen daman. it's good to hear you are
doing fine. but i have put the accident
behind me. we don't need to be friends. we
don't need to 'catch up'. it was just an

unlucky car ride. please don't mail me in
future. take care and take your pills.
    also i'm sorry again. bye. have a good
life.

From: damanroy111@gmail.com
To: shreyasibose07@gmail.com

I tried not mailing you. It's been six months
since your last mail. This might be my last
mail to you as well. I just wanted you to
drop in to this link—http://bit.ly.rytm. I
started writing a couple of months back and
some of my posts are getting traction. I
took the liberty of using your name and mine
but it is all fiction, don't worry. I keep
clarifying to people if they ask. Let me
know if you read them?
    Bye.

She hadn't replied to his mail. There were a few other mails
he had sent after his last but they sounded desperate. He had
deleted them in the course of time so he wouldn't have to
read them. He logged out of his mail and started browsing
through random blogs to take his mind off. He was reading
an article about how goldfish flushed in the toilets grow really
monstrous in the open lakes, often invading entire water bodies,
when his shoulder was tapped.
    'Hi.'
    He turned. 'Hey?'
    'I'm sorry for intruding. Ummm . . . I have been watching
you for the past hour and I was wondering if you're Daman?
Are you? YOU ARE! Aren't you?'

It took him a split second before he nodded. He wasn't sure how to feel about it—a little proud, a tiny bit bothered, a part of him even thought it could be a prank. He had seen the girl walk past the coffee dispenser about twenty minutes ago.

'Oh. Do you mind if I sit here?'

'Sure.'

'Do you come here often?'

'Sometimes, yes,' he said, wondering if this was supposed to be a long conversation or short, an exchange of ideas or small talk.

'I'm sorry I'm intruding on your space.'

'No, it's okay. Tell me?' said Daman, lowering the lid of the laptop.

'Actually, I read your book a couple of weeks back. It was good!'

Thank God! Daman smiled.

'It was recommended by a girl who followed your posts on Facebook. She really loved them. She told me you had written a book stringing them all together after an editor spotted you. That I thought was really cool. Now how often does that happen, right?'

He felt tiny bit proud that this girl—she was beautiful and smart—was a reader of his. The girl continued, 'I'm also a writer of sorts. Well, I don't know if I can call myself that yet. I write blogs and poems. My friends tell me they are good. Oh. Don't worry. I won't ask you to read them or review them. I know how irritating that can be for you. But I was intrigued by how you started out. So I picked up the book.'

'That's nice of you,' said Daman, not knowing what else to say.

'Oh no. The pleasure was all mine. But can I ask you a question? If you don't mind?'

'Sure.'

'Umm . . . my friend sent me a few posts from Facebook as well, the ones she copied on her laptop.'

Jayanti had asked Daman to delete the posts once the deal was signed but they had been copied and shared on other platforms before he could do it.

Daman said, 'And you find those posts better than the book, I suppose?'

'You have been told that before?' asked the girl, curious and miffed that he'd wrested away her critique.

'Yes, I have been told that. Many reviews say the same thing. People who had read my posts don't actually like the book. But people who hadn't don't really see the difference. Many of them even like the new Shreyasi.'

'You don't seem too happy about it?'

'Because I'm not. Because I could run a marathon on burning coals to get the first draft published instead of the crap that's *The Girl of My Dreams* right now. But the book is apparently working so I guess it's a good thing. Maybe I will be more careful with the next one,' said Daman, sighing.

'But does this kind of this happen a lot?'

Daman frowned. 'Editors making the writers change the characters they write?'

'No!' She laughed. 'Like people coming to you and telling you they have read your book? It must, right?'

'It hasn't really happened except once,' he said.

'What was it like?' she asked, inching closer.

'The reader actually met my sister, not me,' said Daman. And then said with a finality, 'It was okay. She ended up bothering my sister a bit. So I am not sure how it was.'

She frowned. 'Shouldn't you be more respectful towards your readers? She must have been in love with you and your work and wanted to be closer to you. Shouldn't you be thankful for that?'

'Maybe.'

'That's better. I take offence if a writer makes fun of his own readers,' she said.

'My bad,' said Daman and raised his hands in mock surrender. 'I'm sorry I didn't ask your name.'

She was Reya, a first-year literature student, Hindu College. Daman reintroduced himself and she laughed at his cheekiness. They walked to the coffee dispenser, talking.

'I don't know if this writing thing is even a real dream, I just like writing,' she said. 'You're lucky though. Um . . . not lucky, I guess talented is the right word.' She offered him a coffee and he refused. She continued, 'There was something I was curious about.'

'What?'

'Is the main character of the book, Shreyasi, inspired by someone?'

Daman shook his head. 'Both Shreyasis—the one in the book and the one I wrote about in my Facebook posts—are fictional. The one in the book is inspired by my editor's wet dream of turning every book into a formulaic bestseller. But the one I first wrote was totally fictional.'

'Then I have another question, if you don't mind. What would you choose? The old Shreyasi and a flop book? Or your Jayanti Raghunath's Shreyasi and the hit book like it's right now.'

Daman weighed the options. The pause made the answer obvious.

'You don't have to answer that,' said Reya. 'Maybe you didn't like the previous Shreyasi that much?'

'Umm, I actually did—'

'It's okay. Let's just assume that Jayanti Raghunath is a whore, okay?'

Daman didn't know what to say to that. But soon, they were both laughing. They were sitting on either side of the corner table of the reading room, allowing themselves long stares at each other. Daman had sensed where it was going. Reya was beautiful! Slender, long hair streaked in dark brown and blue, a perfect tan, and she was interested in his writing. For the next half an hour, they talked about whether writing can be taught, and if a time will come when books will be a thing of the past and writers will be confined to telling entire stories in 140 characters, amongst other things.

'Daman? It was so nice to meet you. But I have to go now. Do you mind if I ask you for your number? So we can catch up later?' she asked, getting up, collecting her books.

Daman nodded and rattled off his number. He wrote down hers.

'But that's just nine digits?' Daman noted.

She peered into Daman's phone and giggled. 'There's a double 22 at the end.'

'Oh. My bad.' Daman corrected the mistake and saved her number. He walked her to the exit of the library. Slowly, the words dried up and there was an awkwardness in the air. There was an all too obvious sexual tension between them but both of them knew it would head nowhere. He turned towards her as she waved down an auto.

'Hey? There's this book launch on Saturday at Oxford Bookstore for *The Girl of My Dreams*. You should come.'

'Is your girlfriend coming?' she asked with a faint, naughty smile. Daman smiled back at her. 'Careful what you wish for. I might just come and get a book signed,' she said.

They hugged, wished each other the best of luck for their writing. The auto drove off. Daman went back to his desk thinking about the girl. He opened the lid of the laptop and loaded Microsoft word. His thoughts still lingered on her. He found himself smiling, thinking of the conversation; it played on a loop in his head.

And then, it struck him.

His smile evaporated. How did she know? Did I tell her? He went through the conversation again his head. He had never told Reya what his editor's name was and yet she knew. Had she read it in a newspaper? Curious, Daman dialled the number the girl had given him. The voice recording from the other side told him the number didn't exist. Fifteen minutes of googling 'Reya, Hindu College, first year' yielded no results. Intrigued, he checked the entry register of the British Council. No one with the name Reya was in the register. There was one name written in the most beautiful cursive handwriting that stuck out amidst the hurried scrawls.

Shreyasi.

The last three books she had issued were *Jerusalem: The Biography*; *India's Wars: A Military History, 1947–1971*; and *The Algorithm Design Manual*. This made no sense.

He fumbled with his phone, his fingers trembling. He typed out a mail to Shreyasi, something he hadn't done in almost a year.

From: damanroy111@gmail.com
To: shreyasibose07@gmail.com

Are you back???!?!??!?!?!??!?!?!?!?!?!
  Daman

From: shreyasibose07@gmail.com
To: damanroy111@gmail.com

YES. And now you know what I look like. Sweet dreams.

11

Shreyasi Bose, twenty-six, had just cleared the empty beer bottles, used glasses and plates left strewn over the couches, tables and floor of the living room of her sprawling three-bedroom house in East of Kailash. She stacked the bottles near the door and dumped the rest in the sink as quietly as she could. She didn't want her husband to wake up from his drunken slumber. Once done, she lit a few scented candles to ward off the smell of food and alcohol from the house. The tub in the bathroom was now filled with hot water. She latched the washroom door and slipped out of her clothes. The bathroom was her sanctuary whenever her husband was back. She smiled at her reflection in the mirror. Her breasts were firm and her thighs were getting muscular and shapely from the squats she did every morning. Her hamstrings were still sore from the jumping lunges she might have done too much of. From the medicine cabinet she took out a bottle of bath salts her husband had bought for her from Jordan (or was it Chile?) and added a handful to the water. She dipped a toe in to check if the water was hot. Then slowly, she slipped in. The water was warmer than she had expected. She liked it. She lay there, submerged, with only her nose protruding out of the water and closed her eyes. The tiredness seemed to wash away.

It had been a long day. Back from his six-month-long assignment, her husband of nearly two years had asked five of his friends and their wives to watch the Indian Premier League match at their place without consulting her. The food and the alcohol were ordered in but she'd had to do all the serving while her husband lay spreadeagled on the sofa and guffawed loudly with his friends. She had asked him to help her just once when the wife of one of his friends had chipped in, 'He's away at sea for six months. Let him rest a little.'

Shreyasi had wanted to break the bottle on her head, shove the rest down her throat and watch the blood gurgle out and choke her. *And what do you think* I do *for those six months, you whore!* Out of spite and habit, Shreyasi later flicked the woman's phone while she was in the washroom. She connected a little OTG connector and a tiny data cable to the phone and dumped the data from the woman's phone into hers. She kept the phone back where she had picked it up from. While flicking through the data she found a string of emails and pictures the woman had sent to her boyfriend. Shreyasi saved them all in a folder and named it.

'You're such a nice couple,' Shreyasi had told the woman. 'May nothing come between you guys.'

The woman had clutched her husband's arm and smiled. Had the woman not been nice to her for the rest of the party, she would have sent those pictures and sexts to her husband and ruined their marriage.

Shreyasi never trusted the words that came out of people's mouths. She believed what people wrote or texted or mailed or WhatsApped, things they hid behind a password, were what revealed the true self of a person.

By the time they wound up, she had something on everyone who had come to the get-together in the little folders on her phone. The folders were organized alphabetically with chronological details—with the addition of the eight people from the party the number had swelled to 643 names/folders. The more people get drunk and tired, the less careful they are with punching their passwords in. Once you have their phones, it's a matter of a couple of minutes, an OTG connector and another phone. That's it, all their dirty secrets they hide behind a four-digit password—phone logs, pictures, chat histories, mail, browser histories—are yours. It is so simple, it is laughable, like taking candy from a kid. While her husband's friends had all sat laughing and talking like their lives were so perfect, she knew who was cheating on whom and with whom, who had unpaid bills, who had had an abortion, who was bulimic and who made his wife fuck him with a strap-on. She knew everything; she had always made it her business to know everything. Because, who knows? There might come a time when she might need this information. It was a wonder she had nothing against her beloved husband of two years. This marriage would have never happened if she had found something against him like she had found against all the prospective suitors she had met before him. But her husband was careful . . . and her parents' patience had worn thin. There was no way out. The doctors had given no hopes of Daman waking up from the coma; there was no point waiting, he was as good as dead; eventually, she agreed to the wedding. But Daman did wake up . . . and he remembered a name. Just her name—Shreyasi.

She picked up one of the little burning tea lights from the edge of the bathtub and put it on her palm. The aluminium casing was scorching hot and it singed her skin. Lazily, she flicked the wick with her index finger before extinguishing it. She hadn't noticed how cold the water had got. Her shrivelled skin prickled with goose pimples. She stepped out of the tub and towelled off the water from her skin. She put on her SpongeBob night suit she had bought only a week back. It brought a smile to her face.

She walked to the living room next, switched on the TV and got comfortable on the couch. She took out her phone and began to scroll through hundreds of folders of people's data she had downloaded from phones she had stolen or borrowed over the years—of her teachers, colleagues, friends, even strangers. She could wreck hundreds of relationships, jobs, friendships and lives with the press of a few buttons.

While sifting, she found one of the first folders she had ever made. Rudra. The boy with floppy hair and the most charming smile, her first true love, her only love before Daman. She was in eleventh standard and he was a new admission. He had shifted to Delhi from Bengaluru and had a peculiar accent which everyone made fun of, but not her. The first time she saw him she knew they had to be together. The voice inside her head asked her to possess him, to love him, to take care of him, to save him from the world and so she did. What had she not done for that rotten boy? Rudra would not have become the prefect had she not planted porn CDs in the bags of the entire Student Council. He would have never made it to the volleyball team had she not mixed ground glass in the team's drink. And yet, he had called her crazy when she first professed her love for him.

Of course, he saw the truth in Shreyasi's love and came around. He told her he loved her, and because he loved her, she let him put his soft hands under her skirt on the school bus every day. But when she thought all was good, he had dared to go against her and talk to Kriti. She did what any girl in love would do. The last day before the summer vacations, she called Rudra posing as Kriti to the men's bathroom in the far corner of the basement where no one ever went. It was four days before anyone found him locked inside. He was emaciated and was found eating his own shit. Kriti was expelled and Shreyasi never saw Rudra again in school. Rudra lost two years of his school. The last time Shreyasi checked his profile, he was in Coimbatore, floundering in an MBA college. *First loves are always complex*, Shreyasi thought.

She exited the folder. She had just kept her phone aside when her husband came stumbling into the room, rubbing his eyes. Shreyasi asked him if he was okay. He smiled at her, his eyes glinting naughtily. He was still drunk. For the last six months, she had slept alone in her bed (their bed) with

thoughts of her and Daman. But now her husband was here.
Her husband stretched his hand, that silly smile still pasted on
his face. Shreyasi switched off the television. She gave him
her hand and realized how cold her own hand was. He led
her through the corridor to their bedroom. She slipped into
the blanket, her body turned away from him, almost teetering
on the edge of the bed. She heard him fumble with his clothes
before clambering on to the bed. Not long after she felt his
naked body against her. He turned Shreyasi towards him and
put his lips to hers. He pried them open with his tongue.
The stench of alcohol in his breath was overpowering. 'I
love you,' he said. *You're lying. I know. There's someone. I just
haven't found her . . .*

His tongue inside her, she tried to think of the time she was
in love with her husband. All she remembered was that it wasn't
for a long time and she had no memory of it now. However
little she liked him was washed away slowly. Now she only
remembered her festering loneliness, the sheer lovelessness and
the growing resentment of the last two years of their marriage.
His coarse marine-engineer hands were inside her night suit.
Slowly and clumsily, he got her naked, kissing her all the time.
She bit him on his lip and tasted blood. It didn't deter him. His
hands went south and found her dry and cold. She thought he
would react adversely but instead he winked at her and crawled
down inside the blanket. *He's drunk.* She felt his lips against her
dry self. He spat and licked. She moved her head to the side.
On the bedside table, lay a copy of Daman's book, *The Girl
of My Dreams.* The cover page was curled into itself and the
author photograph was half visible. A faint smile came over
her face. She half closed her eyes and imagined it was Daman
between her thighs, like she had done all those nights in her
bed while touching herself. Almost instantly, her body reacted
and shuddered. The thought of Daman woke up her senses

and made them surface like a kraken. Suddenly, it was like she
was made of nerve endings. She moaned. It encouraged her
husband. He licked vigorously, thrusting his tongue inside her.
She held his hair and shoved him deeper. She gasped. He held
her other hand. It wasn't a sailor's rough hand but Daman's. She
removed her other hand from her husband's head and turned
over the cover page. Daman was staring at her from the book.
Her toes curled and her eyes were half closed. Her husband
tried to move up but she pushed him down again. He was now
shoving a couple of fingers inside her. She was soaking wet.
She panted. But before she could sense it, her husband had
crawled right back up. His cock rubbed against her belly and
he wanted to kiss her. 'Not like this,' she said and pushed him
away. She turned away from him, her ass bumped against his
thighs. Her husband took the cue. He held her by the hip. She
stationed her eyes at the inside cover of the book. Daman's eyes
danced under the night lamp. Her husband slapped her with his
cock and with one quick thrust, he entered her. He mounted
her and fucked her like a rabid animal. Shreyasi bit the pillow
to keep herself from taking Daman's name. 'I love you,' her
husband said. *You don't.* 'Shut up and fuck me,' grumbled
Shreyasi. He did exactly that. But not long after, she felt his
thighs shudder. He grunted loudly and came inside her. Once
done, he slumped to the side, giggling and panting. 'It was
good, yeah?' he asked. Shreyasi nodded.

Shreyasi slipped out of the bed. He called her name out.
She didn't look back. Instead she picked her clothes and hurried
to the washroom. She washed herself, took a long hot shower,
thought of Daman and made herself come. Once done, she
dried herself, sat on the commode lid and buried her face into
her palms. The men in her life had always disappointed her.
Her husband and Daman.

She cried thinking of both of them.

12

She's at the wheel of the car. We are laughing about something she said. A jute bag filled with bottles of vodka, whisky and tequila clangs loudly at her feet. She picks it up and keeps it on her lap. She takes out a bottle of vodka and wiggles it in front of my face. I shake my head. But Shreyasi has already unscrewed the cap. She's now drinking from it. Before long, the bottle is on my lips as well. I try to shake it away but Shreyasi keeps pressing it on to my lips. The alcohol burns a path to my stomach. Finally, I manage to sway away from the bottle's mouth. A little vodka spills on to my T-shirt. We both giggle. I haven't eaten anything since morning and the vodka goes straight to my brain. I start to feel a little woozy. My eyes water. I bend towards her. She gives me a little peck on my lips, wetting them, her hand on my chest. I try to lean in more but she turns her head towards the road. It's too late. A pair of headlights shine at us. She swerves towards the railing and slams into it. The car flips . . . Seconds later, bloodied and broken, we are looking at each other but we are smiling . . . We are alive . . .

Daman woke up panting in his drenched bed. *Fuck*, he thought. It was the seventh straight day he had pissed his bed. He chewed his pills and smoked three cigarettes by the time he walked out of the washroom. He had been smoking like a steam engine for the past week, running through four packets in a day just to calm his nerves. He had been grappling with his nightmares and the freakish reappearance of Shreyasi. On the day he met Shreyasi, he called Puchku and asked for the description of the girl who had met her on the way back from school. It matched with the girl he had met at the British Council. He wondered why Shreyasi wouldn't just meet him. Why would she play these games, meet under changed names, go and see his sister of all the people? It scared him a bit. He wondered if she was Shreyasi at all. Shouldn't he have felt something if he saw her after all these months? He wondered if she was an 'off the rails', unhinged pretender. Someone who read the posts and the book and was now pretending to be Shreyasi. He considered it as a real possibility but then she had used the same email ID as Shreyasi's. Moreover, apart from his family and Sumit, no one knew of Shreyasi's existence, not even Avni. This girl knew about Goa. It had to be *her*.

Since that day in the library, he had frantically mailed Shreyasi without much success.

From: damanroy111@gmail.com
To: shreyasibose07@gmail.com

Where were you?
    Daman

From: damanroy111@gmail.com
To: shreyasibose07@gmail.com

Why are you back?
    Daman

From: damanroy111@gmail.com
To: shreyasibose07@gmail.com

Why not meet me properly? We can sit and talk.
    Daman

From: damanroy111@gmail.com
To: shreyasibose07@gmail.com

?
Daman

From: damanroy111@gmail.com
To: shreyasibose07@gmail.com

What the fuck is going on? Why are you
playing these games?
    Daman

It had been three days since he'd sent the last mail and she hadn't
replied to him. As Daman brushed his teeth, his phone beeped.
Shreyasi had finally replied. His heart thumped and toothpaste
froth dribbled out of his mouth as he read it.

From: shreyasibose07@gmail.com
To: damanroy111@gmail.com

Why play games? Because why not? What fun it
would be if we are like the others? Sitting and
talking isn't really our thing, is it? Would
you have appreciated it had I just waltzed
into your life and said, 'Hi, nice to see
you again?' No, that's not the Shreyasi you
love. Do I need to remind you what kind of a
couple we really were? Please find attached
the 860 posts you wrote on us. Do you know
my favourite Daman-and-Shreyasi story? It's
the one where we, me and you, Daman and
Shreyasi, tail my petulant, insufferable
and arrogant ex-boyfriend, corner him,
threaten him, torture him, and leave him
inches from his death, tied naked outside

the reception of his office. It might have
never happened but it could have, had the Goa
trip ended differently for us. So kudos to
your imagination. Read them again and you
will know why we were different before you
dared to put that crap about us in the book.
But I still love you, baby.

    Shreyasi, *The Girl of Your Dreams*

Daman read the mail and saw the truth in it. She couldn't have just walked in and said she was Shreyasi. That would have been such a disappointment after months of romanticizing her. What she was doing here was at least getting his attention, bothering him, reducing his brain to mush, making him piss his bed and smoke like a chimney, consuming his time and mind, and that, he was sure, was what she was aiming at. Shreyasi from his posts would have done exactly this. The behavioural patterns of this girl who called herself Shreyasi were just like the one he had written about in the posts. She was exactly like the girl he had constructed in his head from little snippets of conversations, in those numerous nightmares. It had to be her, there was no doubt any more in Daman's head. Only a little dejection.

Sitting on the bed, reading her mail again, he wondered why he questioned Shreyasi's resurfacing and even her existence despite the obvious markers that proved it was really her. He realized that it was because he had expected his memory to respond to the real Shreyasi. But he had felt nothing. Nothing. No floodgates of memory had opened. It just left him with an emptiness where the fantasies of Shreyasi lay. Shreyasi had come back and spoilt everything.

He closed his eyes and heard the last words she had said.

'Careful what you wish for. I might just come and get a book signed.'

13

Avni banged head-on into two of her co-workers, making them spill the files they were carrying. 'Sorry!' she muttered and ran towards the washroom. Closing the door behind her, she fumbled through her handbag and backpack and placed her clothes and make-up on the ledge of the basin. She was already late for Daman's book event. He had called twice to check where she had reached. She had selected a pretty little black dress for the evening. Hurriedly, she applied the foundation and while it set she put on her dress. *Breathe, Avni, Breathe.* It took her fifteen minutes to change and do her make-up. She stuffed her office clothes into the two bags and ran out of the washroom. She could change out of her comfortable shoes later. She took the stairs to the parking lot two at a time. She threw her bags on to the back seat and jumped into the front. She revved the engine and backed out of her parking space. She had just moved a few metres when she heard a loud thump and a shriek. She braked hard. Her heart leapt to her mouth. *Fuck.* She clenched the steering wheel. *Not today. Not today. Not today.* She turned to look at the damage. Much to her relief, the girl whose scooter she had hit was already standing, rubbing herself off. Avni hopped out of the car and ran towards the girl.

'Are you okay? Let me help you,' Avni said and helped the girl who was trying to get her scooter upright. 'Listen, I'm sorry, I didn't look while reversing. I am ready to pay for any damages.'

'It's okay,' said the rattled girl, not looking at Avni.

'Are you sure?'

The girl nodded and dragged her scooter away from Avni's car. 'I'm okay. I will be fine,' she said.

Avni stood there awkwardly for a few moments, and then walked back to the car. She closed her eyes and said a little prayer before turning the engine on. She put the car in gear and backed out slowly. She drove towards the exit. It was already 5.40 p.m. There was no way she would get to the event on time. She was paying the parking fee when she spotted the girl she had hit in her rear-view mirror, standing with her hands on her waist. Every few seconds she would kick the scooter but the engine would gurgle and stop. After a few tries she put her hands on her head, exasperated. Avni switched on the blinkers and parked the car on the side. She ran towards the girl. 'Hey?' She waved at the girl as she walked towards her. 'Can I help you?' The girl looked at Avni blankly. Avni reached the girl and asked her, 'Can I drop you somewhere?' The girl shook her head but Avni insisted. 'Look, I'm sorry for this. You can park your scooter here and call the mechanic tomorrow? You can send me the bill,' she said and gave the girl her business card. 'Let me give you a lift. Please.'

And just like that, the girl was in tears.

'Hey? Hey? It's okay. I'm sorry. We can go to the mechanic right now. If your parents are the problem I can talk to them and tell them it was my fault. Don't cry,' said Avni, holding her hand. 'Let me talk to them?'

The girl wiped her tears. 'It's not about my parents. It's just that . . .'

'What?'

'I needed to be somewhere,' mumbled the girl. She now looked embarrassed to have cried.

Avni smiled. 'Boyfriend, haan? Where are you meeting him? I will drop you wherever you want to go.'

'I had to meet someone much more important than a boyfriend,' said the girl, blushing like a new bride. 'My favourite writer—'

Avni asked, 'Who?'

'Daman Roy, the author of *The Girl of My Dreams*. He has a book event today in Connaught Place. He's the love of my life,' said the girl, smiling widely. Avni covered her face to suppress her smile. *So cute*, she thought. The girl continued, 'It starts at six and the invite said he will be signing copies. I was already late and then this . . .' She pointed to the scooter and her face scrunched up into a little ball. She continued, 'I also wore this new top I bought yesterday for the event.'

The childlike enthusiasm in her eyes, the longing to meet her favourite author, was so heartening that Avni wanted to hug her. Like her, the girl too had dressed to impress and had done a better job of it. In her short white top and shiny faux leather pants she looked gorgeous. Avni felt proud to see Daman have legitimate fans, people who had gone out, spent money, bought and read the book, and longed to meet him.

'I can drop you there,' said Avni. 'I am going the same way too. Connaught Place, you said, right?'

'I hope I am not imposing?' she asked, her eyes glittering with innocent hope.

'Not at all.' Avni laughed. The girl parked her scooter and followed Avni to her car. Avni drove out of the parking lot weighing when she should tell the girl who she was. *I'm the author's girlfriend. Actually, I am more like his fiancée.* 'So where's the book event exactly in Connaught Place?' asked Avni.

'It's at Oxford Bookstore,' she answered, her eyes stuck at the car's clock. 'I'm so late! I wanted to get my book signed and click a picture with him. What if there are too many people? What if he leaves?'

'He won't.'

'What if he does? He's so pretty. I want a picture!' squealed the girl. She took out her well-worn copy of *The Girl of My Dreams* from her backpack and showed the picture to Avni. 'Isn't he cute? Look at him!'

'He's okay.'

'Please. He's so cute. You should read the book. Or better still, read the stuff he posted online before he wrote the book. He deleted everything now but I have it copied on my laptop. It's so good! I read it every day,' she gushed.

There was a long drive ahead of them so Avni asked her in good humour, 'Hey? I just remembered. I think I know this author. He's dating a friends' friend. I don't remember his girlfriend's name though.'

'You can't be serious? Can you make me meet him?' Before Avni could answer, the girl asked, 'Is his girlfriend's name Shreyasi?'

'No.'

The girl frowned. 'It doesn't matter to me who he's dating. For me, he will always be in love with Shreyasi. She's his one true love. Don't you know that they are inseparable? Other girls are just distractions,' said the girl clutching the book to her chest like a schoolgirl.

'You know she's a fictional character, right? She's just someone he probably made up for the book,' said Avni, scowling.

The girl retorted sharply. 'True, the Shreyasi in the book is clearly someone he made up but the Shreyasi from his posts is real. They were in love and the stories about him and her are all true. I will make you read all of them, all 860 of them. You will know that it's all real. He loves her.'

'Fine,' said Avni. 'I will read them. I'm sorry I didn't tell you my name. I'm Avni.'

'I am Ashi,' said the girl. And then suddenly, the girl's expression changed. She kept looking at Avni. Something had clicked inside her. 'Hey? Are you? Are you? No! No!'

'Yes.'

'You're Daman's girlfriend!'

Avni nodded, smiling.

She buried her face in her palms. 'Oh. My. God. I am so sorry! I am so sorry! I am so sorry! I just remembered a picture he had posted of the two of you. You two look so good together,' she gushed.

'Ah, too late,' said Avni and winked at her.

'Can I have a picture together? I want it for my Snapchat! This is unbelievable!'

'Why not.'

The girl whipped out her phone and clicked three pictures. For the rest of the drive, she couldn't look at Avni, too embarrassed for what she'd said. 'So you like Daman a lot?' asked Avni.

'I don't like him. I love him,' said the girl while she checked her hair in the mirror. 'Do you think my hair looks all right? I had gotten it streaked brown and red for a couple of days. I didn't like it and reverted to black. I hope Daman likes it.'

14

'Did you update your Facebook profile today?'

'Yes.'

'And Twitter?'

'Yes.'

'And Instagram?'

'Yes, Jayanti. Now stop it. It's only six right now. Avni texted me that she's stuck in traffic. Maybe others are too. The idea of this book launch was yours. Don't sweat me over it if no one turns up.' The book launch was supposed to have begun and there were only about fifteen people waiting for Daman which in Jayanti's words was a catastrophe. Daman took out his phone and called Avni to check where she had reached. 'Hey? Where are you?'

'I just parked the car. Will be there in ten minutes. And I'm getting someone with me! She's a big fan of yours and I just met her,' she said. Daman heard some scuffling from the other side of the phone. Avni continued, 'She wants to talk to you. She's freaking out. Will you talk to her?'

'Of course,' said Daman, scratching his head. He heard Avni pass the phone to the girl with her.

'Hello.' The voice of the girl trembled. 'I'm such a big fan of yours! I . . . I can't believe I am talking to you.'

'Hi! What's your name?'

'Ashi.'

He heard the girl say to Avni, 'Can you please not look? I'm already nervous! Walk a few steps ahead of me!'

Daman heard Avni mumble a 'fine' and walk away from the girl. Daman continued, 'It was really sweet—'

'Look at you, acting like the courteous writer acknowledging the love of a fawning reader.'

'Excuse me?'

'Spare me the bullshit, baby,' said the girl. 'I will see you in a bit. You have a bit of answering to do at this book event.' She whispered it like a threat. 'I know you have been looking forward to seeing me, haven't you? Well, your wait ends, baby,' said the girl. 'The battery is low.'

She cut the call. Daman tried calling Avni again but the phone was switched off. Daman's heartbeat quickened. The voice was unmistakably hers. He called on Avni's number again. It was still switched off. What is she doing with Avni? He heard a knock on the door of the back office and the bookstore owner, Ram Prakash, a fat, jolly man walked in. He told them that the crowd had swelled to about thirty people and they could start any time they wanted. 'Just a few more minutes. I'm waiting for someone,' said Daman, his fingers quaking.

'I will go and make the announcement,' said Ram Prakash. 'Daman? There's one request. You can't smoke in there. There are smoke detectors—'

'Got it,' said Daman and he left.

'Have you started writing the second book, Daman? I'm trying to make the calendar for the coming months. So I need to know,' said Jayanti.

'Can we please not talk about it right now?' snapped Daman.

'This can't wait, Daman. Karthik Iyer's next book's date is going to be finalized. We don't want your book to be placed around his. It would kill your book, so we need to be careful. The earlier we sign the book, the better. And before you start again, Bookhound Publishers will have the final say on how the book will shape up. I hope you understand that now. The book has worked and there are thirty people outside—things are going well for you.'

'Weren't you calling this event a disaster a few minutes earlier?'

'Because it was and because I thought you didn't do all that I told you to. But seems like you did and see? Anyway, let's not keep them waiting. Let's start. I don't think that girlfriend of yours is coming.'

'What the fuck are you talking about? Of course she's coming!' said Daman.

A little later, Daman followed Jayanti towards the little stage that was built for the book launch. He worried for Avni's absence, his right hand firmly inside his pocket, waiting for his phone to ring.

15

Daman Roy and Jayanti Raghunath sat on two red couches on an elevated platform discussing how Daman's first book, *The Girl of My Dreams*, now a well-loved bestseller, came into existence. Jayanti talked about how she had spotted Daman on Facebook and thought he had the spark and the intelligence to be a successful writer. She peppered the story with juicy anecdotal lies and conversations they had never had. 'Oh, he would not pick up my calls! But he was always good with deadlines! Daman is a joy to work with . . . I remember this one time . . .' Daman had looked nervous for the first fifteen minutes and had searched for a familiar face in the crowd. He breathed easy when in the far corner of the room he found Avni looking on with a proud smile on her face. She was alone.

Daman fake-smiled and fibbed about how he saw a mentor in Jayanti Raghunath, and was thankful for everything she had done for him. Avni kept distracting him, blowing kisses and winking from where she stood in the crowd. Unlike everyone else, she didn't have a copy of *The Girl of My Dreams* in her hands. 'I will read it as soon as the project ends,' Avni had said when Daman had given her the book weeks ago. He would never ask her again to read the book. Not after he'd read this anonymous one-star review on Amazon which had kept him awake for a week.

Review submitted by FDKJHFDSH:

> The author is a narcissistic prick. Why would he use his own name? As far as my friends tell me, Shreyasi is fictional, so shouldn't the author have used a name that isn't his? Is the

author trying to mislead his readers into believing it's a real
story? It's clearly not a real story. I feel it's a dick move by
the author. Also I feel sorry for his real girlfriend. How
unfair it must be for her? I will not give this book more
than one star. It might be a great story but it's principally
wrong.

Daman had bristled when he'd first read the review. What the
fuck does this reader know about what goes into completing a
book? Naive bastard. He couldn't even write his name, bloody
FDKJHFDSH. It would have remained just another review
to be read and forgotten if he hadn't clicked on the username
FDKJHFDSH. The user had reviewed two more items—a
Panasonic microwave and a charger for iPhone 6s. Avni had
made both these purchases last month. Daman had helped her
pick the microwave. FDKJHFDSH was Avni. Even so, Daman
couldn't bring himself to confront her. 'Also, I feel sorry for his
girlfriend. How unfair it must be for her?' It wasn't a review of
the book. It was Avni venting out.

A little later, Daman was asked to read from the book.
The audience chose the passage—a page-long confession of
Daman's love for Shreyasi, edited heavily and almost rewritten
entirely by Jayanti.

'I'm bad at book readings so bear with me. Here goes:

'I never thought I would fall in love. Maybe I was just
scared to imagine the possibility of not being loved back.
You changed all that, Shreyasi. Am I scared? Yes, I am. Do
I deserve you? Of course not. But the fact that you walked
into my life when everything had gone to shit and made me
look forward to every new morning is something I can never
forget. You can walk away today. It will rip a huge hole in
my heart but I can't stop you. But even if you do walk away
you will always be a huge part of my life, the most important

part of my life. Will it be hard? Only if dying is hard. Just to think of spending a day without you crushes my heart. To live without you is a fate worse than death but I'm ready for it. I had decided that the day I made up my mind to let my guard down. And now, I'm in love and there's no going back, Shreyasi. I will always love you . . .'

Daman read on till he reached the end of the page, despite wanting to gag on the cheesy lines. The audience applauded. Daman smiled back at them. Avni clapped the hardest but her eyes gave her away the truth. She hated Shreyasi.

'That was beautiful,' said Jayanti. The crowd nodded in affirmation. 'We will now take questions from the audience.'

Daman had enjoyed most of evening and wondered why he had been so against the idea of doing a book event in the first place. The questions from the audience were more or less generic, nothing Daman hadn't expected. A couple of people asked why the character of Shreyasi had changed so drastically in the book and it was handled by Jayanti who talked about the need to tell stories which were more identifiable. Except a handful, most of the readers liked the new Shreyasi. A girl who had been blushing all this while got up and asked, 'Why is the main character's name Daman? Is it because you love your name? Or it's because the character is based on you? Is the story real? I love the book by the way!'

'Thank you for your question,' said Daman. 'It's a bit of both. When I started writing I picked up traits that I had and put them in the book and so I kept the main guy's name in the book as Daman. It made the writing process easier. I just never happened to change the name. Also, it doesn't matter if the story is real. Because if the story made you feel something, it's real for you, isn't it? For me, the story happened in my head. So it's all very real to me. I can imagine the characters and situations and I feel like I was there when it was happening. Thank you for the question.'

The girl nodded brightly and sat down.

'We will take one last audience question,' said Jayanti. 'And then we will have the author sign the books. Everyone who wants to get a book signed can form a queue on the left. Daman will not leave till he has signed all the books. Thank you.'

Daman waved at Avni as the crowd started to move towards the dais to get their books signed. People jostled and pushed to get in front of the line. Avni was caught between two overenthusiastic readers.

'Jayanti,' Daman whispered. 'Take Avni to the back office?'

'You will be okay here?'

'It's a book signing, Jayanti. What can go wrong?'

The microphone was passed to a girl in the second last row for the last audience question. Daman had noticed her before because she stuck out like a sore thumb. She hadn't once looked up and spent the entire time peering into her phone. Daman wondered if she was here with a friend.

'Hi, Daman?'

'Hi.'

'I don't know if I should ask you the question I have in mind,' said the girl. The coldness and the anger in her voice was unmistakable. She was now the only one sitting amidst the empty chairs. She looked familiar. And then it struck him where he had seen that face. *Ashi. Reya. Shreyasi.* Daman squirmed in his seat.

The girl noticed his discomfort. 'Should I?'

'You can ask whatever you want,' said Daman, composing himself.

'Are you a coward, Daman?' she asked, crossing one leg over the other. Her leather pants glistened under the lights of the bookstore. A silent murmur filled the bookstore. All eyes turned towards her. 'You changed the character of the book because you had to tell an identifiable story, sell more books, isn't it?' She air-quoted the word identifiable. 'You wrote a book you didn't believe in. Why are you even a writer then?' she asked. 'Don't just look at me. Answer my question.'

Daman got his voice back and said, 'I changed the character for the betterment of the novel. The neurotic, deranged, sociopathic, depressed Shreyasi wouldn't have worked so I chose the option I felt would be more interesting to read for a large section of the audience. I don't want to write in a bubble. I want my books to be read, liked and sold because that's what allows me to do what I like to do best—write. Because, believe it or not, you need to earn to get by and writing doesn't pay much anyway.'

The crowd giggled.

'So what you're—'

Ram Prakash cut her off. 'Young lady, that was the last question.'

The girl shook her head in defiance. 'With all due respect, Daman still wants to answer my counter question since he hasn't put the microphone down. He's answerable to everyone connected to the book and God knows I'm connected to the book,' said the girl with an authority that surprised everyone. The girl spoke again, the threatening bass of her voice now filling up the entire bookstore. She wasn't loud yet her voice seemed to hit Daman at the bottom of his stomach. It made him nervous. She continued, 'My second question is what happens to the muse, the girl who served as an inspiration behind that character? What should she think of you for what you did with her for money?'

'There is no muse. And even if there was, she should be happy I used the name,' he said.

The crowd giggled again.

'Happy? She would have been happy had you stayed the damn away from her name. Why did you insult her by changing everything about her? WHO THE HELL GAVE YOU THAT POWER? DON'T LOOK AT ME LIKE A DEAD DUCK. USE THAT TONGUE AND ANSWER ME—WHAT ARE YOU IF NOT A PIMP?'

Her voice crashed against the walls and echoed. A pin-drop silence descended to the room. She kept the microphone on the chair next to her, and looked at Daman calmly.

'Your hypothesis is incorrect. The previous Shreyasi and the one in the book are both fictional so the question doesn't arise—'

The girl got up and left mid-sentence. An awkward silence followed. It took a few seconds before everyone recovered. Readers swarmed him in groups of four and five and got their books signed, asked him a few questions, posed for pictures and selfies, and thanked him for making time for them. The girl's presence still hung in the air like a corpse's stench. Daman followed Ram Prakash to the back office after the signing was over. Ram Prakash apologized to Daman for the girl's behaviour. He told him that she was a regular customer and hence he couldn't chastise her more than he did.

'It wasn't your fault,' said Daman.

Avni lunged at Daman and hugged him as soon as he entered the back office. 'That was so good!' she said and kissed him on his cheek. Daman kissed her back.

'Are you okay?' asked Daman.

'Yes? What would happen to me?' asked Avni, surprised.

Ram Prakash, Jayanti and Daman sat in the back office and chatted about the session over cups of coffee. No one mentioned the unruly girl from the Q/A session.

'So when's the next book coming?' asked Ram Prakash. 'You should hurry up. Public memory is short.'

'See? That's what I have been telling him. He should finish it quickly and sign the contract,' said Jayanti like a concerned parent.

Soon, the conversation drifted to the one Daman thought of as the Justin Bieber of Indian literature—Karthik Iyer—and his next book which was due to come out in the next few months. Another tasteless love story about him and girlfriend for life, Varnika.

'Has he finished writing it? He's a very good writer. My customers love him! Some even buy multiple copies of his books. They are crazy about him,' said Ram Prakash. Jayanti told Ram Prakash that Karthik hadn't finished writing the book. Ram Prakash continued, 'We are waiting for it. If it's big like the last book was, we will have some money rolling in after all.'

Daman excused himself, told them he needed to visit the washroom. What he really wanted to do was vomit because all the excitement around Karthik's impending book made him sick. He desperately needed to smoke; he wondered where Shreyasi was.

16

Daman washed his face. He hadn't realized how exhausting book launches could be. But mostly, he felt drained thinking of how to deal with the Shreyasi issue. He was drying his hands when over the din of the dryer he heard someone giggle and whisper, 'Stop. Stop. Not here. STOP.' He turned. The voice came from inside the stall. The very next second a couple tumbled out and Daman looked away.

'Hey?' the man was next to him, drying his hands with a tissue, a silly smile pasted on his face. 'I am sorry about that.'

'I hope it was fun.'

'My wife is a big fan of yours,' said the man, nudging Daman with his elbow.

Daman looked over his shoulder. The girl had disappeared inside the stall. 'That's sweet.'

He had just turned to leave when the man called out. 'Hey? Daman?' Daman turned. 'I haven't read anything of yours but my wife has. But she was late and couldn't get her book signed. Do you mind?'

'Of course not,' said Daman.

'She's just fixing herself up,' said the man, ruffling his hair, embarrassed. They both stood waiting awkwardly for the man's wife to come out of the stall. In the dim lighting of the washroom it took Daman more than a second to realize who had stepped out of the stall. *She's married!*

'Shreyasi! Look who I caught here,' said the man to his wife.

The girl clasped her mouth in shock. Her eyes grew wide and she looked at Daman with amazement. 'OH. MY. GOD,' said the girl, gasping.

The man looked at Daman and said, 'Didn't I tell you? She loves you. Your book is always on the side table. No one dares to move it from there. She reads it every day.' The man kissed his wife on her cheek. The wife, Shreyasi, smiled at Daman. 'Now get it signed, will you? Don't complain once you get home that you couldn't get it signed,' said the man, nudging her ahead. 'I'm Akash, by the way.' He shook Daman's hand. 'Your hands are so cold,' he remarked. Daman smiled weakly at him.

Shreyasi clumsily fumbled through her handbag to fetch a book and a bundle of papers. 'Can you sign them all?'

Daman tried to form a sentence but words failed him. He nodded. *It's all an act. This man is not her husband. This is another trick of hers. She's playing another role. If she is Shreyasi, why don't I feel anything? Why did you have to come back?* Daman spoke, 'Listen—'

Shreyasi kept the pages and the book on the sink ledge and handed a pen to Daman. 'Sign them,' she said. The awe of a star-struck fan had dried from her voice. The coldness in her eyes was unambiguous. 'Can you sign every page? Would mean a lot to me!'

Akash muttered to his wife, 'You're making him sign these in a washroom? At least let's just go out?' The man put an arm around Daman's shoulder like they were brothers and walked him out. Shreyasi followed them, cradling the book and the pages in her hands. 'Keep them here,' Akash said to Shreyasi pointing to the cashier's table. He looked at the cashier and said, 'We just need to sign some papers.'

'Of course,' said the cashier and looked at Shreyasi. '*Kaisi hai ma'am aap?* (How are you, ma'am?)'

'I am good. And you?'

'You don't come here often any more?' asked the cashier.

'I have been a little busy,' said Shreyasi.

And while the cashier and Shreyasi talked, Akash whined to Daman about how Shreyasi would drag him to bookstores and the British Council Library every now and then. 'She knows everyone here,' said Akash. 'I am not into books though. I am a seaman. A sailor. A modern-day pirate.' The man giggled like men ought not to. 'Just kidding, I am a marine engineer. And the little time I do get on land, she drags me to these bookstores. No offence.' Daman was hardly listening to the man. He looked over his shoulder trying to make sense of it all. Along with the cashier, another helper of the bookstore had joined the conversation now. They were chatting as if they were long-lost friends. A little later, she introduced Akash to the employees of the bookstore. Daman started signing the pages, doubly aware of Shreyasi's closeness to him. The pages were printouts of the posts he had put up on Facebook.

'Are you done yet?' asked Akash.

'No,' said Shreyasi. 'Just this terribly written book is left. But I don't want to get this signed. I will get it signed when he rewrites it or redeems himself in the next book.'

Akash frowned. 'That's no way to talk to someone.'

Just then, Ram Prakash came looking for Daman. 'Oh, you're signing books here. We were waiting for you inside.' That's when Ram Prakash noticed Shreyasi. They exchanged smiles and shook hands. 'What you did at the book launch was uncalled for, Beta. He's a new writer, why heckle him with questions?'

'I am sorry, Uncle,' she said.

'I haven't seen you in days. I hope you're not buying e-books, are you?'

'No, Uncle. Never,' said Shreyasi. 'And I am sorry I took away your author. I was just getting something signed.'

Ram Prakash looked at Daman and said, 'I told you, she's one of our most regular customers. That's why I couldn't shut her up there. She was really excited when your book came out. But I don't think she liked it.' The man laughed throatily. He looked at Shreyasi and told her, 'I have asked him to write the second book quickly.'

'I hope he doesn't make the same stupid mistake again.' She looked at Daman. 'I will be looking forward to it. Try not to screw that up or . . .' she said. 'Anyway, I won't take any more of your time. Can I hug you before I leave?' Before Daman could say anything, she had already stepped forward. As she hugged him, she whispered, 'Best of luck, baby. I hope you will give me what I want.'

'Me? Is that what you want?' whispered Daman into Shreyasi's ear.

She whispered back. 'I could have you any moment I want to, Daman. You're not difficult to get. What I want is to have our love story back, not this pile of garbage you wrote. I live for our story. Do you understand?' She stepped away and smiled at Daman.

Akash remarked, 'Happy now?'

'Yes.'

Akash thanked Daman for his time and left with his wife, Shreyasi. Ram Prakash and Daman returned to the back office.

'Have you met her husband before?' asked Daman.

'Yes, a couple of times. I went to their wedding reception as well. He's a nice, cultured guy. Her parents were concerned about her marriage for a long time. People say she had a boyfriend who was in the hospital and that's why she was stalling the marriage for a long time even after being engaged to the boy. They are a lovely couple though. God bless them.'

17

'So where do you want to go?'

'Anywhere other than Summerhouse,' said Avni, pre-empting Daman's choice. 'I heard you were mobbed by a girl when you left the back office? Celebrity, eh?' She nudged him mischievously. 'Was she hot? Did she make you sign her cleavage?'

'She was with her husband,' clarified Daman. He toyed with the idea of coming clean about Shreyasi, and telling Avni about the reappearance. He dropped it when he thought that word might reach his family and Sumit. All hell would break loose then. He decided to wait till he figured out what was it that she really wanted and where she'd been all this time. He needed to talk to her, sit with her, and figure this out.

Thirty minutes later, Daman and Avni were in the parking lot of Hauz Khas Village drinking warm vodka and coke out of plastic tumblers. Daman just had the one peg. He had to drive later, he said. Together, they checked the pictures Daman had been tagged in from the book launch.

A little later, Avni said, 'I gave my mother your book.'

'It will not make her like me.'

'You never know.'

Daman rolled his eyes.

'Don't spoil your mood. It's your day, Daman,' she said.

'Fine. So you tell me about yours? How did it go? Did you make a lot of money?'

Did you make a lot of money? He always asked her that. Avni lied and told him a story about a merger her company was working on. In truth, Avni was out on a business lunch with a senior executive from Barclays who had shown interest in recruiting her. The hike was substantial and the profile was exciting. Avni had already decided she would take the job. This would place her years ahead of her peers. Sitting there on the bonnet of Daman's car, she wondered if she should tell Daman about her decision but decided against it. After a long time, it was his day.

'Am I meeting your parents soon?' she asked.

'Yes,' said Daman. 'Let me sign the next contract. They worry about me. First I want to get my finances in place and then broach the topic of us. It's been a tough couple of months. I'm a little short on money.'

'Did you pay off your credit card bill? Do you want me to—'

'I will do it this week. There are a few cheques from the articles I wrote. I haven't cashed them but it will be a substantial amount once I do. I'm covered for three months.'

She didn't say anything. Instead she leant over slowly and kissed Daman on his lips. His mouth was bitter but just how she liked it. Ten minutes later, they were inside his car, the seats laid flat, his hands under her T-shirt grabbing and fondling, her both hands stroking him before she went down on him. Avni started by teasing him, licking him slowly, and was about to take him inside her mouth when the window was knocked on urgently. Startled, they sat up straight and quickly dressed up in full view of two Delhi Police constables.

'*Bahar aaja qb, ladke* (Come out now, boy),' said one of the men.

Daman asked Avni to stay in and stepped out of the car. The constables took Daman to a corner and issued standard threats of dragging him to the police station and booking him on charges of public indecency. But soon enough, they were discussing money and Daman took out his wallet. He offered the 1500 rupees he had on him but the constables wanted more. Avni watched helplessly as he negotiated impatiently and poorly. They walked towards the car. Daman tailed close behind, grumbling. Avni was asked to roll down the window. Avni gave them another 1500 rupees and they let them go. During the drive back to Avni's house, Daman had said nothing but one sentence, 'You didn't have to give them anything. I could have gone to the police station and sorted this out.'

He dropped Avni home and then drove back to his house. Once on his floor, he switched on the gallery light and reached for the keys in his pocket. *Fuck.* He noticed that the lock had been changed. Daman's landlord, Sharmaji, lived at the other end of the apartment complex, on the sixth floor. Daman was out of breath and simmered in a murderous rage when he knocked on his landlord's door. It was already eleven in the night.

'Yes?' said the landlord as he opened the door.

'The lock has been changed. I need the key. I don't have time for this, Uncle. I have had a long day.'

'Your cheque has bounced again, Beta. I need the rent first and the other post-dated cheques you had promised. I can talk to your father—'

'Tomorrow. I will give it you tomorrow. It's late, Uncle. Can't I just get the key right now?'

'See, Beta, you asked me not to talk to your parents about money and I respected that. But you need to pay me in time,' said the landlord. He unhooked a key hanging from a nail near the door and handed the key to Daman. 'Next time, I will have to talk to them. This was a warning.'

'Thanks,' said Daman. He turned to leave.

'Beta?'

'Yes, Uncle?'

'Why don't you go back to your old job? All this writing business is not good for young people like you.'

Fuck you. 'I will think about it,' said Daman and walked down the stairs, even angrier than before, with half a mind to go back up and bash him up. Once home, Daman dialled Jayanti's number. If whoring out his book was the only way to keep a little bit of honour intact, then so be it. *Everyone works for money, why shouldn't I?* But even as he dialled Jayanti's number, Shreyasi's unspoken threat rang clear in his ears.

'I hope he doesn't make the same mistake again . . . I will be looking forward to it. Try not to screw that up or . . .'

18

When Jayanti's phone rang she was tucked in bed, reading on her iPad with the bedside lamp on. She had just got done with her emails. It had been a good day for Jayanti. Daman's book launch had gone better than she had expected. He was still holding out on his second book but she was sure he would come around soon. Stupid idealism always loses to an empty bank account. Karthik had just submitted the first few chapters of his book and if he kept up the pace, Jayanti could push for a launch within this year. She looked at the clock. It was late. She picked up the call after three rings.

'I hope I didn't disturb you?'

'No, tell me, Daman.'

'I want to sign the next book with Bookhound.'

'That's great news! I'm glad you turned around. I'm so happy for you. This is so thrilling!' She kept the iPad aside.

'But this time I want more advance money and a 5 per cent bump in royalty payments. I want the advance to be split 50–50—50 per cent when I sign and 50 per cent when I submit the manuscript.'

'Daman, I will have to talk to my seniors about it. You're asking for too much,' said Jayanti.

'It's a straightforward deal. You can make it happen.'

'Fine. You have it your way. But Bookhound Publishers will have the last creative call on the book. We can't give up on that. Is that okay?'

'You will have the right to turn my book to shit. You can make it into a joke book for all I care.'

'We need to work out what's best for you.'

'People around me need to stop thinking about what's best for me,' said Daman.

'Excuse me?'

'Nothing, Jayanti. Just figure things out and let's lock this as soon as possible. I need the money in my bank as soon as possible.'

Jayanti could smell the stink of Daman's desperation. She smiled and said, 'Sure. And I'm glad we are working together again. Just give me a broad outline of the story, something I can pitch to the editorial team . . . and I will start working on the contract.'

'Give me two weeks.'

She disconnected the phone soon after. Daman had turned around like she had expected. Daman was her trump card. After his last bestseller, Karthik Iyer was now an unmanageable success, a beast of an author with a commanding reader base, and with that came the opportunities for him to move to another publisher. She had already heard whispers of him being courted by Silver Eye Books and Purple Pen Publishers, amongst others. Daman's books were her fall-back plan. She could make him into another Karthik if he let her. All he needed to do was write eponymously named characters and whoever he would be dating at the time, sprinkle a little bit of 'Based on true events . . .' type bullshit and he could even beat Karthik in time. Jayanti had some ideas for the next book. One idea in particular had been festering in her mind for quite some time now, but she wouldn't share it with Daman till he signed on the dotted line.

She had just got back to reading when her phone beeped. It was a match on Tinder. A smile crept up on her face. She thought she deserved a celebration tonight. She opened the app. She had been on the app for over a year but had been on only five dates—two women and three men. Half an hour later, she was in a pretty red dress and pointy heels, on her way to Starbucks, Greater Kailash. She found her date in her pyjamas sipping on iced tea and poring over a book.

'Hi. Are you Shreyasi?'

She looked up from her book. 'Hi.' She put the book aside and hugged Jayanti. 'Nice to meet you.'

'Likewise,' Jayanti said as she settled in. *She's beautiful,* thought Jayanti.

'Do you want something?' asked the girl.

'I'm good. I have had too much coffee for one day. You look younger than the pictures.'

'Instagram filters change people.' She smiled. 'So do you do this often? Try to find love on dating apps?'

'Am I being judged by a teenager on my dating choices?'

'I'm twenty-three.'

'I'm ten years older.'

'And yet we are here.'

'So we are,' said Jayanti.

'And you are in a dress and heels,' remarked Shreyasi.

'I like to be dressed well.'

'Your dress is hot,' said Shreyasi, biting her lip.

Jayanti flushed. She wondered if her apartment was clean enough to invite her over. 'Thank you. I would say something about your pyjamas but they are pyjamas.'

'You can say something about me,' said Shreyasi and leant forward.

'You're gorgeous. Would that suffice?' Jayanti smiled.

'For now, yes. Are you dating someone?'

'Why would that be any of your business?'

'Isn't this a date?' asked Shreyasi.

'I wouldn't take it that far. I am not sure if I like you yet. I don't even know if Shreyasi is your real name.'

'How do I know if Jayanti is yours?'

'You don't but I am sure I don't give the impression that I would go to the length of changing my name for meeting someone,' said Jayanti. 'So what do you do? Or you're still a student hopping from one date to another?'

Shreyasi laughed heartily. 'So you take me for a dumb teenager.'

'I also said you're hot. Don't forget that.'

'Oh yes. That does oodles for my self-esteem. Should I record that somewhere? I will listen to it on days I cry myself to sleep,' said Shreyasi and sipped on her iced tea. 'I work in an IT company.'

'Is that interesting?'

'Sometimes, it is. What do you do?' asked Shreyasi.

'I edit books.'

'Ah, nice. So did you notice me reading? Will it better my chances with you?' said the girl, winking as she blew air into the straw and bubbled her drink. Before Jayanti could say anything, she added, 'I was just kidding. I have a husband.'

'You do?' said Jayanti. 'Why are you on Tinder then?'

'I didn't say I have a wife.'

Jayanti reddened. How long has it been since I last had sex, she wondered glumly. The last time she had someone in her bed was six months ago. It wasn't even good, she remembered. The guy had no idea what he was doing so she had finished him off quickly, rolled over and slept.

'So your husband is out of town?' asked Jayanti.

'No, actually he just came to town. He's a sailor. Marine engineering. He's out with his friends getting drunk silly so I thought I deserved to get a girlfriend of my own.'

She smiled at Jayanti. Jayanti could feel her eyes linger on her legs. 'So we are friends, are we?' asked Jayanti.

'Of course, if you want us to be, that is,' said Shreyasi. 'But for that we would want to know each other better. So tell me, what books have you edited? Anything I would have read?'

'Have you heard of Karthik Iyer? I edit all his books.' The girl's face scrunched. Jayanti continued, 'Not a fan of romance, it seems?'

'I would say the exact opposite. If I were not a fan of romance would I be seeking romance in a friend despite having a loving husband? I just don't like Karthik Iyer's brand of romance. The limiting, monogamous, gender-defined romance. It's too . . . banal for me. I am sure people like it. But to each their own. Though I do like this guy . . . his name . . . Yes, Daman! He wrote these crazy stories about himself in some Facebook posts. I only noticed because I read my name in the stories.' She giggled. 'They were quite entertaining and zany and wild and mad and passionate. That's the kind of love that never dies, the only kind on which books should be written. Immortal, eternal, whatever you might call it. He wrote a book too I heard but I haven't got hold of it yet.'

'I will get you a copy. I am his editor as well.'

'Ah! Are you? Am I sitting with someone really important?' said the girl, grinning. 'I should be more courteous then. Maybe wearing these pyjamas wasn't a wise choice.'

The girl laughed and covered her lips with her fingers. She might have been in her pyjamas but her lipstick was precise and hot. Jayanti wondered what it would be like to kiss her. Her mind went to the first time she had kissed a girl. She was in eighth standard. It wasn't sexual. It was just a thing to do. It felt thrilling and nice and wet and warm. It was long after that that she kissed her first boy. She had kissed both men and women since and had not been able to tell apart which was more fulfilling. She stared at Shreyasi's full lips as she spoke.

'I will look forward to the copy,' said Shreyasi. 'It will be fun to read my name in print.'

'Though you might not like me after,' said Jayanti.

'Who says I like you now?'

Sharp girl, thought Jayanti. 'Okay, let me amend that. Like is a soft word. Instead, you will hate me. I edited the book to make it read more like Karthik's books—the constricting, limiting love you mentioned. The brand of books you don't like.'

'But you already had Karthik Iyer? Why would you need two?'

Not so sharp now, thought Jayanti. 'For the same reason you are here despite having a man to go back to. I like to keep my options open too.'

The girl lifted the empty glass of iced tea in the air as if to toast her. And then she asked, 'Are you sure you don't want anything?'

'Actually I wouldn't mind another coffee,' said Jayanti.

They both got up and walked to the counter. Jayanti ordered herself a latte and the girl asked for another iced tea. While they waited, the girl put a casual hand over Jayanti's right shoulder and asked, 'So it must give you a lot of kick having these authors and their stories by their balls, right?'

'No one has anyone by the balls. They can walk out, choose a different publisher any time they want to,' said Jayanti. She was doubly aware of Shreyasi's lingering hand over hers. Slowly, she started to draw little triangles on Jayanti's hand with her nails.

'And yet, they are with you, willing to change their books for you. Aren't you a witch?' said the girl and winked at Jayanti.

'Witch is one of the better words that have come to describe me.'

'Don't forget me when you successfully make Daman into a Karthik Iyer clone,' said the girl.

'I didn't think we meant to remember each other,' said Jayanti. Just then their drinks came. As they walked back, Jayanti put her hand on the exposed small of Shreyasi's back. She wouldn't have stopped at that if they were back at her place. She would have pushed her on to her bed.

'I get lonely when my husband travels.'

'And when he doesn't?' asked Jayanti.

A smile passed between the two of them. They spent the rest of the night together.

19

'Did you read it?' asked Daman, too excited to sit.

Daman's fingers still ached from all the typing. The pain was sharp in the first week and he would have to dip his fingers in hot water to rest the joints. But by the second week it had reduced to a slow, niggling thrum. It was like a little taste of arthritis before time. He had typed furiously for a fortnight, hunched over his laptop, leaving his writing post only to shit and bathe and collect food from the door. He hadn't visited his parents or seen Avni. He had switched off his phone and all his calls had gone to voicemail. He hadn't checked his mails or Facebook or Twitter. The newspapers lay stacked and untouched in the corner. The kitchen stank from the mould that had gathered over the unfinished pizza slices. Once finished, he had read and edited and rewritten endlessly till his ten-page synopsis of the sequel to *The Girl of My Dreams* read like a story. After running a spelling and a grammar check, he shot it across to Avni.

He couldn't wait to hear what she had to say about it. 'I did,' said Avni. 'It's very good.' She stared at her coffee, stirring it.

'You don't have to lie. It's only an abstract. I can still juggle a few things around. What's wrong with it? If you can just tell me I will mark it out.' Daman took a pad and a pen out of the drawer and sat next to Avni. He scratched out NOTES in a scraggly hand on the page.

Avni took the pad from his hand and kept it away. 'I'm not a writer. Whatever I say might not be of any value.'

Daman took the pad again. 'But you are a reader and that matters. Now tell me?'

'Daman. I should first probably apologize. You're a good writer and I should have read your first book earlier. The synopsis was brilliant.' She smiled.

'Are you serious?'

'I loved it. Apart from certain stretches which I think can be made crisper, it was extraordinary. I wanted to read more.'

Daman saw Avni's eyes light up when she said that. Daman didn't think her words would matter as much as they did. He felt confident, happy.

'But then I read it over and over again,' she said in a small voice.

Of course she did, she's a stickler, thought Daman. No wonder she took so much time to revert.

'I also read a few other books in the same genre, books that have sold millions of copies worldwide and have good reviews.'

'You did that for me?'

'Of course I did. Who else would I do this for?' She smiled and put her hand on Daman's. 'Anyway, I made a list of things I thought worked for me in those books and what didn't. I picked the books that were closest to your genre and I made some notes. I will mail you the other points. But there's just one glaring problem with the book and I know you're going to flip when I say it.'

'What is it?'

'Shreyasi.' Daman rolled his eyes. 'See, you're already getting defensive. Hear me out . . . Don't walk away. The girl Shreyasi isn't the problem.' Daman turned. She said, 'The problem lies somewhere else.'

Daman's face darkened. He pulled a chair and sat down.

'I read *The Girl of My Dreams* as well. Both the book version and the one in the posts. Do you know some forums have all those posts? Anyway, I never thought I would say this but I actually liked Shreyasi's character. She's fun, she's crazy and the main guy seems to be in love with her. It's all a little mental but it works.'

Daman was surprised to see her smile; it was hard to digest she was the one who wrote a scathing review of the book a few months ago.

'Then what's the problem in the sequel?'

She sighed. 'The guy doesn't seem to be in love with her. The first book was perfect. But the conviction seems to be missing in the second. I read through the synopsis over and over again. I thought I was being biased because, you know, reading your boyfriend's name with another girl isn't every girl's dream. But I loved the first book, the posts, everything. All that is missing in this synopsis of the second book. Daman isn't in love with Shreyasi. It couldn't feel it at all. It felt like you're trying too hard. It just feels a little clunky. The character is still brilliant, it's their relationship that's the problem. It feels a little make-believe. Maybe you will iron it out when you start writing the chapters.'

She's got it right, thought Daman. This thought had bothered him as well when he wrote the synopsis. The first few days he had been sporadically distracted by thoughts of Shreyasi. He had battled, often fruitlessly, to not think of Shreyasi's face when he wrote about the character. He had thought he had done a decent job keeping the real person and the character separate but it looked like he had failed. *There's no conviction because Shreyasi is back and I'm not in love with her*, he thought.

'Is there anything else?' asked Daman.

'Yes. Now I was thinking about the book over the past few days and I might have found an answer to the Shreyasi problem.' Daman leant forward. She continued, 'Keep Shreyasi as she is. Don't change her. Let her be in her own space but add another character. A nice girl. Beautiful. Lovable. I'm not saying you have to love the character but put it in because people will like that. Think of it like an insurance, even if they don't like Daman and Shreyasi in the book, they might like Daman's new best friend. What do you say?'

This would please Jayanti, thought Daman. For the next half an hour, Avni sold him the idea even better than Jayanti could. *But what do I do about Shreyasi? Why the fuck did she have to come back?* Avni pressed on.

'It's not that bad an idea,' said Daman. 'All I need to do is make the main guy like this new girl and we are done.'

Avni blinked at him. 'I have thought of a name as well for the new character. It starts with an A. Just saying.'

'Oh, c'mon.'

'What? That's the least any boyfriend could do!'

'Fine. I will think about it,' said Daman.

An hour later, Avni left Daman so that he could start rewriting the synopsis with two aims in mind—to make the love story of Daman–Shreyasi credible and add a new character, Avni. The first few sentences were tough. After thirty minutes of tapping around unsuccessfully, he started writing about Avni. It came easy to him. The character Avni, the supposedly perfect girl—loosely based on his girlfriend— was sweet tongued but opinionated, wily but cute, ambitious and successful, and she was in love with the main guy. He spent the next few hours writing feverishly to fuse Avni into the storyline without changing the DNA of the book. It was morning by the time he finished writing it. The first thought that came to his mind was what Shreyasi would think about another girl stealing the thunder from her. After unsuccessfully trying to shake that thought off, he logged into his mail and checked if Shreyasi had mailed him in the preceding days. And there it was, buried between mails from Amazon, Flipkart and every website he had ever made an account on, a mail from Shreyasi.

From : shreyasibose07@gmail.com
To : damanroy111@gmail.com

Hi.
    I hope you do a good job with the synopsis.
Don't disappoint me. Don't listen to Jayanti
or Avni. Do justice to my character and our
love story. That's all I ask for. Best of
luck, baby.
    Shreyasi, *The Girl of Your Dreams*

Well, fuck her, he thought and went to sleep.

20

'Is she there yet?' asked Avni.

'She's stuck in traffic. Where have you reached?' asked Daman. 'You better reach here before I sign the stupid contract.'

Avni laughed. 'You will be okay, Daman. I will reach there in fifteen. I can see a constable staring right at me. Bye.' She disconnected the call.

Daman kept the phone aside and buried himself in the book he had brought with him. He had been on the same page for long, reading and rereading a certain passage when his concentration, or the lack of it, was punctuated by the sound of the chair scraping against the cold, hardwood floor. He looked up. Before he could form a sentence, Shreyasi had already slipped into the chair, her bag was on the table, and she was sitting cross-legged in front of him.

'You?'

'C'mon. You can't be completely surprised to see me. I'm sure a day doesn't go by when you don't think about me. You have been waiting for us to meet and talk, haven't you? You must have questions. Many, I suppose.'

'Shreyasi, you—'

'I'm a little overdressed for this cafe. Akash and I are going to his friends' house for a lunch. I didn't want to be the bedraggled wife. Being married is quite tiring. Tell me, are you having those nightmares still?'

'That's none of your business,' said Daman and slammed the table with his fist. 'You shouldn't be here. It's too late for whatever you're trying to achieve. You can't just walk out and walk into my life whenever the fuck you want to. I don't remember anything about you and I don't want to. Do you get that?'

Shreyasi's brows knitted together. She breathed in, her face flushed with anger. She smiled beneath the anger and said, 'You're angry because of those mails I sent you when you woke up from the coma? Or are you pissed that I'm married now?'

'All I know is you shouldn't be here, okay? You presence is fucking jeopardizing my book. Whatever the fuck happened between us, it's too late now. Just leave and don't ever contact me again.'

Shreyasi's eyes had turned red. A tear escaped one of her eyes and traced its way from her cheek to her chin. She said, her voice low as a whisper, sodden with guilt, 'I know you're angry with me, baby. But I was engaged when I met you in Goa. You were dying the time I left the hospital. I tried my best to stall the wedding but my parents didn't listen. You were still in a coma when I completed four months of my marriage. The doctors said you could wake up as a child or a paraplegic if you do at all. What was I supposed to do? I prayed to God every day for you to wake up. And then you did and remembered my name. Since then all I lived for was what you used to write in those stories using my name and yours. The Shreyasi in those posts was me, Daman was you. I thought that's going to be our love story.'

'What does this even mean now?' said Daman. 'I just used your name. That's it. That's where it ends. I wasn't thinking about you when I was writing before, okay? I don't remember anything about you. You need to stop doing whatever you are doing.'

She shook her head and wiped her tears. 'Daman, how much do you remember from the night of the accident?'

Daman looked at her. Every time their eyes met, he searched in vain for a trigger that would fill all the blank spaces in his memories, open the floodgates of lost time, and remind him of what exactly happened that night. For months he had sought a face in those faint remembrances, the dreams, the nightmares, but now when the face was staring back at him, he couldn't place it in the stories in his head. It was peculiar and disappointing. The girl he had fantasized and dreamt about, with whom he had imagined a vivid love story, with whom he had conjured up a past and future, made him feel nothing. NOTHING. Except a little niggling fear.

'I remember most of it.'

'Who was driving?' asked Shreyasi.

'You were,' said Daman. 'If you are Shreyasi that is.'

'Why would you still doubt that I'm Shreyasi if you remember most of it?'

Daman felt trapped. He said, 'I just don't remember your face.'

Shreyasi shook her head derisively. 'And what do you remember from before the day we went on the drive?' Daman drew a blank. *We just spent a little time in the car. Nothing more. Or did we?*

'You do remember, baby. It's all in your subconscious, hidden,' she said. 'Otherwise how did you write what you wrote in those Facebook posts? The ones that were set in Goa? Those precise incidents?'

'I imagined them. That's what writers do.'

'Yes, writers imagine but not you. The nightmares aren't the only dreams you see about me, am I right?'

Yes. I have other nightmares. Or dreams if you can call them. But I don't see your face in them either. 'I think you should go,' said Daman.

The waiter got Shreyasi's coffee and placed it in front of her. 'I am here to tell you something,' she said. Her phone beeped. She took it out from her handbag, replied to the text and put it back in. 'That was Akash. He was asking me if I was done. He's picking me up in five minutes. I don't want to be late and you wouldn't want Avni to catch me here with you. How embarrassing it would be for her to know that she's just a mistress and that the girl she thought was a fan was your muse and soulmate and lover.'

'And what does that make your husband?' retorted Daman.

'A fool. He thinks I'm in love with him and I'm fine by that. As long as you keep our love alive in the books you write I want nothing else, baby. Even if it means spending the rest of my days with a man I don't love or even like. That's all I want, baby,' said Shreyasi and then added after a pause, 'And so when Jayanti is going to offer more money than you had asked for you're going to turn her down, do you understand?'

'What are talking about? How—'

'She will ask you to drop my character in the next book. She will ask you to stop writing about me.'

'That's preposterous. She is the one who suggested to keep Shreyasi and Daman as the names in the first book,' argued Daman. 'All this is nonsense, Shreyasi. No one cares whose name I use in the book!'

'Didn't she make you use my name in the first book? Today, she will make you use Avni's and Avni is going to support her. Isn't Avni too coming today?'

'What has that to do with anything?'

'Who suggested that Avni be a part of this meeting? You? Avni? Or did Jayanti plant the seed inside your head? Think? What did she say? Was it . . . "Why don't you get Avni along? We can sign the contract and then head over to a nice place for lunch. It's a Saturday so she wouldn't be working." Is that what she said? Or was it . . . "Go through the contract thoroughly this time? Make someone read it? Someone from your family? Or maybe that girlfriend of yours?" Who planted the idea?'

'I wanted Avni to be with me,' lied Daman.

'It's a surprise you're a writer when you make for such a bad liar. Anyway, let's just assume Jayanti puts forward the notion. What will your answer be?'

'I don't know.'

'Your answer will be NO, baby. Are you not listening to me? Didn't you just hear what I said before? I will not suffer the humiliation again. Do you hear me, Daman? I will not have that bitch replace me in the book. I will—'

'ENOUGH! That girl is my girlfriend. And you're . . . no one,' grumbled Daman.

'No one? I'm the love of your life, Daman. You know that. I love you, baby. You're the only part of my life that I like and treasure. What will I do if even your words abandon me? That's all I care about.' Her eyes burned red and glistened with tears.

'What are you even talking about? I will do whatever I feel like.'

'No, you won't,' said Shreyasi, her voice stern. Tears streamed down her face. 'I'm asking you nicely to not test my patience and my love for you. Don't make me the bad person in this. I'm trying to help.'

'You should leave.'

'You don't have any manners left now, do you?' said Shreyasi, picking up her bag. She wiped her tears. She got up and took a step closer to Daman. She bent and placed a soft kiss on Daman's right cheek. 'I love you, baby. Reject her proposal or . . .' she whispered in his ears. Then she turned and left the cafe, sobbing. Daman remembered what his mother had told him continually over the months—getting into that car with her was a mistake. Shreyasi was crazy.

21

When Avni walked in and sat where Shreyasi had fifteen minutes ago, she didn't notice the cup of coffee Shreyasi had ordered and not touched. The waiter whisked it away at Daman's behest.

'Are you nervous?' asked Avni.

'A little.'

Avni shifted her chair close to Daman and warmed his hands till Jayanti came striding in twenty minutes later and apologized profusely for being late. She told them she got caught in an early-morning meeting with her boss.

'Do you want something?' asked Avni.

'I'm good. It's so good to see you again, Avni. How have you been? Good?'

Avni nodded. 'I hope you have got good news for us.'

'Only good news,' said Jayanti and smiled at Daman who grinned weakly. She continued, 'I talked to my seniors and we are committed to making Daman our next big author. The first book is doing well and all we need is to work towards making sure all the subsequent books work. You are one of our biggest talents and we want to treat you as such.'

Avni sensed Daman's discomfort at the nonsensical jargon Jayanti spewed.

'We have decided on an approach on how we treat you as an author,' said Jayanti. 'The earlier we fix on a direction the better it will be for us. Marketing wise, we will put all our efforts in that direction. Of course we understand monies will be a major concern so we have taken care of that. I made my team and my seniors understand that the payment terms need to change and that we need to give you all the support you need.'

Look at her talk. One might be fooled into believing she actually means these words, thought Avni. Avni looked at Daman who was staring stone-faced at Jayanti, unmoved by her drivel.

'So you asked for 10 per cent royalty, a 5 per cent bump over your current percentage, and believe you me it was tough for me to get them to agree to it—'

Avni interrupted Jayanti. 'Isn't 10 per cent the royalty for the majority of your authors? Why would that be hard for Daman to get? That should be a given.'

'It was tough because I wasn't aiming for 10 but for 12 because he's so important for us,' said Jayanti with a self-satisfied smile.

Avni had walked right into the trap. Not wanting to get beat, Avni asked, 'And what's the advance money?'

'He asked for 10 lakh, we are ready to offer him 14. And we will back him with whatever is needed.'

'What's the bad news?' asked Daman, scowling. 'You're not this benevolent. What are you asking of me instead? Do I need to wear an anklet? Submit my passport?'

'You insult me, Daman. I am just looking out for you. You're my author—'

Avni cut in. 'Let's not do this. Can we talk specifics? We don't want to get sucked into something we will regret later.'

Jayanti looked away from Avni and towards Daman. 'Look, it's nothing we hadn't discussed before. The night you called me and said you wanted to sign up you agreed to making some changes to the book. That's all I want from you. There will be no hidden clauses in the contract.' She looked at Avni and said, 'You can read it too if you want to.'

'But what kind of changes in the book are you looking for?' asked Avni.

Jayanti leant into her chair. 'Oh, it's nothing major. We all know the problems and the arguments we had regarding

Shreyasi. The entire editorial team read your synopsis. And we all thought that—'

Daman softly muttered, as if almost to himself, 'We should drop Shreyasi from the book?'

Jayanti was taken by surprise. 'Yes, exactly! Now that we have Avni's character in the book we thought keeping Shreyasi is superfluous,' said Jayanti. Avni tried hard not to smile but she suspected Jayanti noticed it. Jayanti continued, 'People lapped up the first book because they thought it was all true.'

'And now you want Avni in the book because my readers know I'm dating her,' said Daman.

'Daman, you know it's a good idea,' said Jayanti. 'The entire editorial team backs it. They love the story otherwise—'

Daman slammed the table. 'Who the fuck cares who I am dating and who I write about in the book? I'm not doing what Karthik does. I'm not going down that path. I can't do it,' said Daman.

Avni clutched his hand. Why, her eyes seemed to scream.

'The deal hinges on that,' said Jayanti.

'Daman, let's think this over,' implored Avni, still reeling from how quickly Daman had turned it down despite the money. 'There's no need to rush into it. We can go back home and think about it.'

'My seniors want an answer today,' insisted Jayanti.

Daman frowned. 'You are your senior. You answer only to the CEO, so stop saying things like the editorial team and your seniors. You're just arm-twisting me into this. Why don't you write the book yourself?' spat out Daman.

'I am not the writer, you are.'

Avni interrupted, 'Jayanti? Can you give us a second alone? We will—'

Daman shot Avni an icy look. 'There's nothing to talk about. I won't be another Karthik Iyer.'

'The deal won't stand without it.'

'Fine,' said Daman. 'I will find another publisher.'

Jayanti suppressed a smile. 'No one has the resources to do what we can do for you. We are also committing to a marketing plan of almost the same amount to build you as a brand. So effectively, that's a lot of money we are spending on you as a writer to make you into a brand.'

'Fuck your brand,' grumbled Daman.

Avni felt a growing tightness in her neck. *How can he turn this down? Is he blind to see what he stands to gain out of this? Why can't he get over the godforsaken name?*

'I think it's a great opportunity,' said Avni, steeling her voice. 'It could change your life. It's a lot of money to turn down, Daman'

'She's right,' said Jayanti. 'I need to leave this meeting with an answer. It's either this way or that.'

Daman buried his face in his palms and rubbed his face. *Please say yes*, thought Avni. He then leant back in his chair and stared listlessly at his hands. A little later, he agreed to the proposal.

22

Daman had thought of the freedom that awaited him when he first signed on with Jayanti. No bosses, no deadlines and no presentations—he would be paid to tell stories. How swiftly things had changed. He had left his job, fought with his parents and moved out, all to be a pawn in Jayanti's list of authors. A second Karthik Iyer, a knock-off. *At least the money is good*, he told himself. He put his arm across Avni and hugged her close. They had come home tired from their meeting with Jayanti. Avni had promptly fallen asleep. Daman had stayed up and stared at the ceiling.

'Are you awake?' asked Daman.

'Hmmm.'

She turned and buried her face in Daman's chest. She kissed him softly. 'Do you remember the first time I lay naked in your bed?'

'You were a shy little thing,' said Daman, twirling the smooth curls of Avni's hair.

Avni smiled. 'It was my first time.'

'You came over your shyness really quick,' remarked Daman. 'Not that I am complaining.'

'Only because I had imagined us a lot of times before it happened,' said Avni and turned away from him.

Daman's nakedness pressed against her. 'And was it just like you imagined it to be?' He cupped Avni's bare breast and drew circles around her nipple.

'More or less.' Daman frowned. She said, 'It wasn't anything to do with you. I had dreamt and thought and worried about what orgasms would be like. I read somewhere that it was like waking a dragon in your loins, others said it was like slipping into deep sleep, some even told me it was like space travel, weightless and limitless . . . there were no boundaries to my imagination. So no matter what you did, it would have been a little underwhelming. The standards I had set in my mind were humanly impossible to match.' She turned and slipped her hands south. She stroked him slowly. Daman kissed her and she put the free arm around him. She continued, 'Is reality underwhelming?'

'Why are you asking me that?'

'Are we underwhelming? You and me together? Is what we have less, compared to what your characters have in your book? Are you disappointed in us?'

'Avni, you can't think like that,' said Daman.

'It is just what it is. Sometimes I wish we had met in a more interesting fashion, something you could have written about. No one is going to be a big fan of, "Oh, they met in front of their office buildings, started talking, and just kind of started going out."' She chuckled pitifully.

'I will come up with something,' said Daman.

'But will I ever beat Shreyasi?'

Daman held her tighter. Daman thought of telling her where Shreyasi's name came from. *But will her questions stop then? What possible good will come out of her knowing that I believed Shreyasi was the love of my life till I met Avni? What will she think when she knows Shreyasi's back and that she loves me? Will she believe that I don't love Shreyasi?* Before Daman could say anything, his phone rang. *Jayanti Raghunath calling.* 'I need to take that.' Daman answered just before the last ring.

'Hello?' he said sitting up on the bed. Avni pinned her ears to the phone.

'Hi Daman. Is it a good time to talk?' asked Jayanti.

'Yes, tell me?'

'I was sitting with my marketing team and we were ironing out the deal and the timelines. We were thinking of

placing your book towards the end of next year. Will that be
okay by you?'

'What are you talking about?'

'It will give us some time to manage the marketing around
your book, that's all.'

'Are you fucking kidding me?' Daman got up, his free
fist clenched, blood running to his face. 'Why would you
need eighteen months to publish a book, Jayanti? What on
earth could you be doing sitting on the book for eighteen
months!'

'We need to—'

'Don't give me the marketing bullshit. At least try and
come up with a pretext that's more real. What is it?'

There was a small pause. And then she said, 'It's Karthik.'

'What about him?' probed Daman.

'He has pledged us two books in the same time period.
We need to push his books. He needs an open window both
before and after the second book. He has specifically asked for
your book to not coincide with his.'

'What does his books have to do with mine? What the
fuck does that even mean, Jayanti?'

'I would understand if you took your book elsewhere.
Things changed at the last moment. I tried convincing Karthik
but he's adamant.'

'What are you saying, Jayanti? What was all the garbage
you spewed in the morning about me being your top author
and what not? You're such a—'

'Daman, just check yourself there and think before you
say anything. Publishing is a small industry. Let's not say things
to each other we wouldn't be able to take back. Sooner or
later, we will have to work together.'

'Doesn't stop me from telling you that you're a fucking
slut—'

The line was disconnected. Daman let out a hoarse cry and swung wildly to throw his phone away. He restrained himself when he saw Avni's terrified face. Daman was still heaving from the anger, his blood boiling when his phone rang again. It was an unknown number. He received the call.

'Hello?'

'Are you with her?'

'Excuse me?'

'You can't even recognize my voice? Walk away from that whore of yours. I need to tell you something,' said the voice.

Daman walked to the washroom. He hadn't noticed the tears in his eyes. 'It's a literary agent,' Daman told Avni and locked himself inside. He lowered the lid of the commode and sat on it.

'Yes?'

She spoke in an urgent whisper, 'What did I say will happen? I had asked you not to test my patience. Jayanti pulled the plug on the deal, didn't she?'

'How . . . how . . .'

'You have to listen to know why Karthik did what he did. Check your mail. I have sent you a little video,' said Shreyasi.

Daman did as instructed. He downloaded and played the thirty-second video. It was grainy and shot from an awkward angle but Daman knew who it was in the video—a drunk, slurring Jayanti Raghunath. He put the phone to his ear to listen closely to what seemed like a conversation between Jayanti Raghunath and Shreyasi.

'Karthik is good but I don't see him going anywhere in the long run. Readers will tire of him. That's why I'm trying to push Daman.'

'You think Daman is a better writer than Karthik?'

'Of course. Though Daman needs to learn a few things, nothing a substantial hike in royalty can't take care of.'

'So you're thinking of making him bigger than Karthik?'

'Why not if he can be? He just needs to listen to me. That Shreyasi girl? She needs to go from his book.'

The two women laughed and the video abruptly came to an end. He played it again.

'Hello?'

Daman put the phone to his ear. 'Karthik saw this?'

'And pushed you out of the equation. Didn't I tell you to not test my patience? Rather than write about Avni, instead of me, you don't write at all, baby. It's better this way.'

'Why are you doing this?'

'For love, Daman.'

The line was disconnected.

23

Daman had been waiting for an hour for his turn at the Vodafone outlet before his token number flashed on the LED screen and he was summoned by a tired-looking customer service executive who had a rehearsed smile on him.

'How can I help you?'

'Hi, I'm Daman. I need a little help. Here's a number,' said Daman, and slipped a piece of paper in front of the woman. On it was written the number Shreyasi had called from. It had been three days and all the calls to Shreyasi had gone unanswered. Daman had to undo this. He needed the deal to go through. 'I need to know where the person who owns this number lives.'

The woman looked at the piece of paper and then slid it back towards Daman. 'Sorry sir, I can't reveal names or addresses of our customers. It's against the company policy. Is there something else I could help you with?' The woman smiled at him.

'I understand but this is a special case. I got a call from this number and I need to know who has sent me the text.'

The woman shook her head. 'I can't do anything, sir. Is there anything else I can help you with?'

'Are you not listening to me? I got an important call from this number. I'm asking for specific help and you're asking me if I need help with anything else? No, I don't! I just want to know the address of the crackpot you sold this number to. Can I get that information, ma'am? Because that's clearly your responsibility.'

She smiled again. Daman wanted to knock out her perfect set of teeth.

'No, sir. I'm not at liberty to disclose that.'

'Are you out of your mind—'

'There's no need to raise your voice, sir.'

'I will do whatever the fuck I want to do. Just look into your laptop and tell me who this person is and I will be on my way, okay? It's not that tough,' said Daman with as much calm as he could muster.

'I can't do it.'

'No one will know. I will pay you for it.'

The girl looked around, leant forward and whispered, 'Three thousand.'

'Done.'

The woman tapped an awful lot of keys for fetching a simple piece of information.

'What's your name, sir?'

'I'm Daman. What do you need that for? Just tell me the address,' he said, pulling out the wallet from his back pocket.

There was a pause before the woman spoke.

'This number is registered to you, sir,' said the woman.

'What! What are you talking about? Are . . . are you sure!'

The woman turned the computer screen towards him. She also showed the scanned copy of the document submitted, Daman's driving licence, and a signed form Daman had apparently filled up. It had a close copy of Daman's signature but he knew it wasn't his. Daman wiped the astonishment off his face, lied and apologized to the disgruntled woman, how all of it was a big misunderstanding, and left the place.

Just as he stepped inside his car, his phone rang. It was the same number.

'Hello?'

'I see that you have missed me,' said Shreyasi.

'Listen.'

'I can meet you tomorrow evening if you feel like. It's not as if you're busy.'

'Where?'

'Karthik is doing a book reading at Oxford. Come? It will be fun and we can talk things out.'

'Okay, but—'

'We will talk then. Got to go. Bye.'

24

The next day, Daman was in the metro hurtling towards Connaught Place. He wasn't even at the venue yet and he had already spotted two groups of giggly teenagers talking about how exciting it would be to see Karthik Iyer in flesh and blood. Daman thought they would break down in tears any moment. Daman reached the venue at 5.45 p.m., fifteen minutes before the event was supposed to start, but the bookstore was already chock-a-block with little girls jostling for the best view of the stage. There were a handful of guys who looked like they had been forced by their girlfriends or sisters to get a book signed by this demigod who moonlighted as an author. He stood at the far end of the room, staring at his phone. The calls to Shreyasi had gone unanswered. The couches on which Karthik Iyer and Jayanti Raghunath would sit, where he sat a few weeks earlier, were barely visible from where he stood. After twenty minutes, Karthik Iyer walked in amidst feverish cheers and gasps from the crowd. Daman thought he spotted a few girls with tears in their eyes. Another bunch professed their love to him in sentences from his books. Karthik smiled, winked and nodded at them. Karthik Iyer wasn't a bad-looking man and he seemed to know that. He stood at 6 feet 1 inch. Dressed in a crisp blue shirt which strained against his heavy biceps, navy blue denims and brown loafers, he looked as if he had walked out of a magazine shoot. But most of all, he had a pleasant face—a non-threatening, calm, smiling face. *So he's the guy who fucked me up. Insecure bastard*, Daman thought.

The session started. Karthik was a better speaker than him, more seasoned, and knew how to work the crowd. Every answer of his ended with applause or poignant nods. He regaled the star-struck crowd with stories of his childhood and of the days he had spent working as a botanist before he turned to writing full-time. The crowd lapped up his rehearsed words like thirsty crows. Daman searched for Shreyasi's face in that bustling scene to no success. When the conversation between Jayanti and Karthik ended on the stage and the microphone was being passed around, Daman raised his hand the highest. He was looked over a few times but the emcee finally noticed and the microphone was passed on to him. Jayanti shot Daman a look which he ignored.

'Hello, I'm Daman,' he said. 'Congratulations for the books you have written in the past and the one you're writing. I'm also a writer, though infinitely less successful. But don't you think that the success of your mediocre books is the reason why other authors don't get a chance to prove their worth? Like Jayanti Raghunath here, who's my editor as well, told me a couple of days back that they will have to shift my book's release to next year because they want to concentrate on yours. Do you think that's fair? That's my question.'

He passed the microphone back to the emcee. The crowd muttered profanities. 'Asshole!' 'So rude!' 'Jealous!' The girls in the crowd looked at Daman like they wanted to pull him apart limb by limb. He stared at Karthik who brought the microphone up to his beautiful face and chuckled.

'I'm a writer, Daman,' said Karthik. 'I write books. That's all I do. My job ends there. What happens after the book leaves my computer is not my business. If tomorrow my book is being read by just one reader, I would still write. So if you're asking me to stop writing and stop publishing my books, I think that's unfair. Also, I don't have any say . . .'

Daman had stopped listening at this point. Amidst the many people staring at him, he found Shreyasi's smiling face. Then she turned and left. Daman tried weaving his way out of the crowd but he was stuck.

He heard Karthik end. 'I hope I have answered your question.'

'THANKS!' Daman shouted back and started pushing his way out the crowd. In his anxiety to catch Shreyasi, he stepped over a few girls' toes. They cried out, 'Jerk!'

Finally, out of the crowd, he could breathe again. He looked to his left and then to his right. He found Shreyasi entering the little cafe adjoining the bookstore.

'Sit,' she said when she saw Daman. She was looking remarkably calm. 'Will you have something? You look like shit. When was the last time you took a shower?'

Daman pulled out a cigarette and lit it.

'You can't smoke in here,' said Shreyasi. Daman put it out. She continued, 'It is nice to see you again. I was glad to know we share our hatred for Karthik Iyer. He's just a . . . never mind. I'm sorry your book is getting pushed because of his—'

'It's getting pushed because of you!' snapped Daman.

'You're getting into semantics now. Their tea is good. You should try it.'

'How did you register this number under my name?'

'Always the curious writer, you,' said Shreyasi and laughed. 'But let's talk about what we are here for. I—'

Daman interrupted her. 'Before you say anything, I want to make it clear for once and all that I might have used your name, maybe conjured up the character of Shreyasi thinking of you, but there's nothing between you and me now. Whatever happened in Goa ended there. I got past it, Shreyasi, and you should too.'

'It's easy for you to say that.'

'Shreyasi . . .'

'You're not the one who remembers everything so stop telling me what to do.' She sighed. She took out her phone and tapped on it. 'Check your mail,' she said. 'Don't look at me. Check your phone.'

Daman fished out his phone and opened his mail. 'What is this?' he asked, seeing the attachments.

'These are my flight tickets and the hotel reservations of that trip to Goa,' she said. 'If you call Sumit, he will tell you that these are the same days you were in Goa as well. This was the same hotel you stayed in.'

Daman kept his phone aside. 'What's your point, Shreyasi?' he said.

Her eyes went soft. 'It wasn't just a car ride, baby.'

'What does that mean?'

'Your friends and mine put up at the same hotel in Goa. You and I didn't spend an hour but three days together falling in love. We hid from our friends and sneaked out. We went on never-ending drives, drank under the stars and made love, held hands till they were clammy and hoped time would stand still. I was already engaged so I thought of it as a last fling before marriage. Little did I know I would fall in love with you,' she said. 'Tell me, do you really think your friends sent you alone to get drinks for them?'

'Why—'

'You volunteered because you wanted to spend time with me. Okay, tell me this. Have you seen the pictures of your trip to Goa? In how many of those are you with Sumit? Did you never ask yourself why you were missing from those pictures? Because you were with me all the time.'

'There are no pictures. Sumit's data card got corrupted.'

'How convenient.'

'Oh please, Shreyasi. I am aware he might have deleted them to keep my PTSD at bay,' he said. 'Anyway it doesn't matter whether we spent a few hours or three days, you're married now and I don't feel the same any more. We should move on with our lives now and find our happiness elsewhere.'

'I don't wish to move on.'

'What will you have me do then?'

'Baby,' she said and reached out to hold his hand. Her eyes glistened with tears. 'While you lay sleeping in the hospital, there was a strange man in my bed, spreading my legs and thrusting himself inside me day after day. You know what kept me going? Your name, your memories, your face.' Tears streamed down her face. She wiped them and continued, 'And then you woke up and remembered me, my name. I came to see you but—'

'You never came to see me! They told me you had left the country,' grumbled Daman.

'Because they hated me. They believed it was because of me that you had almost died so they didn't let me meet you. They figured you would get to know the truth if I met you.'

'What truth?'

'What do you see in your dreams, Daman? Who drove that car? You or me?'

'It changes but mostly it is you,' said Daman.

'It was you. You drove the car. You drank and you looked at me and didn't notice the taxi on the wrong side,' said Shreyasi, matter-of-factly. 'Two people died that night.'

'But—'

'Every time you had a dream about you driving the car, your therapy was set back by five steps. You had a hard time dealing with the deaths. That's why they trained you into believing it was me who was driving that night. They lied to keep you sane,' she said. 'Don't they keep telling you that it was I who drove?'

'They do.'

'I don't blame them for wanting to keep me away from you,' she said. 'They wanted you to get better and so did I. They thought if you saw me you would remember that I wasn't driving, you were. If my absence helped you recover, so be it, I thought. I disappeared. I didn't want to worsen your illness.'

'Even if what you say is true, what do you want from me now?'

'Your words, baby. That's all I had,' she said. 'Despite my absence, you used my name and wrote about me. I knew I couldn't be with you but when I read those little stories, I could imagine being with you again. You were my happiness, you were everything to me but then . . .'

'The book came out with Jayanti's version of Shreyasi,' said Daman. 'Look, Shreyasi. I apologize if the book offended you but you have to realize I didn't know.'

Shreyasi frowned. 'You think I was offended? I wasn't offended. I felt bereft, I felt like something had died inside of me,' she said and threw him an icy look. 'And yet you were about to sign a book deal with her. One that doesn't even have me.'

'This is my career, damn it!'

'Don't raise your voice at me. You should know better than that,' Shreyasi warned.

Daman lowered his voice, 'I understand where you're coming from but what's in the past is best left in the past. We can be friends and put this to rest. There's no point dwelling on it any more.'

She laughed mirthlessly. 'We will never be friends. We are lovers and we will always be that. Here's what I want you to do. It's the same thing you want as well. Write Shreyasi well in the next book and it will make me very happy.'

Fuck her, he thought, *she's crazy*. To her he said, 'Firstly, there's no book contract yet, and secondly, I don't have creative control of the book.'

'You should concentrate first on writing the book. Jayanti comes later. The book contract will happen. I give you my word. Have some faith in me.'

'It's actually Karthik who—'

'He will be taken care of, love. Just write the book.'

'What if I don't?' asked Daman.

She got up. 'You will,' she said. She ran her fingers through Daman's hair. 'Because I love you very . . . very much,' she whispered in his ear and walked away.

25

It was a Monday morning and Avni found herself crouched in one corner of a bathroom stall, crying. It felt like she had been knifed in the back and it was slowly turning and twisting with every second that passed. This wasn't her. She was to be the model, non-intrusive, fun, one-of-the-guys kind of girlfriend who the other boys wanted for themselves. And what did she not do for Daman? She suffered his inane ambition to be an idealistic writer, put up with her nagging dad asking her to find a guy who worked a stable job at KPMG or Ernst & Young, and even refrained from texting Daman or calling him for days on end lest she disturb one of his creative outbursts, even when the pain of missing him was almost physical. That's what relationships are about. That's what loyalty is about. That's what life is about. You hammer away at it, you work at it, and you get results. *After all the nights I have spent worrying about him since his deal fell through, this is how he repays me?*

The previous evening she had met Daman after ten days. He looked like a shadow of himself, scrawny and shabby, his cheekbones protruding and his eyes sunken. He had aged years in a few days. Along with the deal, he had also crumbled. She could make out that he had been smoking way too much, and sleeping very little. It had taken a lot of coaxing for Avni to drag him out of his apartment that evening. He had mostly kept quiet, nodding and smiling weakly at whatever Avni said. He looked hungry but he ate little.

'It will be okay,' Avni found herself telling him over and over again.

When Daman excused himself to visit the washroom, Avni had checked Daman's phone. She hadn't meant to do it. But his phone beeped incessantly and she only wanted to silence it. She would have just done that if she hadn't read the beginning of a text that flashed on the screen. Curiosity and fear got the better of her. She swiped open the phone and read the string of texts from an unsaved number.

Don't write about her.
I love you.
It would kill me to see someone else's name in print other than me.
I love you, Daman.
She doesn't love you the way I love you. If you write about me, I will make this thing with Karthik go away.
And the last one. I love you. Always yours, Shreyasi.

She didn't question Daman when he came back from the washroom. She told him some work had come up and left.

Twelve hours later, she was still trying to fight the truth she had learnt. She toyed with her phone, trying to think of what she would say to him. She couldn't even bring herself to be angry at him. *I'm so stupid! How could I believe that Shreyasi wasn't real? She was there all the time. How could I have been so blind!* She mustered up the courage to dial Sumit's number instead. They decided to meet in an hour. Avni left the washroom stall, washed her face, and reapplied her make-up before she left the office. Sumit was waiting for her when she reached the cafe. It was the same cafe Daman and Sumit would wait for her to come to after she wrapped up work when they had first started dating. She would change out of her office clothes and into little black or silver or yellow dresses in the washroom to go clubbing with them. The latch of the washroom had always been suspect. Once Daman had opened the door and clicked a hazy, unrecognizable picture of her peeing. For the next week, he had been insufferable, threatening to send it to all her colleagues. The joke went stale soon enough, but after that it would always be Sumit who stood guard at the door as she changed.

'Hi,' he said and got up to hug her.

'Hi.'

'What happened? Is everything okay?'

'Did you tell Daman we are meeting?' asked Avni.

'No, but—'

'Thank you.'

The waiter placed two menus in front of them and looked on expectantly. Avni ordered two cappuccinos for them. It took her all her might not to burst out in little sobs. *Everyone lied to me, even Sumit. I took him for a friend*, she thought before she spoke.

'I wanted to ask you something. And I want you to be true to me. I know the half-truth so there's no point in lying any more.'

'What is it?'

'Who's Shreyasi?'

Avni saw Sumit's face darken. 'Why are you asking me that?'

'She's not just a character in the book, is she?'

The waiter got their coffees and placed them in front of them. They would remain untouched for the rest of evening.

Sumit sighed and spoke, 'I had asked Daman to tell you about the nightmares.'

'What nightmares?'

Sumit told Avni all that he knew, the accident, the therapies, the PTSD and the psychogenic amnesia. Avni listened to him with rapt attention. All she knew was Daman had been in a debilitating accident; everything else was news to her.

'Is that all?' asked Avni.

'Yes, that's all.'

'Are you sure there's nothing more to this?'

'I'm sure.'

Sumit's lies made Avni bristle. 'So you're telling me the girl walked away and never once contacted Daman?'

'No, she didn't.'

Avni slammed the table. 'When will you guys stop lying!' The coffee cups clanked. Coffee was spilt. Her palm stung.

The accusation made Sumit squirm. 'Look, Avni, she didn't, okay! Daman tried to get in touch with her but that's where it ended. The email ID I gave him was the one created by me. It was I who posed as Shreyasi and asked him to leave her alone. I will show you the mails. Wait.' Sumit pulled out his phone from his back pocket and tried signing into a mail ID, shreyasibose07@gmail.com. The mail ID spat out every password combination Sumit tried. Incorrect password. 'I must have forgotten the password. You've got to believe me. I'm not lying. I hated that whore and wanted Daman to just stop fucking obsessing over her. It wasn't worth it. The girl nearly drove Daman to his death!'

Avni watched Sumit carefully. *He's not lying*, she thought. Sumit's face had turned scarlet in anger and the vein on the side of his forehead throbbed visibly. The mail ID had been auto-filled as he started to type 'shr' . . . that meant Sumit had at one point in time signed in using the name.

Sumit continued, 'Why are you asking me all this? Did he tell you something?'

'No.'

'Then?'

'It's because Shreyasi is back.'

'How is that possible?'

'She's in love with Daman. She wants him back.'

'What nonsense is this? She can't do that! There must be some mistake,' Sumit spat angrily.

Avni shook her head. 'I read texts from her on Daman's phone.'

26

'Do you love me?' she asks. The words come out in a gurgle of blood and tissue. Her jaw is broken and twisted in places. The car is suspended mid-air. It's the second flip. I'm still in the driving seat. My hands are off the steering wheel. I'm bracing myself for the impact. My leg is broken and twisted at an awkward angle. A searing pain grips me. The car lands on the roof and spins. The jerk nearly snaps my back. She reaches out for me. A bone has splintered in her forearm and broken the skin. It juts out grotesquely. I want to touch her. 'I do,' I say. But before my words can reach her she's thrown out of the car with a violent jerk, like a fired cannonball. The wind is kicked out of her. The car turns again. I lose sight of her. And then, everything catches fire.

A startled Daman woke up to the thundering horn of a passing truck. He was drenched in sweat and his hands shook like a tuning fork. His car was parked on the side of a busy road. But . . . He was driving to the British Council. He had no clue how he ended up there. It was sundown and the traffic was on the rise. He started the ignition and throttled the air conditioner. With a rag he found in the glove compartment, he wiped his seat and then himself. He had just put the car into drive when he noticed the missed calls on his phone. Avni. He would call her later. *There's no need to bother her with this. She's worried enough.* The last time they met Avni had been scared shitless seeing him unshaven and weak. 'It will be okay, something better will come along,' she had said a thousand times that evening. Little did she know that it wasn't the deal but the nightmares that had been wringing Daman like a washerwoman's coarse hands. For the first time, there was something consistent in all the dreams and the nightmares. He was driving. Ever since Shreyasi had told him this little detail it was like his body was physically trying to not accept the possibility. *So what if I was driving? What changes?* He ran a fever on most nights but it would subside in the mornings. He had dared not tell his parents about it or they would descend to his apartment like the army and get him admitted to a hospital.

By the time he reached home, there were fifteen more missed calls from Avni. He parked the car and climbed upstairs to his apartment. Even as he jumped the last couple of stairs, he could sense something amiss. As he took a few steps closer, he noticed that the door was ajar. Clenching his fists he tiptoed to the door. His heartbeat quickened, beads of sweat trickled down his forehead. He pinned his ear to the door. Someone was inside. He looked around for a bat or a rod or anything and found a piece of wood. Positioning himself a couple of yards away from the door, he kicked the door open and shouted something unintelligible in the air and then stopped mid-shriek . . . He dropped his hands.

'Fuck! What are you doing here? How . . . How did you get in?' asked Daman.

Her face was ice, her voice steel. 'Where's your phone?' Avni asked, her eyes sore from crying.

Daman flapped around for his phone and took it out. 'Must be on silent,' he said after looking at the screen.

Avni dialled his number and the phone rang. Daman disconnected the call.

'Silent, huh?'

Daman fumbled an apology.

'What's this, Daman?' asked Avni, pointing to the sheets of papers kept on the table.

Daman picked them up. They were the printouts he had taken of the synopsis of his next book but . . . He flipped through the sheets of paper. The lines had been brutally cut and censored. Big cross marks in black marker crowded the pages.

'Who's done this?' Avni asked aloud. The name Avni was systematically blacked out and the words SLUT, BITCH, WHORE, were written everywhere where Daman and Avni appeared in the same sentence.

'What . . . how . . .' He knew.

Avni's eyes smouldered. 'Please don't lie to me any more.' Her body shook with little sobs. She wiped off the tears on her sleeve. 'I know about Shreyasi. Sumit told me everything.'

'Let me explain—'

'When did she come back?' she mumbled. 'When were you thinking of telling me? She was here, wasn't she? She's the one who has called me a slut, hasn't she?'

Daman frowned.

Avni couldn't even bring herself to look at him. 'I read the texts from her. Have you guys slept together? How often does she come here? You still love her, don't you? How—'

'Enough.' Daman cut in. 'No one comes here, okay? I didn't cheat on you. And I didn't know about this fucking synopsis till you showed it to me!'

Avni wiped her tears with the back of her hand and looked at him. 'How much of a fool do you think I am? You go missing for days on end, don't pick my calls, and then there's this.' She pointed to the pages and looked back at him with questioning eyes. 'What did I do to you to deserve this?'

'Avni—'

'What kind of a person are you?'

'I'm not lying about anything, okay? Will you—'

'It all makes sense now,' she muttered, her words slurring between the sobs. 'This is why you didn't want to make me meet your parents. I'm so stupid. I'm so, so stupid. Shit.' She buried her face in her palms.

'Let me expla—'

'I should have listened to my friends. He's a writer. Don't date him. I made a fool out of myself, didn't I? I should have just said yes to the guy—'

'You need to stop crying and listen to me.'

'WHAT—'

'Don't shout, Avni. And FUCKING LISTEN TO ME. Yes, SHREYASI is back but I'm NOT dating her. I have met her only thrice.'

Avni threw her hands up. She picked up her bag to leave. Daman held her. 'Listen to me for five minutes,' he said. 'You remember the girl whom you gave a lift to on the day of the book launch? Ashi? It was Shreyasi, not Ashi. She met me with a different name at the British Council before that but I didn't know she was Shreyasi. Yes, I do get nightmares about her but I didn't remember her face. Didn't Sumit tell you that? I hardly remember anything from Goa. She stalked us. She stalked you. She even got to Puchku. She pretended to be a fan and walked her home one day from the metro station.'

'Why . . . why would she do that?' asked Avni, her face still blank.

'She didn't like the book. She thought I disrespected her in the book.'

'This makes no sense,' she said. Daman made her sit down and told her everything that had happened till then.

'How can you not remember anything from Goa?'

Daman told her about the PTSD and the dissociative amnesia. While Avni googled, he told her, 'Sometimes the mind locks away painful memories so that the body is saved from the trauma. It's a coping mechanism. It's common in kids who are molested by their relatives. The memories are locked so that their relationships with the perpetrators aren't affected.'

He told her how his family and Sumit had constantly reminded him that it was Shreyasi and not him who was driving the car. 'But she told me it was I who was behind the wheel. I can't seem to take it well.'

Avni closed the browser and put her phone away. 'So you're not in love with her?'

'Of course not.'

'But that means she also broke in here,' said Avni, looking at the synopsis of the book.

'It seems like she did.'

'This is serious,' she said. 'What are we going to do? Come sit here. Stop walking around. It's freaking me out even more,' said Avni. She took his hands into hers and rubbed them. She continued, 'I had no idea. I just—I'm so sorry. I just got so angry. I shouldn't have said those things.'

'I should have told you. I just thought it will pass.'

'So what are you going to do about her, Daman? She ruined your deal. God knows what she will do next.'

'We will have to talk her out of this somehow,' said Daman.

Avni sighed. She put her head on his shoulder and slipped her hands around him.

'Sumit was quite shocked to know that Shreyasi is back.'

'He hates her.'

'I sensed that,' she said. She added after a pause, 'Is there any way she is not Shreyasi?'

'What do you mean?'

'What if she's just a reader obsessed with you and your character? What if she modelled herself on the character once she found out that they shared the same name? Maybe she's just some random Shreyasi who's pretending to be the girl in the car.'

'I thought of that as well but that can't be,' said Daman. 'She mailed me from the same email ID that Shreyasi used to.'

'Daman? There's something you should know about that email ID. Maybe Shreyasi isn't back.'

27

A couple of hours after his numerous texts to Shreyasi had gone unanswered, Daman's phone rang.

'Hey. Hi, Shreyasi. I have been texting you all morning!'

'I know. I was out somewhere. What was so urgent?'

'I want to talk about us,' he answered.

'About us? This is a welcome start. So tell me, what do you want to talk about us?' she said.

'Not like this. I want to meet you. I want to do this in person.'

'Whoa. Tiger. Slow down. What happened? You're scaring me now. Did you remember something?'

'No, I didn't. It's still the same,' said Daman. 'Can you meet me right now?'

'I like whatever's gotten into you, baby. Where do you want to meet? Hey? Do you want to come over? Akash has gone to the embassy to sort out his visa. We will have a couple of hours. If you don't mind you can . . .'

'Umm . . . I don't think that would be wise. It would . . . feel wrong,' said Daman.

'Look at you, all morally upright. Fine, you pick a place and I will be there. Maybe I will tell you all that we had done together. You won't behave like such a goody two shoes then.'

'Hmmmm . . . Do you think you can come to South Extension? The Costa Coffee on the first floor in about an hour?'

'. . .'

'Are you there Shreyasi?'

'Yes, I'm here. I'm just a little overwhelmed . . .' Her voice trailed off. 'I'm just so happy that you came around, baby. Thank you so much, Daman.'

'So you will be there?'

'Of course I will be there.'

An hour later, Daman was waiting for Shreyasi at Costa Coffee, South Extension. He wore a crisp white shirt, blue trousers and a pair of black loafers. He tried Sumit's number again. All his previous calls had gone unanswered but this time Sumit answered the call. 'Hey? Where the hell were you? I've called you a hundred times at least since morning.'

'Only like ten.'

'Okay, listen. This is really important. First of all, I know Avni came to you and you're an asshole for not telling me that. Secondly, she also told me about the fake ID you created under Shreyasi's name. Now—'

'She asked me not to tell you. And you know I made that email for your good. You needed to stop thinking about her,' grumbled Sumit.

'Yeah, whatever, Bhaiya. But Shreyasi is back now.'

'Avni was telling me the same nonsense. I told Avni that the girl must be some obsessed reader, that's all. It couldn't be Shreyasi in a hundred years.'

'That's what we are beginning to think as well. If this Shreyasi is an imposter, there must be a real one out there, right? Avni and I spent the entire morning trying to get to some official of the hospital Shreyasi and I were taken to so I could get some records.'

'Did you find something?'

'The hospital shifted somewhere else and they only have records going back six months.'

'Oh.'

'We also tried contacting the police. But the FIR registered only had Shreyasi's first name. So we kind of hit a roadblock. But then, Avni suggested something. You must have seen Shreyasi in the hospital, right? If I send you a picture of Shreyasi, you can tell us whether it's her?' asked Daman.

'Um . . .'

'Please tell me, you would be able to recognize her,' urged Daman. 'Otherwise it's going to be a wild goose chase trying to confirm this girl's identity.'

'I . . . I . . . think I do remember her,' said Sumit.

Jackpot! Daman smiled. 'That's awesome! You fucking made my day, Bhaiya. Okay, look, I'm seeing her in a few minutes. I will try to click a picture and send it to you. If she's the girl, let me know ASAP, okay?'

'But I don't understand why you are doing all this? Are you still in love with Shreyasi?'

'Me? I broke out of that fantasy the minute it got real,' said Daman. 'Oh shit. She's here. I will just send a picture if I manage to get one.'

28

He noticed Shreyasi outside the coffee shop, looking at her reflection and fixing her hair. Dressed in a striped shirt and black pencil trousers, she looked striking. Pretending to look into his phone, he clicked a picture and shot it across to Sumit. Shreyasi smiled brightly when she noticed Daman and waved at him. She trotted towards him and hugged him. Daman placed his hands on the small of her back. She didn't let go for a few seconds. Daman waited for the picture to reach Sumit. The network was weak.

'Sit?' said Daman and pulled the chair back for her. She had been crying, he noticed. 'Did you have any trouble finding the place?'

Shreyasi giggled. 'You really remember nothing,' she remarked. 'This is the one of only two places you could sit and write. You told me that.'

'Did I tell you I wanted to be a writer?'

'Yes, you did. You never thought you would actually manage it but look at you now!' She beamed and held his hand. 'Do you want to eat something?'

They ordered a couple of wheat-bread sandwiches and coffee to go with it. While chewing through a big bite of her sandwich, mustard dripping from her fingers, she asked, 'So what did you want to talk about us? The sandwiches here are so good! Eat.'

Taking a small bite from sandwich, he asked, 'I want to know about us. Like you said, I remember nothing. How did we start dating? We were at the same hotel, right? But how did we start a conversation? Who approached whom? Who said the first line? You or I? What did we talk about?'

She has to slip up somewhere, Daman thought as he waited for her to answer. She smiled again, covering her teeth with a tissue. 'Is there a list of questions you have written down? I can mail my answers across if that suits you.' She licked her fingers and then wiped them clean.

'I want to reconstruct the events and chronology in my head. So what if I don't remember? I can imagine. I'm good at that,' said Daman and winked at her.

She held his hand and kissed it. 'Yes, you are. But I'm so happy we are doing this. Does Avni know that you're breaking up with her?'

Daman frowned. 'I never said I'm breaking up with her, Shreyasi. I have been with her for over a year. That's a lot more than the three days I spent with you. You asked me to write about you and not her. Isn't that why you slashed out the parts of the book?'

'That's true but—'

Daman cut in, trying to be as soft as he could with her. He kissed her hand and said, 'I don't see any reason for me to break up with her to achieve that, just like you don't have any reason to leave your husband. Am I right or am I missing something here?'

Her face hardened. 'There's a difference. You love her, you are attached to her, I know that now. I feel nothing for my husband. He can drown in his next posting for all I care,' she said coldly.

'Avni has given me a lot of her time and care and I can't be unfair to her,' argued Daman. 'You can understand because you have been in love—'

'Correction. I'm in love.'

Be gentle, Daman reminded himself. *Let her make a mistake.* 'Yes, you are in love and so you know how crushed she would feel. Both of you love me, but what I want to understand here is why I should give you precedence over her in my life and my book? Three days, that's all we shared. Make me understand what was it in those three days that should make me put you ahead of her?'

'. . .'

'Oh, c'mon. You can't cry. I'm just trying to reason with you,' said Daman and raised his hands.

'It was much more than three days.'

'Yes, I know that after—'

Shreyasi cut him. 'I have been with you longer, Daman. I have been in the shadows but I have always been there, guarding you, loving you, watching you. Before Avni, even before the accident, before Goa, before everything.'

'What are you talking about?'

With sad eyes and a smile on her face she said, 'You always wanted your love story to start in a library, didn't you?'

I never told anybody that. 'Yes. How do you know?'

'And that's exactly how we met in Goa.'

'So? What effect—'

'It wasn't by accident, it was planned. For you our love story in Goa must have been serendipity, a start of something wonderful, but I had planned it months in advance.' She ran her fingers over the side of his face. 'You might have met me for the first time in Goa but I had met you before. Several times. You might have just spent three days with me but I had spent months with you before that. Do you know where we first met?'

Daman shook his head. 'No.'

She smiled softly and looked around. 'Here,' she said. 'Three years ago. A year before the accident.'

'What do you mean?' asked Daman, totally at a loss.

'Remember your last year in college at DTU?'

'What has that to do with anything?' he asked.

'You used to come here quite a lot. You would finish the classes at your college and then take the 769 bus here. You could have taken the metro every day but you always chose the bus. It gave you an uninterrupted two hours to read the books you carried in your backpack.'

'How do you know all this?' asked Daman, shocked.

'Will you let me complete or are you going to keep interrupting me?'

'Go on.'

'More often than not, you would be in frayed grey T-shirts which you had too many of, jeans and chappals. You would get down at the bus stop and head straight to this coffee shop. Earlier, you usually ordered Americanos because they used to be cheaper. Sometimes you would get your own coffee sachets and add it to the water here when no one was looking.' She pointed to a desk with a couple of public computers on it. 'You only used to sit on that one. This is where I first saw you, hunched over a computer, typing the entire time I was here. Unlike the others, you didn't need anyone. You stared at the screen like no one existed. That's the day I felt something I hadn't ever felt before. I didn't know that feeling was love.'

'But—'

She continued as if he hadn't interrupted her. 'I started coming here more often to look at you. You were just another college boy here to finish your assignments, freeloading on the Internet here. I would sit on this seat where we are sitting now and watch you type endlessly. Sometimes, you would order a coffee and I would be standing right beside you. Sometimes, our bodies would touch. You would smile shyly and apologise. I started stealing the tissues you used, the cups your lips touched, the stirrers you held in your hands. Slowly, a little drawer in my cupboard became a treasure chest of your things. Before I knew it, a month had passed. You were a part of my life, the most important part. I used to look forward to the evenings. I would come here after my office hours and watch you for hours. All my weariness would get washed away by the sight of you. But one day, you just stopped coming. For a week, I sat where we are sitting right now and spent hours waiting for you. My heart broke. I had to do something. I traced you back to your college and found that your library had just got equipped with high-speed Internet. Now being in your college library every day without raising suspicion was tough so I had to lure you back to this cafe. And that's when you won the loyal-member card of this cafe that allowed you free coffee and a doughnut every time you came here. You thanked me for it by never writing in your college library again.'

Wha—How did she know all of this?

'You started coming here once more. We used to spend so much time together. You wrote, I looked at you write. It was a little crushing for my soul because you never noticed me. For months, I used to dress up in my finest outfits and sit right here and never once did you look up and catch my gaze. Maybe you were just shy. Slowly I realized you were trying to write a book. I saw how much you struggled with it. I could literally see the pain on your pretty face. I loved you and I pitied you and I loved you. I wanted to run to you and take you in my arms and assure you, I wanted to take you home, love you, show you the things I had of you, and tell you that you already had one fan for your unwritten book. Just like that weeks passed between us within a heartbeat. You sat there, trying to write your story. I sat here, watching you tussle with it. You never went beyond a few pages. Every day after you would leave, I would fetch your deleted stories from the Recycle Bin of the computer and read them. I would take printouts and take them home. I still have them all in a little file. They were all unfinished chapters, so beautiful, like our story.

'Every time I read them I felt I knew a bit of you and then I wanted to know more. I have never done drugs but I am thinking that's what it must be like. You want to shoot up just once, do just one line of cocaine and pretty soon you want it all the time. There would be a few weeks when you would not come because of your college exams. God's my witness, how badly I suffered during those days. But after the exams, you would always come running back to me. Every day I used to sit here and think of what I would say to you, but I never managed to muster up the courage to talk to you. The heroines in the stories you junked were unapproachable, smart, sexy, and I thought I was none of that.' She chuckled and took out her phone. She showed Daman a picture. 'See! I used to be a little chubby. But no longer, right?' In the picture, Daman noticed that Shreyasi was a little plump. The picture was a selfie. It had been clicked in the same coffee shop. In the background, Daman could see a younger himself hunched over the computer, a coffee by his side. 'I have many more, baby,' she said and clicked on a folder. The pictures were of the same kind, taken from the same angle, and ran into hundreds. Only the timestamp changed. All of them were from three years ago.

'You were watching me?' asked Daman. *She's a stalker.*

'I was admiring you all this time. For a year, I sat where you're sitting and I admired you. Look where we are now. We are finally on the brink of something amazing. The last time we met was a mistake. What happened in Goa shouldn't have happened.'

'How did you come to Goa?'

'I followed you.'

'How did you know?'

'You would often log into your mail account on a public computer and forget to log out. It was that one,' said Shreyasi and pointed to the couple of computers in the corner. Daman looked in the direction. Multihued screen savers bounced around the computer screens. *I'm capable of that*, he thought.

'And you checked my mails?'

'Why wouldn't I? Why would you want to hide anything from me? Anyway, I was just looking for more stories but guess what I found?' said Shreyasi, brightly. 'Plane tickets to Goa. Hotel reservations. I knew this was a sign, this was my chance. Why else would you keep your mail ID logged in? I was so excited.' A smile lit her face up.

'And you followed me?'

She grinned. 'I did. And that's when I met you, baby. After months and months of just staring at you it was finally going to happen. And it was going to happen in the way you had described it in one of your stories. In a little, empty library in Goa.'

Shreyasi had finished her sandwich while Daman had just had a single bite. The coffee cups were empty. Shreyasi asked for another round and instructed the waiter to reheat his sandwich.

'But weren't you engaged at that time?'

'Yes, I was. But what happens in Goa stays in Goa, right?' She pursed her lips. 'You were supposed to be my one last fling before I got married.' She clasped her hand tighter over his.

'You stalked me for over a year and I was supposed to be your one last fling? That seems unreasonable even for you,' scoffed Daman.

Shreyasi sulked. 'I wasn't stalking you. I was looking at you because I loved you. I loved you since the first time I saw you. Sure, it took me some time to realize it and act on it but I have always loved you. You've got to believe that. It's plain as day. Who would do all that I have done for you?'

'By that do you mean meeting my sister and Avni and Jayanti under guise? Wrecking my deal with Bookhound?' accused Daman.

She smiled as if it was meant as a compliment. 'I also met Sumit. They were there for the picking. All four of them were so innocent. Most of all, your best friend and angry-boy, Sumit. How can they just keep their phones lying around when their entire lives, their secrets lay beyond just a four-letter password which they punch in without even bothering to check who is looking over their shoulders. The bigger the phones get the easier they become to get hold of.' She slipped a phone in front of him. 'You're not that different, baby. You never look over your shoulder when you type out your password either.' The phone was Daman's and it was unlocked.

When did she pick it up? 'How did you . . .'

'I have watched you, remember? Also, I deleted the picture you were trying to send to Sumit. You could have just told me. We will click a picture when we finish talking. I know where the lighting is good. I have clicked a lot of pictures here.'

'I was . . .'

'Sumit doesn't like me, does he? That's okay. I don't hold that against him. In all fairness, he's been a good friend to you. But unbeknownst to him, I have done what he should have done or at least wanted to do. Remember the girl you were dating in the final year of college? You were with her for five months. You believed you were in love with her. You even used her name for a few junked stories. I have changed her name to mine. If—'

'What about Ananya?'

'Sumit kept telling you to break up with her. Something about her being the college slut. But you had a propensity to date risqué girls. You always ran after the impossible-to-get, damaged girls and loved them with all you had, hoping to change them, mould them, but also just letting them be, telling them that it was okay to be who they were. Baby, I respect you for that and I love you for that. But you didn't deserve her. She lied to you every day, she cheated on you, she made fun of you, and that I couldn't take. You sat right here in the coffee shop, defending that bitch, taking your best friend on for that whore. He kept telling you stories about her and you refused to believe any of them. Who do you think made you break up with her?'

'. . .'

'You got screenshots of her sexts in your mail. Not with one but a couple of guys. Who do you think sent you that?'

Fuck. 'I got an anonymous mail,' Daman pleaded.

She snickered. 'Of course it was anonymous, Daman. At that time it was, but it was me.' She flicked through her phone again. Within seconds, she'd pulled out the screenshots and showed them to Daman. 'I have always been looking out for you. Imagine if I hadn't mailed you the proof of Ananya's infidelity you would still be dating her. She would still be fooling you. Trust me, it wasn't easy. She guarded her phone with her dear life. Smart girl, that one. Anyway now you know who your guardian angel is. I have always protected you. I don't even want to get to how I saved you from a detention in thermodynamics in your last semester. I will tell you some other time how I dealt with your professor of that subject, B.B. Arora. Don't look at me like that. I didn't kill him,' she said and giggled. 'But forget detention, you got a seventy-three in that subject. I still remember your smiling face when you looked at the result sheet in the administrative department. You looked so gorgeous, baby. I have many stories to tell you but I don't want to digress. You asked why you should give me precedence over Avni. You should because I could have stopped it from happening. Avni and you would have never been with each other.'

'But we are,' mumbled Daman, his wits failing him.

Shreyasi slammed the table. Her lips turned into a snarl. 'BECAUSE I LET IT HAPPEN. Because I let it happen.' She continued, her voice a low angry murmur now, 'I let it happen because I thought she was droll and dull. She was a banker, a far cry from any girl you would ever want to date. Even that slut Ananya was more interesting by a mile. She was the most boring of all three girls you dated before her. Why do you think you were Avni's first boyfriend? Why do you think no one saw what you did in her?'

'Can we not—'

'Because she's dull, Daman. You know that better than anyone. Or else why wouldn't you write about her in the first place? That's a question that answers itself, doesn't it? Or why don't you make her meet your parents? Because you're not sure of her and you will never be. Stop kidding yourself, Daman. I have watched you on your dates with her. You look bored with her.'

'That's not true,' defended Daman.

'Look, I know Avni is a compromise like my husband is.'

'But—'

'Okay, have it your way. Let's choose a middle path. Where will I go after disappointing you, baby? My fate is forever entwined with yours,' she said. 'I will not mind the two of you being together, just like you shouldn't mind my husband, as long as you stay committed to me as I have been to you. I reserve the right to be your one true love, your inspiration, your muse. Do you get that? We will be like the writers Sahir Ludhianvi and Amrita Pritam, who never got married, stayed with different people, and yet loved each other till the very end. You know about them, don't you, baby? We are just like them, you and me.' She blushed, her cheeks turning light crimson. It seemed like she would curl up in the chair like a little baby.

Daman just sat there, his face contorted in disbelief, looking at her, still like a statue.

She continued, 'I know it can be a little hard for you to process, baby . . .'

'Hard for me to process? What are you talking about? What you did is illegal. I can get you jailed for this,' Daman seethed.

Shreyasi leant away from him, shocked. 'Why would you do that? Do you not see my love for you, baby? I did everything for us. Surely you can feel that, can't you?' Her voice trembled. She looked away from him, wiping the corner of her eye. 'Going to the police won't help. You have no proof and they won't believe you. They would believe me though after I tell them that there's a folder in your phone named Shreyasi with a lot of pictures of mine clicked from a distance. But it hurts me to know you would even think of going to the police, baby.' She clutched her chest and looked up. Her eyes were red and teary.

Daman fumbled through his phone and there it was. The folder named Shreyasi. *When did she do this? Be gentle. Be fucking gentle.* 'Give me your hand,' said Daman. Taking her hand into his, he spoke with as much tenderness as he could muster. 'This needs to stop. Please. I recognize your feelings and I am flattered by them. But this needs to stop. I will go with you to a doctor if that is what it takes. But we need to work our way out of this. This madness has to stop.'

'You're calling my love madness? The last three years were madness?' asked Shreyasi, tears streaking down her face.

He shifted his chair close to her and put an arm around her. 'Shreyasi, enough has happened. But now it needs to end. For your sake and mine. I'm thinking about us. It's not fair to Avni or your husband. All relationships come to an end. Maybe ours ends here. Three years is a long time, isn't it? We had a good run. But this is it. If you say you love me, do this for me. Walk away from this, okay?'

She muzzled her face into his chest and sobbed softly. 'But can't we just stay like this.'

'No, Shreyasi. We can't,' said Daman with as much sincerity as he could gather. 'Please. I'm begging you.'

'No. No. Please don't beg. I will feel bad about myself if I let you do that.' She took a tissue and blew her nose into it. She sighed. 'I will think about it. I have loved you so much. Can you give me some time?'

Daman nodded. 'Thank you.'

She started to laugh despite her tears.

'What?' Daman asked, scared at what fresh hell she would throw at him.

'I thought we would have sex today. It's so stupid of me. Do you know where we went from the library in Goa?'

He shook his head.

'To your room. You were so smooth that day. You told me you could make better coffee in the coffee maker of the room. I knew it was a trick to get me to bed but it was also what I wanted. Once in the room, you didn't even pretend we were there for the coffee. You just . . . kissed me.'

'Did we?'

'Thrice,' said Shreyasi unflinchingly, without a hint of shame.

Did all of this really happen?

She continued. 'Within minutes of being in the room we were naked and you inside me. And within seconds you were done.' She smiled impishly. 'Don't be embarrassed. I was done as well. It was the very definition of a quickie.' She continued unabashedly, wiping the smudged mascara. 'And then we did it twice again. I was still trembling hours later.'

'. . .'

'Do you remember any of this?'

'No,' said Daman. 'But I wish I did.'

Before Shreyasi left that day, they clicked a picture together. After she left, Daman sent it to Sumit who confirmed that she is the girl from the car, that she was Shreyasi. His stalker and his guardian angel.

29

Avni was not a crazy person.

On the contrary, she was often accused of being too rational. But this Shreyasi affair was slowly making her lose her mind. The story had shifted another year back, when Daman was in college, two years before Avni even knew of Daman's existence. They shared a history. Daman–Shreyasi wasn't the garden-variety case of obsession any more, theirs was a perverse love story.

'Avni wouldn't have happened had I not let it happen,' Shreyasi had said that day. These words had kept her awake at nights. Avni had heard the entire conversation between Daman and Shreyasi at the cafe in South Extension, sitting two tables away with her back towards them. She heard Shreyasi threaten, grovel, plead, cry and then promise to think about backing off. And yet, Avni hadn't been able to stop thinking about Daman and Shreyasi, about them. She was sure Daman had been thinking about it as well. After Shreyasi had left that day, Daman and Avni shifted to a coffee shop a couple of blocks down. Daman hadn't said much during the evening apart from how crazy it all was!

Coming from a writer who had loved a crazy girl in his head, had written about her on the Internet and in his book, she didn't know how to perceive his reaction. *How long before Daman finds Shreyasi's love and madness perversely cute and falls in love with her?* Shreyasi's perseverance was as commendable as it was sick. She was the Hannibal Lecter of stalkers. With long, flowing black hair and a deathly pale complexion. Daman told her Shreyasi hadn't contacted him after that day in the coffee shop. But how could she be sure? The past few days she had spent long hours staring at the screen saver of Daman and herself on her office laptop and wondered if Shreyasi had called back. *What if Daman actually likes her madness? What if I'm really boring? What if I'm dull?*

It was a Sunday. She left home dressed in a white suit she had bought the day before from Fab India. She left her hair open and applied a little make-up. She knew Daman wouldn't be too pleased but she was running out of options. It wasn't paranoia. She was just making sure. An hour after she left her house, she stood outside his parents' house. She knew he would be there. When Daman's mother opened the door, Avni pretended like it was a surprise she had been planning for long. Daman's mother welcomed her with a warmth she had not expected.

'*Ei to eshe gache!* (Look, she has come!)' his mother had shrieked and kissed her forehead. His mother poured oil outside the house before she stepped in. Avni flushed when his mother bit of a piece of her nail to ward off evil spirits and her own evil eye. 'So beautiful,' she had said while Daman looked on, annoyed.

He didn't talk to her for the entire first hour. He didn't even look her in the eye. This Daman's mother took as shyness. Avni knew better. But his irritation was something she could take care of if she had Daman to herself in the long run. *This will be a silly anecdotal story we will tell our kids in the future*, she thought. Daman would tell them how their mother had gotten insecure and landed up unannounced at their grandparents' house.

Daman's father asked her a host of questions about her job, the rotting financial state of the country, the fiscal deficit, and nodded appreciatively through her answers. While his father and she talked, at first agreeably and then choosing to argue on a few points, Daman's mother whipped up a nice meal. Avni made sure she laughed at his father's satirical comments on the government. His father returned the courtesy. Once sure she had made an impression on the father, she excused herself and went to the kitchen to help Daman's mother out.

'*Mei to kintu khub bhalo* (The girl is nice),' she heard Daman's father say to Puchku, who for the most part had looked at her inquisitively. Avni had come to Daman's place with one and one purpose only. To entrench herself in Daman's life, to leave landmines for Daman to deal with if he ever retreated from their relationship. She deserved that after all she had put into the relationship. If Daman dared to break up with her, at least he would have his parents backing her up. Daman's mother didn't let her touch anything in the kitchen, so she just stood there, chatting. His mother was a good cook and an even better conversationalist. For a moment there, she almost thought she had never not been a part of this family. She helped his mother serve the food. The mood was generally light around the table and everyone laughed and joked quite a bit. Except Daman who alternated between being annoyed and awkward. Even the sister eased up when Avni offered to share her Netflix password with her. She caught Daman alone while she was washing her hands after the lunch.

'Are you still angry?'

'No,' said Daman, not meeting her eyes.

'I'm sorry. I shouldn't have come,' she said trying to elicit tears but they failed her.

'Yes, you shouldn't have.'

And then the tears came. He was looking away and it took him a few seconds to notice them. When he did he took her in his arms and asked her what was wrong. The first tears were fake but the minute she was in his arms, the real tears came.

'I felt insecure.'

'What? Why?' asked Daman. A flicker of recognition shined in his eyes. 'Oh, because of what she said? Are you crazy?'

'No. But she was right. I am dull, am I not? Maybe that's why you didn't want me to meet your parents.'

'You couldn't be more wrong, Avni. That girl is unhinged. You're not. Why would you do this? You could have just told me,' explained Daman.

'I'm sorry.'

'It's okay, Avni,' he said and kissed her forehead. He asked her to wash her face and fix herself before someone noticed them. 'I don't want them to think I'm a domestic abuser as well. I have a feeling they like you.'

She smiled.

A little later, Puchku dragged Avni to her room and showed her the new *A Song of Ice and Fire* book collection, complete with maps and a digitally signed letter from G.R.R. Martin. Puchku was impressed by how much Avni knew about G.R.R. Martin and *Game of Thrones* despite not having read the books. *Of course I know everything! I came prepared*, Avni thought. Puchku tweeted about only two things—*Game of Thrones* and Harry Potter. Avni had stayed up and read up on both.

'So you guys will get married, haan?' asked Puchku excitedly after a bit.

'It's a little too early to say that.'

'But why get married to my brother? He's a bit of a loser compared to you, Di.' She laughed so much she snorted. She apologized.

Di. Am I family? It warmed her insides a little. It was then that she noticed a framed picture of Daman kept on the side table, right next to Puchku's books on inorganic chemistry. In the picture, Daman was heavily bandaged, his eyes open but blank.

'That's the day after he woke up,' explained Ritu. 'I keep it to remind myself how lucky we were to get Dada back.

Dada didn't even remember me when he first saw me. But slowly, things came back to him.'

'It must be hard for you?'

Puchku nodded, eyes brimming with tears. 'It was worse for Maa. The first couple of months after he woke up were trying. They diagnosed him with PTSD. Sometimes everything seemed to be creeping back to normal but suddenly a mention of the accident or even something random on television would undo days of progress, he would start getting seizures and lose all sense of time and space and people. Twice, he almost choked on his own saliva. They had to cut a hole in his neck.'

I know. I have seen the scars.

'But now he's okay,' she said and touched the side table. 'Touchwood.'

Avni smiled at her. A moment of silence passed between them before Avni asked, 'So what do I call you? Ritu or Puchku?'

'Puchku,' she replied.

30

Radhika, Sukriti and Ananya were the three girls Daman had dated before Avni. He had held hands but not kissed Radhika, had kissed but hadn't had sex with Sukriti, and had lost his virginity to Ananya. But it wasn't until Daman had met Avni that he knew how powerful and intimate sex could be. The ferocity with which Avni approached sex was something Daman had never experienced before. Despite her naivety, everything was just perfect—the moans, the scratches, the little touches, the longer licks, the orgasms. He would never forget the first time he had made her come. It was quick and thunderous. Her body had reacted like she was being exorcised. Even now, she took up the responsibility of making herself come using him, guiding him. She led sex. Today, they had jumped right into bed after lunch at his parents' apartment. Avni's eagerness had been palpable. She had smelt of sex and desperation and blowjobs. 'I love you,' she had whispered repeatedly as she rode him. *She does*, Daman had thought. Avni had never been good with words and displays of affection. She had always relied on him picking up on signals which he did from time to time. But this— coming to his house unannounced and doing everything in her capacity to impress them—was the strongest hint he had picked up. She was really in love with him.

I love her too.

'I fell asleep,' said Avni, stirring up from her slumber. 'Aren't you sleepy? You look like you haven't slept in days.' She ran a loving finger over his face. 'Is she bothering you?'

'Not really.'

'She hasn't called again, right?'

'And that's troubling,' he said as got up from the bed.

He walked around, pressing the side of his temples. 'Isn't that a little strange that she walked away so easily?'

'Maybe she saw the sense in that.'

'She's the not the kind who would leave without as much as a goodbye.'

'Are you missing her now?' scoffed Avni. Daman rolled his eyes. She continued, 'Daman, sit down. We got what we wanted, right? She's off our backs.'

'She's not off our backs, I'm sure of that. She was stalking me, working me like a puppet and now she just gives up? How's that possible? There's something not right here,' urged Daman.

'I don't know.'

'Wait, I will show you something.' Daman opened a drawer and pulled out a bunch of a papers. He gave one of them to Avni. 'Ananya's break-up or the detention wasn't the only time she's interfered in my life,' he said. 'Read this.'

'This is to inform you that I wouldn't be able to be join your company. The salary you offered during campus interviews was below my expectations and an insult to my talent. I won't be able to join your company. Please don't bother sending me the Letter of Joining. Regards, Daman.'

'This is a mail I sent to Larsen & Tourbo turning down their offer.'

'Shreyasi sent this mail, not you?'

'Precisely. Because they would have posted me in Mumbai and not Delhi. And this is not the only one. She has been deleting mails from readers who don't like Shreyasi,' said Daman.

Avni frowned. 'You haven't changed your password for three years?'

'I just change a digit or add a letter when I have to. And how does it matter? She has been looking over my shoulder since forever.'

'But if she were reading your mails, why didn't she read the manuscript when you sent it to Jayanti?' asked Avni.

'I think she was trying to hold out, build up the excitement. Maybe she didn't want to spoil it by reading the unfinished book. She wouldn't have expected I would butcher the character in the book. Maybe that's why she had been so angry. She had slipped.'

'This is so screwed-up.'

'That's why I think she's going to be back,' said Daman.

They sat for the next few hours fruitlessly brooding. They caught up on Netflix but neither of them had their mind in it. Soon, it was time for Avni to go home. 'Don't worry. We will figure out a way,' she said as Daman locked the door to his apartment. She kissed him. He wrapped an arm around her. As they reached the ground floor, they saw a lot of people rushing outside the apartment complex, talking excitedly amongst themselves.

'What is it?' wondered Avni.

They joined the rest of the people as they poured out of the apartment buildings. The minute they stepped out of the building complex a wave of heat hit them. Instinctively, Daman grasped Avni's hand. They jostled through the crowd to the source of the commotion. The heat wave intensified. And as they crossed the last few files of the crowd, Daman noticed something burning. It was not long before he realized it was a car on fire, flames licking at everything, burning through paint and metal. The fire was dying now. The car was slowly being reduced to a blackened shell. Sirens blew in the background. Avni jerked her hand free. She gasped. Her eyes widened and she let out a silent shriek. She looked at Daman. That's when it hit him. Daman's stomach sank to his feet.

'It's my car!' thought Daman. He passed out soon after.

31

'It's common in people who have suffered PTSD. It's not a full relapse though. Take the medicines and you will be as good as new in a couple of months. Just make sure you stay away from scenarios that possibly put too much stress on your mind, or anything that mimics the accident, okay?' the doctor said.

'I'm not planning to see my car burn for the third time, doctor,' joked Daman.

Avni didn't see the humour in it. She was still shaken from what she had witnessed in the last three terrifying days. The doctor signed Daman's discharge papers and they took his leave. Since the time Daman had collapsed and had been rushed to the hospital, he had had two seizures, three panic attacks and a few instances of lapsed memory. While the receptionist readied Daman's bills, Avni said, 'I still think we should tell your parents. Or at least Sumit.'

'Telling Sumit is the same as telling my parents,' he said. 'They are already anxious about Puchku's upcoming exams, I don't want them to worry even more. I'm fine now. You're making too much out of it.'

'Too much? I saw you wake up in a wet bed twice. TWICE! I have never been so scared.'

'It's okay—'

'It's NOT OKAY! I saw your body shake and tremble . . . I thought . . . I was so angry I couldn't help you. You were right there in front of my eyes and . . . I was . . . so helpless.'

'That's why people study for a decade and become doctors so people like you don't have to help.'

Avni handed the file over to the nurse at the reception and turned to hug him. 'What if the next time it's worse?'

Avni cried in his arms. Daman assured her. 'It won't be. Didn't you hear what the doctor said? I don't have a car to burn down.'

They took a cab back to Daman's apartment. He stopped by his car for a moment, now reduced to a black and grey heap of metal, and frowned.

Avni held his hand and said, 'The doctor asked you not to stress yourself. And I'm not losing you over a car. The insurance will cover most of it so stop worrying about it.' She led him away from the rubble.

While Daman had been away, Avni had called a professional cleaning service and got the house scrubbed. The curtains were also changed to a brighter colour.

'It looks like a dollhouse,' said Daman. 'But in a good way.'

'Chai?'

'Sure,' said Daman and followed Avni to the kitchen. He lit a cigarette but she wrenched it out of his hands and put it out.

'What?' Daman protested. 'There's absolutely no correlation between smoking and PTSD.'

'And we are not going to prove otherwise,' said Avni and put the water to boil.

Later he helped her pour the tea into the two new cups she had bought. They took their cups to the living room.

'I'm calling Jayanti tonight,' he said. 'After the hospital bills . . . anyway, I will try to get a better signing amount. It will be a little tight but I will be fine. Those guys at the online magazine have been after my life to write for them. I will take that offer up.'

'You should have let me pay the hospital bill,' she said. 'Have you thought about other publishers?'

'I don't want to. At least Jayanti is a known devil,' said Daman in a defeatist tone. 'I want to just sign this and get back to writing the book. I will take up a few writing assignments on the side.'

I just want to hug him and make all of this go away, she thought. 'Sure, whatever you think will make you happy,' said Avni.

'You sound like my mother now.' He chuckled.

Avni smiled. 'How much time do you think the insurance guys will take to reimburse the money?' asked Avni.

'At least five months from what I know. I will have to check the papers though.'

'Don't buy a car when they pay you back!'

'Of course,' said Daman and chuckled. 'Once burnt, twice shy. Twice burnt, never again.'

A little later, it was time for Avni to go to work. She didn't want to leave. She hadn't been to work for three days and there was only so much work she had done sitting in Daman's hospital room while he squirmed and sweated and trembled. 'I will see you tomorrow,' Avni said.

'I would have dropped you but—'

'We will buy a new car in time,' said Avni. She saw Daman get up and said, 'I will go. You just lie down and get some rest. I love you.'

Just as she opened the door, she found an envelope lying outside, gathering dust, which they had not noticed on their way in. She picked it up.

'What is it?' Daman asked.

'It's a letter,' she said.

She strained the envelope against the light and tore it open carefully. Inside there was printed copy of the insurance deed of the Daman's car. On it, a message in red ink was stencilled.

I HAD TO, BABY. I HAD NO CHOICE.

Daman and Avni noticed it at the same time. The insurance of Daman's car had expired the day before the car caught fire.

32

Two hours had passed since they opened the envelope. Avni had called her office and deferred her meetings.

'You should go. There's nothing you will achieve sitting here,' said Daman.

'I can't leave you like this.'

'I will be fine!' snapped Daman.

'We should go to the police. This is getting out of hand.'

'With what? What proof do we have? This!' He waved the insurance deed of his in his hand. 'Who's going to believe our story?' He shook his head. 'I knew we hadn't seen the last of her, I knew it!'

As if on cue, Daman's phone beeped. It was a text from Shreyasi. COME ONLINE ON SKYPE. GET AVNI TOO.

'Don't do it,' argued Avni. 'The doctor asked you to—'

'And do what? Hide? For how long? She burnt down my fucking car!'

He logged on to Skype on his laptop and found a request from Shreyasi.

'Record everything,' said Daman.

Avni placed her phone at a distance with the video recording on.

'Ready?' he asked.

'Yes.'

Daman called her. Three rings later, Shreyasi picked up. At first her video was pixelated but it cleared out slowly. Shreyasi smiled at them. She had earphones on and was entering the metro.

She said with a bright smile, 'Look who's here. The liar and the bitch. Before we start this conversation, I need both of you to switch off your phones.' Daman and Avni looked at each other. 'What are you waiting for? Quickly now,' urged Shreyasi.

Both of them did as instructed.

'Why did you burn the car down?' asked Daman.

'God! Look at those curtains behind you,' remarked Shreyasi. 'I expected better out of you, Avni.'

'Why did you burn the car down?' he asked again.

Behind her, the announcement rang aloud. She paused for it to stop. 'The next station is Rajiv Chowk. The next station is Rajiv Chowk. Please mind the gap. Please mind the gap.'

'Avni? What would you do if someone calls you terrible? Or a crackpot? Or psychotic?' asked Shreyasi. 'You called me all of these, didn't you?'

'You followed us?' gasped Avni. *She knew I was on the other table. She followed us after she pretended to have left!*

'I only did what you did to me, Avni,' said Shreyasi. 'Did you really think I wouldn't notice you sitting on the next table eavesdropping on my conversation with Daman? I had spent a year sitting in that coffee shop for my baby. I know it like the back of my hand. So yes, I followed you once both of you left the coffee shop, hand in hand, gossiping about me and calling me names.'

Avni composed herself and said, 'You had no right to burn the car down! That's a criminal offence!'

'Creeping into my book trying to take my place, changing the curtains of my baby's flat, that's more of an offence.'

'Why the fuck did you burn the car down?' grumbled Daman, slamming the table.

'Revenge,' snapped Shreyasi. 'And don't ever use that tone with me, baby.'

'That cost me money!'

'The insurance will cover all of it,' said Shreyasi.

'It expired and you fucking know that,' said Avni.

Shreyasi looked at Daman and said, 'Ask your whore not to talk to me like that.'

'Whatever,' Avni retorted and walked away from the computer screen.

'That bitch has a lot of attitude, baby,' scoffed Shreyasi. 'Yes, I knew the insurance was getting over. Remember the day you went for the party at Olive when I drove you home and you were too knackered to remember the next day. The day you found your books burnt? I might have drugged your drink a little bit.'

'You did what?' asked Daman.

Avni got up and shifted close to the laptop screen.

'Rohypnol, I roofied your drink. I really wanted to be the first one to read the book!' she exclaimed. 'Anyway, out of habit, I clicked pictures of all your documents. Car registration card, pollution check, the works. I never thought I would need them but let's just call it a happy coincidence that I did.'

They heard the announcements again. Shreyasi smiled at Daman while the speakers blared behind her. 'The next station is New Delhi. The next station is New Delhi. Please mind the gap. Please mind the gap.'

'What's your point?' asked Avni.

'Oh, you're back? Has Daman ever told you how ugly you look?' commented Shreyasi. 'My point is that I faked your signatures and took out another insurance of the car. You can have the insurance money if you want.'

Avni shifted restlessly in her seat.

'What would you have me do for it?' asked Daman.

Shreyasi grinned. 'You need to break up with the whore sitting next to you. Does that sound simple?'

'No.'

Avni held Daman's hand under the table. Shreyasi didn't fail to make a note of it. She said, 'It would be nice if you don't hold hands in front of me.'

'He won't do it. He won't break up with me,' said Avni.

'I don't see any other option,' said Shreyasi looking daggers at her.

'What he does or doesn't is none of your business,' snapped Avni.

'I wasn't talking to you,' said Shreyasi. 'So Daman, let me sweeten the deal. What if your deal with Jayanti suddenly becomes far more promising than it is right now? An earlier release? More money? More creative control? What if I dealt with Karthik? What if he's no more your problem?'

'How would you do that?' grumbled Daman.

'Leave that to me. But would you like that? I can make it happen. You should know that I can do it, and so does your useless and pathetic ex-girlfriend, Avni. After all, creepy, terrible, psychotic people can do a lot of damage, can't we, Avni?' She winked. 'So what is your decision? Your car, your money, your book, your future or this piece of inadequate shit you call a girlfriend?'

Before Shreyasi could say anything more, Avni cut the call.

'Why did you do that?' grumbled Daman.

'We don't need her.'

'But—'

Avni picked her bag up and left, hot tears in her eyes.

33

Daman waited for Jayanti Raghunath in the conference room of the Bookhound Publishers office. He had emptied three cups of tea in the past half an hour. In his dream last night, Jayanti had walked in, smiled brightly, and told him about how a big guy in the UK office read his books and wanted to take Daman international. His happiness had drowned in the morning sunlight.

He looked at his watch again. Avni hadn't reached yet and neither had she taken his calls. Daman lost it when she finally took his call. 'Where the hell are you? You can't abandon me now!' She told him she will be there in fifteen minutes. 'Is that the metro I can hear behind you? Why didn't you drive, or take a cab?' She panted on the phone and said something about surge pricing. He cut the call.

Between that day and now, Shreyasi had repeated her offer about a dozen times, often picking times to call him when Avni was around. 'Your career in return for a break-up. Are you sure she's worth it?' she'd said again and again.

Avni had started spending more time with him, staying over at his apartment on most nights. She had a toothbrush in the washroom and two sets of clothes hanging in the cupboard. She behaved like a limp horse that was scared it will be put down. But Daman had no intentions to break up with her. He spent a lot of time consoling her when he found her whimpering in the middle of the night. 'I wish I could make it all go away, I wish I could do something for you,' she would tell him repeatedly while sobbing into his chest. 'Let me help you,' she had said and pressed him to take post-dated cheques covering the entire insurance amount. He had refused, of course.

'I'm not a landlord,' he had argued. He felt sorry for how she thought it was her fault. He duly told her it was not her fault every time she brought it up. Which is not to say he hadn't himself stayed up nights thinking about how different things could be if he bowed down to Shreyasi's wishes.

He felt a need to pee. He got up and strode into the washroom. By the time he got back to the conference room, Jayanti was sitting there with another woman whom she introduced as the head of the legal department.

'I'm glad you are signing with us. Your book may release later than you wanted it to but I promise we will do everything to make it a massive success,' said Jayanti.

She then asked Daman to clear all his doubts about the contract with the woman from the legal department. They shook hands and Jayanti and the other woman left Daman to leaf through the contract. Clearly, there was no conversation to be had about monies or timelines. The contract was standard. There were no hidden clauses. Just a simple ten pager and Daman went through it twice in the next hour. Every time he thought he was ready, he would start reading it again, try to find a fault but come up short. He didn't want to sign it before Avni went through it. He leant back into his chair.

He looked outside and noticed a little commotion. Jayanti and a couple of other editors were talking animatedly, covering their faces, shaking their heads, and soon they all huddled into Bookhound Publishers' CEO's office. Whatever they were discussing was relayed around the office. Groups of two and three stood talking and their faces had the different variations of same expression of shock he had seen on Jayanti. Jayanti and the other two editors didn't come out until twenty minutes later. Their faces were sullen, as if all the happiness had been drained out of them, drop by drop. A little later, the woman from the legal department dropped in to see how Daman was doing with the contract.

'I want to take this home and then review it. I don't want to make any mistake,' said Daman.

The woman nodded. 'Okay, I will just inform Jayanti about it.' She was about to leave when Daman called out.

'What happened out there?'

'One of our authors was in an accident. I don't know if you have heard of him. Karthik Iyer?'

'What happened to him?'

'He tripped down a flight of stairs.'

'Shit!' said Daman, imagining him lying dead and twisted in a heap. 'Is he okay?'

'He will live. But there's severe spinal injury and his legs are broken in multiple places. The doctors are saying he might not leave the hospital for the next few months,' said the woman, ruefully.

Daman nodded.

'I will just call Jayanti,' said the woman and left.

Daman wondered if he should visit him in the hospital. Despite the hatred he harboured for him, he felt sorry for him.

'Should I come in?' asked Jayanti. She strode in before he could answer. 'The contract is pretty straightforward. Why not sign it now?'

Daman could sense Jayanti wasn't her usual confident self. Her voice shook and she fidgeted with the pen in her hand. She had aged years in an hour. No matter how much of a bitch she might be, they had worked together for years. Even created magic together, at least in terms of sales.

'I'm not sure—'

'You're testing my patience. You have had weeks to think about this and to go to rival publishers. This contract is important. For you and for us. There's nothing to not

understand. Just sign the damned thing. Do you understand?'
Jayanti slapped the table with the last word. Something clicked
in Daman. *She's desperate.* She had never said the contract was
important for them before today.

'I can't, Jayanti. I might make some people to go through
the contract as well. I don't want to make the same mistake
again.'

Jayanti threw her hands up in exasperation. This was the
most unprofessional Jayanti had ever been. She had taken
Karthik's news pretty hard. And just like that, he knew why.
Her best author was rendered useless for a few months. He
wouldn't turn in the two novels he had promised and had signed
up for. That meant an opening in her publishing calendar.

Daman said, 'This contract undermines my talent and it
doesn't pay me enough.'

'What the hell—'

'Karthik will be in the hospital for a few months, will he
not? Which means there's only a slim chance of him finishing
a book this year. That leaves you with no other major releases,'
said Daman.

'So?'

Daman continued, his voice low and assertive, 'So with
Karthik being out of action for the next few months, my book
suddenly becomes a little more important, doesn't it? This
means you're going to pay me more and shift the release date.'
Daman smiled.

'There's no way—'

'I'm sure you will find a way,' said Daman and slid the
contract back to Jayanti. He got up and walked towards the
door. 'The contract is important to you, as you said.'

Jayanti was still sitting in her chair, fuming. 'I can't believe
you're using a fellow author's misfortune as a springboard for
your contract.'

Daman smiled. 'And weren't you fucking me over because of him? I do feel sorry for him but I'm thankful as well. Maybe I will go visit him in the hospital and tell him that. Please send over the new contract and I will be happy to reconsider.'

'No,' said Jayanti. Daman turned to face Jayanti. She got up and took a few steps towards him. When she had come close enough for Daman to feel her breath on his face, she repeated, 'No.'

'Are you sure you're okay with that?'

Jayanti snarled. 'Yes, I'm okay with that. But what I'm not okay is with my pets growling back at me.'

'I'm not—'

'You're Daman. You're a fucking mongrel, that's what you are. Someone I picked up from the streets! Who do you think would even know your name if it weren't for me? So fuck you, fuck your books, and fuck your contract. Walk out of here with your tail between your legs like the dog you are. You thought you would steamroll over me? Use my author's condition against me?'

'Jayanti—'

'What were you thinking in that stupid little head of yours? You're a writer but I didn't think you were into fantasy. When did you think you had become that important to me? To this office? And this publishing company?' She snapped her fingers and grinned. 'I can make another one of you in a month. You should have never quit your job. Because now not only will you never get published here but I will call every one of my editor friends and tell them about your little stunt. Let's see who publishes you then, Daman. Your writing career is over as you know it.'

34

I shouldn't have done it. I shouldn't have done it. Why did I do it? Shut up. It's done. It's for the best. You can't think about it now. It's done. Avni's conversation with herself was cut short rudely by the driver when the auto stopped in front of the coffee shop Daman had asked her to come to when she was on her way to the Bookhound office. *He must have signed the deal,* she figured.

'Seventy-eight rupees,' said the driver.

She paid the driver and wiped clean the smudged kajal with her handkerchief. Her hands were shaking. It was only a few minutes ago that the tears had stopped and they threatened to come back every time she thought about what she had done. *What I did was horrible, but I did it for you, I'm not the inadequate, useless girlfriend.*

'What happened?' she asked, when she saw Daman's bloodshot, furious eyes. 'Did you sign the contract?'

Daman shook his head. 'Everything's finished. I fucked up. I destroyed everything.' He added after a pause, sighing, 'Do you know Karthik could have died this morning and I fucking tried using it?'

Yes. I was there. I saw Karthik tumble. I heard his bones crunch. 'What are you talking about?' asked Avni, feigning innocence. *It was only to help you.* 'I don't know what came over me but I did it for you,' she wanted to say.

He went on to tell her the long and short of it. The news of Karthik's accident, the desperation in Jayanti's voice and his deplorable decision to take her on.

'The more I think about it the more wrong I think I was,' said Daman. 'I was using Karthik's accident.' He massaged his temples with his fingers. 'It seemed the right thing to do at the moment. But now it seems so . . . evil. How could I stoop so fucking low?'

'I'm sorry,' said Avni. *No. No. It can't be. It wasn't supposed to end like this. You weren't supposed to threaten Jayanti. Why did you?*

'Where were you?' asked Daman.

'The metro was stuck.'

'It's done,' he said, stirring his coffee. 'My writing career is finished. She said it in so many words.'

Avni's stomach churned. The words hit her like a physical blow in her guts. *I'm so sorry. I did my best. I thought I will make things all right.* Avni said, 'Maybe she was just scaring you. It could be possible that she doesn't have the kind of influence over other publishers as she's making you believe.'

'But they would know of my situation. How much do you think they would pay me when they know how desperate I am?' he asked. Avni didn't have an answer. 'That's what I thought.'

They sat in silence.

A few minutes later, Avni said, 'I have three fixed deposits and one recurring one. Also, I'm meeting the recruiter from Barclays again. Things are looking positive. We can tide you over.' She reached out and held his hand.

Daman retracted his hand and leant back into his chair. He muttered, 'I know you will always be there, Avni. But I can't just sit here and do nothing, right? God. Why the hell did I have to take that chance? I should have just signed the contract and walked out. Why did Karthik choose today of all the days to fall to his death?'

'He's not dead,' said Avni sharply.

'But he could have been,' said a voice. Daman and Avni both looked up to find Shreyasi smiling at them. 'Thanks to your ex-girlfriend he could've been in a morgue, not a hospital.'

'Shreyasi?'

'Hi, baby,' Shreyasi said and ran her fingers over Daman's face as he flinched. 'Is this seat taken? May I join you guys?'

She pulled the chair and sat down before any of them could answer. She kept her handbag on the table. She continued, 'I apologize for intruding. We should do this more often. The three of us having a coffee rather than one of us girls just spying from a distance.' She threw an accusing look at Avni.

The waiter approached the table. 'Give us ten minutes,' she said. The waiter walked away.

'So I heard what happened with you and Jayanti, baby,' Shreyasi addressed Daman, 'but I didn't hear Avni's part in the entire story. I don't particularly relish unfinished stories. That's why I never found the taste for short stories. There's way too much subtext and suspense at the end of it all. But we don't want any of that between us, do we? So do you wish to share your part in this story, Avni? Or should I tell him?'

She knows, thought Avni. *She knows what I did.*

'What are you doing here, Shreyasi?' grumbled Daman. 'You need to leave. It's all your fault.'

'My fault? That's a bit of a stretch, baby. You're the one who went all ballistic on Jayanti today. I was the one trying to help you, remember? You didn't listen and look where it has taken you, *shona*.'

'You should go,' said Daman.

'I will but I really want to know where Avni was this morning.' Shreyasi looked at Avni. 'Will you tell him or should I?'

She knows.

'What is this? What's she talking about?'

Avni felt the world spin around her. *She knows.*

'Avni? Don't stare at me like that! Look at him and tell him what you did? He's waiting and so am I,' said Shreyasi.

'Let's hurry up and end this facade of a relationship between the two of you.'

'I . . .'

'What?' he asked.

'Tell him, Avni. Where were you this morning?'

Avni wringed her clammy hands. 'Metro station.'

'Yes, now we are getting there. What were you doing at the metro station? Who was you with?'

'Did you cheat on me?' questioned Daman.

Tears started to streak down Avni's face. She shook her head. 'No.'

'Oh, baby. Be more inventive. Cheating? For that she would have to find someone who likes her. And as I told you before, she's a bit dull.' Shreyasi reached out and held Avni's trembling hands. She said, 'Stop crying and tell him what you did, Avni. He's so eager to hear. He looks tortured.'

'I pushed him,' Avni whispered between the soft sobs.

'What? He couldn't hear you. Say that again?' urged Shreyasi.

'I pushed Karthik,' said Avni and buried her face in her palms.

Daman gasped.

'Oh, c'mon. You nearly killed a man and you're crying. I expected better of you,' said Shreyasi. She passed a tissue to Avni. Shreyasi looked at an aghast Daman and explained, 'She followed Karthik to a metro station and pushed him down the stairs. It was crowded and no one saw her.'

'No one but you,' mumbled Daman.

'Right, no one but me,' Shreyasi admitted.

Daman looked at Avni. 'Avni? Why would you do that? What could possibly—'

'I just . . . I just . . . wanted to help,' whimpered Avni. 'I thought . . .'

Daman held his head in his palms. 'He has spinal injury, Avni. Do you understand what that means? How could you do that? Did you really . . .'

'Because of her!' shrieked Avni and pointed at Shreyasi.

Shreyasi grinned. 'Well, I think both of you need to iron out your issues.' Then she caught Daman's gaze and said, 'I will suggest you break up with this girl, baby. She called me terrible, creepy and psychotic, did she not? But what's she now? Also, she did cheat on you.'

'I DIDN'T!'

'Oh yes, you did, sweetheart. She has played you, baby.'

'I didn't!'

'How?' asked Daman, still reeling from what he had heard.

'Do you remember who told you to insert Avni's character into the synopsis?' asked Shreyasi. 'Who was the first person you sent the synopsis to?'

Daman looked at Avni.

'Now ask Avni if she had sent that synopsis to Jayanti. Ask her if it was Jayanti's suggestion to add Avni as a character. Jayanti sold the idea to her and she sold it to you. Ask her if she sent it to her?' said Shreyasi.

'Did you send it?' asked Daman.

Avni nodded.

Shreyasi continued, 'Both Avni and Jayanti were late for that meeting, weren't they? That's only because they were with each other, deciding how to dupe you into cutting my character out and getting hers in. They colluded against you. Now decide who the bitch is?'

'I just wanted the contract for you—'

'Shut up, Avni. It's over,' grumbled Shreyasi and looked at Daman. 'Jayanti and Avni had been meeting behind your back ever since the talk of the new contract came up. I was pleasantly surprised to see her name on Jayanti's phone, to be honest.'

'Jayanti called me!' protested Avni but her words were drowned in sobs.

'How did you get Jayanti's phone?' asked Daman.

'Aw, baby. I like how I can still surprise you.'

Daman found it hard to breathe.

Shreyasi continued, 'Tell us Avni if any of this is untrue?'

Words died in Avni's throat. *I did it for us. I wanted you to get the contract.*

'I will leave you guys to it. I hope you make the right decision, baby. I could have told you earlier about this but I wanted you to see how treacherous she is. I love you. Always remember that,' said Shreyasi, picked up her bag and left.

An hour later, Daman told Avni it would be best if they broke up for a while.

35

'We aren't leaving this room till we sort this out,' said Sumit, hands resting on his waist. 'Look at the two of you. You look like shit without each other.'

It had been an hour since Avni and Daman were sitting opposite each other in Sumit's living room and neither of them had uttered a single word. Daman tried his best not to look at Avni, who resembled death. Her eyes were red and marked with dark circles. Her hair was tied neatly in a pony. It highlighted her skin's pallor and her painfully protruding cheekbones. She looked stripped of flesh, her wrists and arms gangly. He wondered if he looked any better. His sleep in the last few weeks had been sketchy at best. The nightmares and the nausea had been back in full strength. The bed-wetting had come back. Only this time around, sometimes he would see Avni's face instead of Shreyasi's in the car, crying, laughing mirthlessly, and then dying. The doctor had bumped up his dosage of anti-anxiety pills but it only brought a few hours of sleep every day. He would spend the rest of the day walking around undead. Daman had been avoiding Sumit's furious calls all these days but today he'd threatened to tell his parents about his three-day visit to the hospital. The maid fetched biscuits and sweetened tea. Sumit lived alone in a rented two-bedroom house, fitted with air conditioners in all three rooms, and had a full-time maid to tend to his needs. He had just paid the down payment for an SUV.

'When's the car's delivery?' asked Daman. *I could have had all this*, he thought.

'In three weeks,' answered Sumit. 'Can we talk about the matter at hand?'

'I need to get some work done. I will have to leave,' said Daman. 'I respect you for trying, Bhaiya, but this is a waste of time. Nothing is going to come out of it.'

'You're not going anywhere,' snapped Sumit. 'SIT THE FUCK DOWN. You guys have to talk. You can't just throw it away like this.'

'Let him go,' said Avni.

'Avni—'

She interrupted Sumit. 'He's right to do whatever he's doing. I don't blame him.'

'You only did whatever you did to protect him. He has to see that,' protested Sumit.

Daman stiffened. 'What I see is that she went behind my back and conspired with the person I probably hate the most. And the lesser we say about Karthik the better.' He turned to Avni. She cowered. 'I visited Karthik in the hospital yesterday. And you know what? I didn't feel all that bad about him. I was thinking that jerk deserved what came to him. He won't be able to write another book for months. But you know what else I was thinking? What if he had died?'

'It was just a small flight of stairs—' mumbled Avni.

'And yet he's lying broken in a hospital bed. Would you have told me had he died? Would you have told me had Shreyasi not told me?' asked Daman, scowling. 'A person would have been dead because of me, Avni! I have the blood of two people who died in the accident on my hands. You almost added another person to it. You—'

Sumit cut in. 'The accident wasn't your fault, Daman.' Sumit placed his hand over Avni's to keep her from answering. 'And let's not speculate here. She was desperate and she did it for you. Maybe she wouldn't have done it had you come to me with what was happening between you and this Shreyasi.

I thought she was just a troublesome stalker. And why didn't you tell me about the anxiety attack?'

Daman sniggered. 'Okay, so now that you know about the Shreyasi problem, Bhaiya, what have you done about it? What can you possibly do? And what exactly did Shreyasi do that is so unforgivable? Avni has done much worse!'

'You can't compare her with Avni. That's—'

'Why not?' he asked. 'If I were to choose between two unhinged girls I would rather choose the one who has been loyal to me for three years and the one who—'

'Loyal? SHE'S MARRIED FOR FUCK'S SAKE! Do you understand that? I told you not to engage that girl in any conversation and yet you did!' Sumit argued. 'She's insane, she's dangerous.'

Daman rolled his eyes. 'Maybe it's your fault, Bhaiya. Had you given me the right email ID, none of this would have happened,' Daman complained. 'As a matter of fact, had I talked to her then, who knows if I would have ever met Avni?'

Sumit's face darkened. 'She's here to apologize and this is how you treat her? Have you lost your mind? Who was with you when you were floundering—'

'What she did was unforgivable,' growled Daman.

Avni finally looked up and caught Daman's gaze. 'Are you talking to Shreyasi?'

'Why shouldn't I? She's the one who can set all of it right. I know she would never betray me.'

Sumit looked at Daman, appalled. 'WHAT THE FUCK—'

Avni picked up her laptop bag from the side of the table and got up. 'Best of luck,' she said and forced a smile.

'You're not going anywhere,' said Sumit. 'THIS BASTARD HAS TO UNDERSTAND—'

'He has made his decision. It's done. I wish him the best of luck. If that's where his happiness lies. Who am I to stop him?'

Sumit blocked Avni's way. 'What? What happiness? What the fuck is wrong with you two?'

'I need to leave,' said Avni and nudged Sumit out of the way.

Sumit exhorted Daman to stop her, to talk to her, but an unmoved Daman sat there fiddling with his phone. Avni left without a word.

'YOU'RE MAKING A BIG MISTAKE,' Sumit shouted. 'Give me the girl's number.'

Sumit walked towards the table and reached out for Daman's phone. Daman wrested it away before Sumit could take it. Sumit asked for the phone politely. Daman got up, told him he needed to leave. Sumit tried to block Daman's way and get the phone from his hand. Daman refused. Sumit tried snatching it away from him. Daman resisted for a bit, warned Sumit to back off but when he didn't, he swung at Sumit's face and got him square in the jaw. Sumit stumbled backwards but didn't let up.

'I don't want to hit you,' warned Daman.

He came back at Daman. Daman grabbed him by the shoulders and rammed his knee into Sumit's ribcage. Sumit crumpled and fell to the ground. He writhed on the ground holding his chest. Sumit tried getting up again. He hadn't even been on his knees when Daman rammed his feet into Sumit's chest again.

'I won't let you spoil the only chance I have,' said Daman, standing over Sumit, and left.

36

'Take a right from the next turn,' Avni instructed the cab driver.

It had been a month since Daman and she had found his car smouldering in the parking lot of the apartment, and three weeks since Avni had last talked to him at Sumit's apartment. He hadn't reached out to her since. Not even a text to ask her if she was doing okay. *Fuck him, I don't need him!*

Over the last few weeks for which she had been depressed, a number of thoughts had crossed her mind. The two on the top of the list were either 'kill that bitch' or herself, both of which she soon realized were juvenile but things she was capable of. *I almost killed a man.* The feeling would always remain with her. Slowly, she had felt she was losing control over her own life; she was becoming one of those spineless, weak people who subconsciously start a self-destructive life after a failed relationship. *He was my first love.* Self-pity and disgust had threatened to slowly consume her. The pain had engulfed her.

'Yes, just stop there on the left. Wait for fifteen minutes,' said Avni. 'I'm leaving my bag here.'

She stepped out of the car and headed straight to the ward where Karthik lay. Dressed in a short red dress, she looked out of place in the hospital. A few heads turned. Amongst them was the nurse at the reception who smiled at Avni as she walked past. *She doesn't know what I did.* In the past few weeks, she had often visited the hospital and loitered outside Karthik's room, trying to catch a stray glimpse of him. Most times, he would be fast asleep, knocked out from the morphine. But today a girl sat beside him. She recognized her immediately as Varnika, Karthik's girlfriend, the girl he wrote a few books on.

They were holding hands and Karthik was laughing his head off. Far from feeling any relief from the guilt that ate through her, it worsened. *He could have died. I could have killed him.* She marched away from the ward, wiping her tears. *How did it come to this? When did I start loving Daman so much that I became prepared to lose all for him?* After taking a lowdown on Karthik's condition from the nurse, who called her the sweetest fan of Karthik, she walked back to the cab and left for her date.

After Daman had blocked her from his social media profiles three weeks ago, she had applied for a sick leave and started tailing him, unaware of what she wanted to get out of it. She would dress up for office, take her car , and sit in it all day with wafers, Diet coke and water, outside his house and follow him around when he stepped out. At the end of every day, she would go back home, her back crippled with pain, her bowels sick, and break down into a puddle of tears, question and curse herself, but the next day she would do the same. The first few days of following him around yielded nothing. He would stay at his apartment all day and come down only for a brief walk and smoke in the evening. Sometimes he would go to the British Council for an hour in the mornings to issue books. There were moments she even felt sorry for him, moments when she wanted to rush out of the car and embrace him. She even had a little hope. But whatever hope she had was dashed the next week when she found Daman meeting Shreyasi almost every other day. They would go to the same coffee shops, the same pubs and the same movie halls that Daman and she used to frequent. He would even take care to shave. They would laugh, hold hands and be happy. It shattered her heart. After the fifth day, she couldn't take it any more. *I'm Shreyasi now, hiding in the trenches, looking on. I'm the stalker.*

But no more. The crying, the moping, the blaming herself had to stop. This wasn't her. Tonight would be the day she moved on and reclaimed her life. She had no tears left for him. All the anger, the rage, the despair had tapered off, leaving behind a gnawing hollowness. Tonight she would fill that hollowness. Or if she failed, at least exact a little revenge in case he cared. She deserved someone better than him. *I won't love him any more.*

She was meeting a friend from work—Karan. She couldn't tell whether Karan genuinely liked her or just wanted to get into her pants, but if it were the latter he had been at it for a really long time. For months, Karan had timed his coffee breaks to sync with hers, offered her chewing gums after lunch and shared his phone charger so many times that she didn't get hers to office any more. His workstation had shifted too, from being at the far end of the room to now just two seats away. He had lost two staplers and countless pens to Avni who would borrow and lose them. Not once had he complained. In the past few weeks, it had been he who'd double-checked Avni's presentations or ironed out the errors before she mailed them to the seniors. Last week, when she told Karan they should go out some night, like a gentleman it was he who had suggested coffee and not alcohol. But she had wanted to get hammered.

Karan had come dressed sharply in dark a pair of trousers and a crisp white shirt. He looked younger than he did at work, she noticed. They hugged and Karan pulled a chair for her. *This is the guy who deserves me.*

'Do you want to drink something?' Karan asked.

'Of course, aren't we here for just that?' she said.

She wasted no time in getting drunk while Karan pulled out all the stops to impress her. He was funny, charming and courteous. If she had paid attention, it would have been a nice date. She didn't listen to half the things he said but she noticed he was handsome and attentive.

'So did I tell you he is a big prick?' slurred Avni.

'About ten times, yes. This will be the eleventh,' he said. 'Do you really think you need to drink that? You have had too much already.'

'Of course I do! I can handle alcohol quite well. It's him who couldn't handle it at all,' Avni chortled. 'Do you know he had an accident when he was drunk?'

'You told me that.'

'Like he hadn't even drunk that much. So stupid. Imagine! Now take this into consideration and tell me, do you think he really needed to break up with me?' she asked.

'I don't—'

'No, do you really think? Tell me? Tell me very honestly? Do you really think? The NATION WANTS TO KNOW! Do you—'

'You're drunk.'

'I'm fine. I am doing totally fine. You know who's not fine? You know?' drawled Avni.

'Let me take a wild guess? Daman?'

'You're a smart man. I knew you were a smart one. I should have dated you. I can still date you. My mom will like you so much better. You know, you're more my type. Let's start dating, okay? We will kiss tonight and make it official? Now you may think it's a rebound but it's really not. Okay? And I promise,' said Avni and put her hand on her heart. 'I promise—'

'You're embarrassing yourself. I should drop you home,' insisted Karan. He waved the waiter for the bill.

'Are you trying to get rid of me? Are you? Why does everyone want to get rid of me?'

'I'm trying to save you from the embarrassment that will come tomorrow. I'm booking an Uber and I'm dropping you home. Do you think you can go like this to your place?' he asked.

'Of course! My parents accepted Daman! That low-life writer with no future! Why wouldn't they accept me drunk? Pfftt. Stupid question! I'm rethinking my decision of falling in love with you. Should I? Should I not? Should I?' She swayed in her seat as she went on. 'Should I? Should I not?'

As Karan cleared the bill, Avni remarked, 'Daman would have never been able to afford this.' She got her voice down to a whisper and said, 'Shhh. Don't tell anyone but he's broke. But maybe Shreyasi will set everything right.'

'Sure,' said Karan, getting up. 'Do you need help?'

'No!' protested Avni. As soon as she got up, she stumbled and Karan broke her fall. By this time, the entire restaurant was looking at them. Avni flashed a middle finger and thrust out her tongue towards them. She wrapped her hands around Karan and kissed him full on the lips. Karan flinched and swayed out of the way. Avni pressed on, scratching his neck and clawing at him. Karan leant out of the way but this time Avni dug her teeth into his neck. Karan wrenched himself free. 'You don't love me?' she asked.

Karan didn't answer. He held her strongly by the arm and led her through the door even as she flailed her hands around and shouted repeatedly, 'I love you! I love you! I love you!'

37

Avni asked the cab driver to park the car a little way from the parking of her office. The driver asked if he should stop the trip and bill it.

'Give me two minutes?' She looked at her office building. She took a few deep breaths. She took out her phone and typed the keywords in Google's search bar. It prompted suggestions in a blue font. She had used these keywords every hour for the past few days.

Indian drunk girl in restaurant
Drunk girl funny
Drunk girl funny restaurant
Drunk girl proposal turned down
Drunk girl Delhi kiss

A few links had thumbnails of a grainy picture of her. It was a video of hers from the restaurant, taken by random strangers and stitched together by someone well versed with an editing software, that had gone viral, and had been shared across social media platforms and aggregator websites. All for a laugh. They reduced her entire personality, years of being a model citizen, a brilliant student, a stellar employee, a good daughter and good girlfriend, to a video and a few unfunny Internet memes. The video was taken down after she lodged a complaint with the cyber cell, citing invasion of privacy, but not before it had raked up over 3 lakh views.

She paid the bill and walked out of the cab. She took a deep breath and told herself it would be okay. She wouldn't be the first one to get drunk and embarrass herself. If they would laugh, she would laugh with them. She strode inside. Heads turned, people sniggered and her boss frowned when she walked in. Some of them didn't even have the decency to not point fingers at her. The girl from the HR department called her into her office for a friendly chat. *I will accept the Barclays offer. Just three months of the notice period and I'm gone from here.* But even then, she didn't want to leave this office with her head hung low and in hiding. So post lunch, she decided to change gears.

She looked people directly in the eye and cracked jokes about the entire episode herself. She flailed her hands in the air and enacted the scene out a few times in front of bemused colleagues. More than her, it was Karan who looked embarrassed. But soon enough, he joined them too. She was no longer being laughed at, they were laughing with her. By the end of the day, instead of frowning and sniggering, her colleagues were winking and high-fiving her. Every time she went up to a colleague and said 'Will you go out with me?' laughter ensued.

On her way back from the office, fuelled by the rush of having tackled the entire thing successfully, she called the recruiter from Barclays. She was told the position had been filled by a more suitable candidate. Why, she asked. The recruiter said that her behaviour had been found unsatisfactory.

38

After their scuffle at Sumit's house a few days ago, Sumit had called Daman numerous times but Daman had ignored him. It was only after Sumit had threatened to go to Daman's parents that he agreed to meet Sumit.

'She embarrassed herself. It wasn't my fault,' said Daman.

'Can't you see what she's doing? She's acting out because of you. Just talk to her. At least be with her till the time she wears off you.' Sumit pulled his chair closer to him. 'Be nice to her. What did she not do for you?'

'If this is what you want to talk about, I should leave. I need to see Shreyasi in a bit,' said Daman. 'I can't keep her waiting.'

'Keep her waiting? Who the fuck is she that you can't keep her waiting? You're seriously not dating her, are you?'

'Why do you think I'm not? And why the fuck shouldn't I!'

'I can think of a thousand reasons but the top one would still be that SHE'S BATSHIT CRAZY.'

'Will you stop fucking shouting?'

'I will not till the time your break up with her.'

'I'm not going to do that,' said Daman and got up. 'If you have nothing else to say, I'm leaving.'

Sumit threw up his hands in the air. 'Go, do whatever the fuck you want.'

'Thank you for your concern,' said Daman and left the coffee shop.

Once outside, he called for a cab. He was shouting instructions to the cab driver on the phone when Sumit came and stood next to him. He disconnected the call. 'What now?' Daman asked.

'Drop me till the office at least?'

'Fine.'

They hopped into the cab. Daman could see Sumit itching to broach the topic again. And he rolled his eyes when he did it.

'I'm not asking you to break up with her, okay? I'm just asking you to hold off for a little while. Avni is going through a tough time. Be a little considerate?'

'Considerate? For someone who nearly killed a person?'

'She merely pushed him.'

'Let me show you something.'

Daman brought out his phone from his pocket and tapped on to the video section. Even before he could push play, Sumit knew what he was going to see. Though shaky, the quality of the video was crisp. He spotted Avni in an instant. She was looking over shoulders and walking with a hasty pace, following someone. The video turned to Karthik talking on the phone, climbing the stairs to a metro station. The video cut back to Avni who nervously fixed her hair and jostled through the crowd to get closer to Karthik. Moments later, she was behind Karthik, tailing him till he got to the top of the stairs. And then, with the slightest of pushes, Avni nudged him down the stairs. The video zoomed in on Avni's blank face, and then on to Karthik who tumbled down the stairs, people stepping out of his way. *Stop*, thought Sumit. The video stopped playing.

'See? It was a small push,' said Sumit, collecting himself. 'She couldn't have anticipated that. She would have thought someone would break the fall. She was just trying to hurt him a little.'

'Are you not seeing what I'm trying to tell you?'

'What?'

'Who do you think gave me this video?'

'Shreyasi,' mumbled Sumit.

'And what do you think she would do if I dump her and go back to Avni? Even if I want to I can't be with Avni, for her sake and for mine.'

Sumit stayed shut.

Daman continued, 'This video can do a lot more damage than a drunken video.'

'But—'

'There are no buts here. I'm with Shreyasi now. I have nothing to lose.'

'SHE'S MARRIED,' argued Sumit.

'Yes, and I'm not.'

'You're telling me what you're doing is right?' said Sumit, losing his patience again.

'It's not wrong, at least. And who knows, I might be able to shake her off in the future,' Daman said, shrugging.

Sumit stiffened. He wanted to smack Daman. 'Have you lost your mind? The girl is crazy. *Vo bitch chutiya bana rahi hai tera*, she's making a fool out of you. You can't be with her,' urged Sumit.

'The girl also has my balls in her palm. Can't you fucking see that? She has the insurance papers, she has the video and she claims she can get me back my contract.'

'And so you decided to be with her? Are you a whore now, Daman?'

Daman scowled. 'I have not slept with her but maybe I will,' shot back Daman. 'I will decide when it comes to that. And what's your problem? She's into me. She will leave me when she gets over me.'

'She has been stalking you for three years. She needs to see a doctor, she doesn't need you,' said Sumit, infuriated. 'Look, I'm only looking out for you. This can't be good for you. How can you not see that? I suggest you leave the city for a bit. I will pay for wherever you go. Tell Shreyasi it's not going to work out. Apologize to her, ask her to go back to her husband. Maybe she won't put the video up anywhere.'

'No.'

'That wasn't up for discussion. You have to do what I ask you to do. As your bhaiya—'

'I said no,' Daman cut in.

'What no? She's crazy! This will destroy you. Well, look at what all she has done till now. THIS GIRL IS DANGEROUS, BHENCHOD.'

'She's setting it right, again. I can't fuck that up now. And who the hell knows what would have happened had I not crashed my car and had you not given me a fake email ID?'

'NOTHING WOULD HAVE HAPPENED, MADARCHOD,' shouted Sumit.

'And you know that because you are an oracle?'

'I know that because I was there at the FUCKING HOSPITAL! I was there when you were dying. I saw Shreyasi too!' shouted Sumit.

'So?'

Sumit hesitated. 'This isn't Shreyasi.'

'What?'

'She died in the car crash, Daman. The real Shreyasi died that night.'

39

There isn't a lot of traffic on the road. Shreyasi is talking about her first boyfriend. Even though I barely know her, I feel envy pierce through my heart. She notices it on my face and holds my hand. She tells me I'm cute. I smile back at her. She looks divine. It's hard to keep looking at the road. I wish she were driving. She asks me about my girlfriends and I tell her about Ananya, the girl who cheated on me. She calls the girl a bitch. I concur. I should have reached my friends but I'm driving around in circles. She knows that but hasn't protested yet. If I may hazard a guess, she has even encouraged it. The bottles in the jute bag clang near her feet. She gestures towards it and winks. I shake my head. She insists. It's hard to turn her down. She takes two beers out but neither she nor I can pry them open with our teeth. She keeps the bottles back in and takes out a bottle of vodka instead. She twists open the cap. She puts it to her lips and takes a long sip. I shake my head. I have to drive, I argue. But she's not one to listen. She pesters with a scrunched nose. Please, she says, don't be a killjoy. She puts the bottle on my lips. I sway away. Vodka spills over my shirt. That's not fair, she cries out. Fine, I say. She puts it on my mouth again. It's bitter. I close up my throat and spill a little out. Yet a little snakes its way to my stomach and then to my brain. I try harder to look at her. She holds my hand. I feel the warmth envelop my body. I look at her. And then back at the road. I slam on the brakes. A loud screech fills up the car. The taxi in front of us brakes too. It's too late. I swerve left. I hit a car. In panic, I swerve right . . . Shreyasi's thrown wildly to her side. She's wearing her seat belt. The car veers towards the divider. I gasp. I should hit the brakes but I would hit the taxi head-on. I notice the taxi driver. I see death in his eyes. The taxi is empty. I swerve farther to avoid the taxi. I push down on the brake. The car hits the divider and flips. I look at Shreyasi. I'm hanging from my seat. She falls head-on to the roof

of the car. The disquieting crunch of her neck fills my ears. She groans.
The car flips again. She's thrown against the window. Pieces of glass
protrude from her face. She bleeds. Her eyes look at me lifelessly. Her
hands flap around limply. She's dead. Before long, she's flung out
of the car. The car comes to a rest. I'm strapped to my seat but I can
see her clearly. Her face, her hair, her mangled body, her dead eyes,
I can see it all. There's fire. Flames lick at her body. I scream. Her hair
singes, her skin turns black. I retch. I can smell her skin burning, I can
see the eyes melt out of her sockets, those beautiful eyes . . . those lips.
I can see the teeth now. I pass out.

Daman woke up with a startle. The bed he was lying in was
drenched in his sweat. He cried out hoarse. All but a silent
scream escaped his mouth. His throat was choked from all
the shouting from the last seven days he had been here in
the hospital, often restrained to his bed. His head burst, as
fever burned through his body. He shook and trembled. Two
ward boys rushed inside, shouting instructions at each other.
Daman swung wildly getting one of the ward boys in the face.
Before he could swing again, the other pushed him down to
the bed, pinning his shoulder under a knee. Having recovered,
the injured ward boy restrained Daman's hands. Daman
writhed in agony and anger, arching his back and kicking his
legs to break free. A doctor and a nurse followed soon after to
sedate him. 'Shreyasi's dead, I killed her,' he muttered, before
he closed his eyes and feel asleep.

Outside the hospital room, Daman's parents sat, his father
sobbing softly and his mother rubbing his back. The doctor
emerged from the room and asked his parents to follow him
to his chambers. They did so quietly. In the cafeteria of the
hospital, Sumit and Avni sat in front of each other. Avni
wanted to cry but seeing Sumit absolutely wrecked, she held
back her tears. Sumit hadn't slept a wink in three days.

'Why didn't you tell me before?' asked Avni.

'Only the family and I knew. I couldn't have risked it. Of course, if you guys were to be married I would have told you, or maybe the family would have but—'

'I know where you're coming from.' Avni sighed. 'So if Shreyasi died in the car accident a year ago, who's this girl?'

'A stalker. That's what I told Daman, and then told you, but both of you had bought her story hook, line and sinker. I didn't know how else to make you believe. And when I did . . .'

'It's not your fault. You couldn't have known he would . . . get this anxiety attack again,' said Avni. 'What is the doctor saying?'

'It's too early to make a conclusive judgement but it's worse than the last time. They have called the doctor who treated him earlier. He will be here in a day or two. But they are saying his behaviour suggests it's a full relapse.'

Avni nodded. 'How did they treat him the last time?'

Sumit leant into his chair. He let out a deep breath. He explained, 'Things were trickier back then. First he had to get his movements back. Both his brain and body were mush. He had forgotten how to even hold a spoon. The doctors had concentrated on getting those back and make him physically capable. It was only much later that he started getting nightmares of the accident and of Shreyasi. He hadn't asked for Shreyasi for the longest time. He didn't even remember much of her except her name and the car ride they took together,' said Sumit.

The waiter got their sandwiches.

Sumit continued, 'When we first told him about Shreyasi's death he had acted the same way as he is right now. Seizures, acting out, running up a high fever . . . the very same symptoms you're seeing right now. He acted out strangely and lost his temper every now and then. Following which he would sit quietly for hours on end. But then suddenly he would have a vision and lash out. Quite often, we would find him huddled into a corner of the room, shouting. We found him on the ledge of the roof once,' said Sumit and sighed. 'We thought we had lost him.'

'How did they finally treat him?' Avni asked.

'Therapy and medication. He responded well to the treatment but just when we would think he was ready to go home, a nightmare or a stressful episode would trigger something and everything would be undone. He would spend days in the hospital room asking for Shreyasi, asking where she was and if she was okay. Every time someone told him or he remembered that she was dead, he worsened. He would start getting fits again. He would pass out and ask the same question. Where is Shreyasi? It seemed like he wanted an answer but not the one we gave him or the one he found in his repressed memories. His mind would continually negate the reality of Shreyasi's death. His body rejected that he was in some way responsible for her death. The doctors realized a strong correlation of his guilt of Shreyasi's death with his seizures; the seizures were how the brain coped. Since the doctors found that his mind was rejecting the possibility of him being responsible for Shreyasi's death they tried to make him come to terms with it,' said Sumit.

'So?'

'The cycle kept repeating itself till the doctor found a breakthrough. He tried a largely experimental treatment called Retrieval-induced Forgetting,' said Sumit.

'What's that?'

'It means creating false memories. If you keep telling a lie to someone who suffers from dissociative amnesia, someone whose memories are repressed because the event was traumatic, he starts to believe in the lie. So the doctor started lying to Daman. Every time Daman asked where Shreyasi was, the doctor lied to him. And then he asked us to corroborate the lie. It worked. Slowly, his dreams started to change. Many times, she wouldn't die in the dreams,' said Sumit.

'You told him the lie that Daman wasn't driving the car? And that Shreyasi survived the car crash and left the country since?' Avni guessed aloud.

Sumit nodded. 'It worked like a dream,' he said. 'Within weeks, it was as if our old Daman was back. Of course, he kept asking me about Shreyasi and whether I had talked to her or if she had reached out. I kept lying about it all. We made him believe that none of us liked Shreyasi because she was the one driving the car and had ended up almost killing him. The more we made him rehearse the lies, the more he believed in them. I should have never—'

Avni shifted her chair closer to Sumit's and took his hand into hers. She said, 'It wasn't your fault. You were just looking out for him.' She asked after a pause, nervous, 'So what will the therapist do now?'

'He will undo what I did. I told him Shreyasi died in the car crash two years ago and brought on the seizures and the nightmares. The therapist will tell him otherwise and get rid of them,' said Sumit.

'But there's a Shreyasi lurking around this time,' muttered Avni. 'Once he makes him believe that Shreyasi is alive, he will think of her to be the same one. He will go running to her, won't he?'

'Probably.'

'Would the memories of the Goa trip come back to him? Is there a possibility that he would recall the face of the real Shreyasi? If he does then he will know that this Shreyasi is an imposter.'

'No. Those memories won't come back. They are long gone.'

40

Avni called for a cab back to office. She had spent a good part of the last three days in the hospital. 'You staying here won't make a difference,' Sumit had said—who had taken a leave of absence himself—and bid her well. Sitting at the back seat of the car, she took out her little pad and started to scribble. She wrote Shreyasi's name, both the one who died in the crash and the one Sumit called a stalker and wondered about the connection between the two. If the stalker was to be believed, she had been around for more than three years, a full year before Daman had even met the Shreyasi who died that day in the accident. And she had proved herself to be in Goa when Daman was. Avni closed her eyes and massaged her temples. Her phone rang. It was Karan from office. She had been late on a few presentations they had to work together on. It was only yesterday that Karan had sounded her off for being lax. She had not fought back because he was right. Ever since the Barclays deal fell through, she had been out of sorts, being late to office, leaving early, spending hours staring at her computer screen. No one talked about the viral video any more and yet it marred her existence there. She wanted to get out. But there were no replies from the places she had sent her résumé to. She stared at the scribbled piece of paper again. It's all because of this stalker—Shreyasi.

The car stopped.

'Why are we stopping?' asked Avni.

'Someone else is boarding the cab as well,' said the driver. 'You booked a carpool cab.'

'Can't we just go? I will pay extra.'

'That's against the company rules, ma'am,' said the driver.

203

Avni sighed. A few minutes passed by and there was no sign of the person who had booked the same cab. 'Are you going to wait here for the entire day?' asked Avni.

'Just a couple of more minutes, ma'am,' he said.

Just as he said this, the door of the car flung open. A girl slipped in next to Avni.

'Hi,' said Shreyasi and smiled at Avni.

Avni recoiled from her. 'What are you doing here?' She fumbled nervously through her handbag and took out two hundred-rupee notes. She flung them near the driver's seat. 'I'm leaving,' she said and opened the door. But Shreyasi held her hand. Avni grimaced. Shreyasi's grip was strong. 'Leave me,' said Avni.

'We need to talk.'

'We don't!' shot back Avni.

'I know that you know that Shreyasi is dead,' said Shreyasi. 'We need to talk about Daman. It's for the good of both of us.'

Avni wrested her hand free and stepped out of the car. She walked away from the car. The car followed.

'GO THE FUCK AWAY!' shouted Avni at the car. The car still followed. Avni strode to the car. 'WHAT DO YOU WANT! YOU ALREADY HAVE EVERYTHING! NOW JUST GO!'

The car still followed.

'I want to talk,' said Shreyasi. She opened the door. 'Come on now. For Daman.'

After resisting for a bit, Avni stepped inside. *I will kill her, that's the only thing that's left. Don't cry. Don't cry!*

'How's he doing?' asked Shreyasi passing Avni the box of tissues. Avni waved it away dismissively. 'I would have seen him but Sumit is guarding him like a hound.'

'He needs to be guarded from you,' snapped Avni.

Shreyasi smirked. 'I would say the exact opposite. He needs me. He needs his Shreyasi.'

'YOU ARE NOT SHREYASI!' bellowed Avni, her hands clenching into fists.

Shreyasi chortled. 'Of course, I'm his Shreyasi. Okay, I'm not the one who died in the accident, I will grant you that. But I'm Shreyasi. The girl he should have always been in love with. And he will ask for me when he wakes up.'

'You're a fraud! That's what you are. You're just pretending to be Shreyasi and you're not. He never wrote the book or the posts thinking of you. That girl he wrote about is dead! You are no one to him,' flamed Avni.

'Says the one who has been with him for just a year. I have been with him for three years.' She raised her hand stretching out three fingers. 'I waited for a year to talk to him! Unlike you, who just saw him and started talking. WHAT I HAVE FOR HIM CAN'T BE COMPARED TO THE FEW MONTHS YOU HAVE HAD HIM FOR!'

'Is that what you wanted to tell me?'

'I didn't mean to lose my temper,' said Shreyasi, softly. 'I apologize. Actually, I had something to offer you.'

'And what makes you think I will take up anything you offer? You're vile and all you know is how to destroy lives.'

'I didn't destroy anyone's life. All I wanted was love. I have that now. And Daman wouldn't be in that hospital room had Sumit not unnecessarily told him about Shreyasi's death,' Shreyasi said. 'But he's going to be fine. He's going to wake up thinking Shreyasi is dead. But the therapist is going to fool him into believing that Shreyasi still lives. That's the only course of treatment which works for him. Retrieval-induced Forgetting? I guess that's what it's called. And when he starts believing that Shreyasi walked out alive from the accident, he's going to remember me, the stalker-cum-guardian-cum-love-of-his-life.

He will connect the dots. The memories will start flooding back in and he will be in my arms again.'

Avni asked what she had been itching to ask her. 'If you weren't in the car with him that night, who was?'

'Shreyasi,' she answered.

'Of course I know that but—'

'The girl's name was Shreyasi,' said Shreyasi. She chuckled. 'It's strange to say her name. Anyway, she tried to keep him away from me and look what happened. Poor girl! She ended up broken and burnt and dead.' Shreyasi looked at Avni. 'Oh, you look confused now. Aw. So sweet.' She laughed. 'Everything you heard that day in the coffee shop was true. I fell in love with him, read his mails and watched him for almost a year. I knew he was going to Goa. I planned my trip too to the last detail. I was going to give him the love story he always wanted and fantasized about. I booked into the same hotel as he did. Everything was fine till she walked in . . .' Her voice trailed off.

'Yes?'

'. . . Shreyasi, the girl who shared my name, walked in,' said Shreyasi. 'The dumb-fuck at the hotel had switched our rooms because our names were the same. She got the room directly opposite Daman's and I was given one on another floor. Before I knew it, they had struck up a conversation. That slut! That fucking whore! I was still fighting for my room when they had started talking! I had waited a year and she . . . right in front of my eyes. Can you believe it? They were smiling and laughing like they had always been friends. I wanted to strangle the girl and tell Daman that he was supposed to meet me here, not some two-bit whore from Bengaluru. I was shattered, Avni, I was . . . For the next three days, I watched on as the wrong Shreyasi shamelessly flirted with Daman! And he had the audacity, the shamelessness to even respond to her! They went out every day, right in front of my eyes. I was there . . . I had done so much for him and yet! He was with the wrong Shreyasi!' She clutched Avni's hand and squeezed. 'You tell me? Was it fair? Wasn't he supposed to be with me? Of course he was. He should have been with me! But he was with her! All the time.' She took her hand off Avni's and stared at her fingers. 'The accident scared me so much. But she died.' She gazed at Avni. 'It served her right. It had to happen.'

'Did you want her to die?' asked Avni.

'Of course! But that accident . . .' She sighed. She took a deep breath and continued. 'I thought he would never wake up. So I got married. I thought I will eventually move on but I couldn't. I kept thinking of him, I kept praying for him. And three months later, he woke up. He was battered and his head was gone but he was alive.' She smiled. 'And then he remembered her. The other Shreyasi.'

She's crazy. Get out of the car. Go as far away as possible. Avni said, 'But you said you were the character from the posts. You did the same things that she did. You said it was inspired by you and that's why you were furious at him for writing that book that didn't portray you well. But you weren't the girl from the posts! He didn't know you.'

'YES, I WASN'T THE PERSON FROM THE POSTS! BUT I BECAME THAT PERSON! I became the girl from the posts. SHE WAS ME, AND I WAS HER! THERE WAS NO DIFFERENCE! I became the Shreyasi he loved, I became who he wrote about, I became the person from the posts, I talked like her, I dressed up like her, I grew my hair long, got the same tattoos. I did all the things he wrote about. I became the person he could have been in love with, the person he would write about . . . and then he betrayed me! I waited for the book for so long. I had imagined the release of the

book . . . I had imagined every reader of Daman asking him
where this girl Shreyasi was, the girl that I had become . . .
and then slowly and steadily I would have revealed myself to
him . . . He would have found me to be the spitting image of
Shreyasi . . . He would have finally found me . . . He would
cry and love me . . . He would embrace me . . . and then he
would reveal me to the rest of the world . . . . But *The Girl of
My Dreams,* the pile of garbage he wrote, mocked everything
I had for him! I had had enough. I had to meet him and set
things right. What if he wrote another one like that? All that I
had done for him would have been for nothing. The Shreyasi
he thought he loved might have died but his love for her could
have lived through me. He could love me.'

'You need help. You are crazy,' said Avni.

'Because I fell in love?'

'Because you're crazy. I am taking no part in this. I'm
out.' She tapped on the driver's shoulder asking him to stop
the car at the next signal.

'You can still be with Daman.'

Avni frowned. 'What?'

'I'm married and that doesn't stop me from loving Daman.
Daman and I don't need to be married to keep our love story
alive. We have talked about that.'

'And Daman is okay with that?' asked Avni, shocked.
Shreyasi nodded. 'And you want me to have a relationship
like you do with your husband? Are you out of your mind?'

'I'm as serious as serious can be.'

'I can't believe this! You're shitting me!'

'I'm not. I just—'

'There's a fundamental difference. Your husband doesn't
know of Daman, he doesn't know you're a cheating whore,
but I know. I know you two are seeing each other,' Avni spat
out. Shreyasi looked on and smiled. 'What?' asked Avni.

Shreyasi pulled the sleeve of her kurta up. On her right arm were three bluish-red imprints. Someone must have held her tightly there. She covered them up.

'He hit you? You should go to—'

Shreyasi chortled and told Avni she was so naive. 'I let him grab me and push me. But this was all before I told him about Daman.' She smiled and continued, 'Marriages are tricky, Avni. Do you know Akash has never been faithful to me? Take a wild guess who he was sleeping with? It's almost like a bad movie.'

'Who?'

'I always knew he had been cheating on me. He was the only one who could hoodwink me all this time. He was more careful than all of you. The girl had been hiding in plain sight,' said Shreyasi and chuckled. She flicked through her phone and showed Avni the picture of the girl. Shreyasi continued, 'You know who that is? Does she look familiar? No? She's my elder sister. She's married too, if I may add. Now you know why I never found any suspicious names on his last dialled list. I wasn't looking for my sister's number.' Shreyasi laughed. 'My marriage was always a lie. And he's still sleeping with her. I just confronted him a few days back and he lashed out at me just like I had wanted him to. He called me a bitch for breaching his privacy and whatnot, that low-life asshole. Little did he know I recorded everything,' Shreyasi said and winked. 'Once I had that I told him about Daman. He could do nothing but listen like a scared puppy.'

She's a witch. 'Why doesn't he leave you?'

'He can't and he won't. His family will flay him. He's so cute. He's totally afraid of his mother. And imagine what will happen when I show the video during the divorce proceedings. He's not going anywhere. He will be my cute husband on the leash. Well, he stands to gain a lot too. He can do whatever he wants to outside of this marriage and I don't have to sleep with him any more. Let my sister have him.'

'But why wouldn't you leave him and go with Daman?' retorted Avni.

'That's something you won't understand,' said Shreyasi. 'There's a subtle difference between a wife and a muse. I'm Daman's muse. He will immortalize us when he writes about me. What does a wife have to gain? A few good years. A few kids. A little security? How's that any good? Writers don't write about their wives, they write about their muses. Wives are nothing more than facilitators in their lives. Wives ground them, that's all they do. Why do you think he didn't write about you apart from the fact that you're dull?'

Avni seethed but kept quiet.

'Because you're too easy. He sees you every day. He talks to you every day. He can have you in his bed every day. Even if you were interesting, you would no longer be after a little while. You're like that song which once heard too many times becomes unbearable. The shelf lives of wives are abysmal. Muses are forever. He will always love me. Till he doesn't totally have me all for himself, he will love me, he will crave for me, he will want me.'

'I think—'

'You can be his wife.'

Avni laughed out mirthlessly. 'So kind of you. But I think I will pass. Bhaiya? Drop me at the next metro station. Take this woman as far from me as possible.' *A wife, and she will still be the mistress*, thought Avni.

'Avni?' said Shreyasi and waited for Avni to look at her. She continued with a deathly stare in her eyes, 'You won't tell anything that I said to Daman about my husband or about my more-than-generous offer to you. Of course, I don't have to tell you what will happen otherwise?'

'I'm not scared of your threats,' snapped Avni.

'You should be. Unless you want to see Daman back in a hospital bed, shackled to his bed, and you in a prison. Wipe that surprise off your face. I have a video of you pushing Karthik down a flight of stairs. It's full HD. I would have showed it to you sometime but it seems like we aren't friends.'

'You don't—'

'I do have it. Daman has seen it too. It serves as a constant reminder for him of why he shouldn't talk to you.' Shreyasi smiled.

'You bitch!' retorted Avni. She said after composing herself, 'Fine, you win. I'm out of this. But before I leave I should tell you that there's just one little problem, Shreyasi.'

'What?'

'Even if the psychiatrist makes him believe that Shreyasi lives and he gets better, he will always know that you're a stalker and that you staged Goa. He will never love you the way you want him to,' argued Avni.

'Oh, how stupid of you, Avni! You still think that these little details can keep Daman and me apart? You don't know anything about love, do you?' Shreyasi smiled.

Avni got down at the next metro station. She asked Shreyasi just before she got off, 'Did you cause that accident?'

'No,' Shreyasi answered. 'I would never endanger his life.'

The cab drove off.

41

He's so beautiful, thought Shreyasi looking at Daman.

'Why didn't you come visit me earlier?' Daman asked.

I wanted to see you, baby. I wanted to hold you and kiss you and make love to you. I wanted to be with you, baby, but your stupid parents . . . Shreyasi pushed the cake in front of him. It had the words 'Welcome back' written on it in red icing. It had been three weeks since Daman had been discharged from the hospital and he had been living with his parents for the first two weeks. 'You think I didn't want to? Your parents hate me. I didn't want to make it worse,' said Shreyasi and held back her tears.

In the two weeks that Daman had been at his parents' house and away from her, she had been inundated with texts and calls from him. He kept telling her they have to meet, that he needed to talk to her, that he *missed* her. His language in the texts was not of a friend or a foe or someone who had been vexed by a stalker, but that of a forlorn lover who had been kept away from his love. Shreyasi had read those texts countless times. She had taken printouts of the screenshots of the texts, drawn hearts around them and had stuck them on her cubicle's pinboard. She would read them every now and then, and blush like a newly wed wife.

'I thought you would never come back to your place,' said Shreyasi.

Daman held Shreyasi's hand and said, 'Maa didn't want me to but I told them I had to finish the book and I couldn't do it in that house. *I only came because I had to see you.* I couldn't have waited any longer,' Daman responded with a gentle squeeze of her hand.

He loves me!

'Why?' asked Shreyasi.

'I . . . I just wanted to hold you. I wanted to feel this,' he said and grasped her hand tighter. 'I wanted to feel you close to me. I had been going crazy in the therapy . . . the dreams . . .'

Shreyasi leant into Daman and kept her head on his shoulder. *He smells like spring.* 'Do I still die in those dreams?'

Daman put his arm around Shreyasi and kissed her forehead.

'Do you remember how you got the first seizure?' she asked.

'I don't want to dwell on that. I want to talk about *us*,' he answered.

'I just want to be careful, Daman. I read everything there is to be read on PTSD. There are certain triggers that bring on these panic attacks. I don't want you to be in the hospital again,' said Shreyasi.

'That's sweet of you but I don't remember. The last I know is Sumit talking to me.'

'Was it something he said?' asked Shreyasi.

'Can we cut the cake? It looks delicious. The hospital food made me want to kill myself.'

'In a bit. Tell me?'

'No, I don't remember. Sumit is the last thing I remember. After that I just remember everything in little flashes. I remember that I was restrained to my bed. I remember hearing my mother cry, the ward boys shouting. I remember seeing Sumit sobbing, my father fighting with the doctors. Then of course, I remember sitting in front of the psychiatrist and crying. I remember telling him how scared I was thinking that I had killed you, that you had died in the car crash. I remember the psychiatrist telling me that you hadn't died and yet the tears wouldn't stop. I knew you hadn't died because I remembered *us*, because I remembered your face . . . yet the feeling was so strong that I kept thinking you were dead. I just wanted to see you so badly. But my parents . . . I was so confused . . . You were alive because I remembered your face and whatever happened between you, me and Avni but in the dreams you were dead, I could feel you die. The doctor kept telling me otherwise, he kept telling me you are alive. I knew it was the truth because I had met you after the accident, I remembered that. I remember telling the doctor about you, how you came back into my life in the strangest way possible. About how you told me you had stalked me for a year.'

'You told him everything?'

'There's patient–doctor confidentiality. He's not going to report you for stalking me,' said Daman and chuckled.

'You still remember nothing of the trip?'

'Nope. It's all gone.'

Shreyasi smiled.

'But I have you to tell me all about it.'

'You have changed,' said Shreyasi, forcing away her tears. *He needs me. He loves me. He wants me.*

'I thought I had lost you,' said Daman and looked away from her. 'Now, can we cut the cake?'

She nodded. *He's trying not to cry, my sweet baby. How much he loves me, my love.* Daman took the knife and cut a small sliver and made her eat it. Then he cut a huge chunk of the cake and gobbled it down.

'Tell me about Goa?' asked Daman, licking his fingers.

For the next half an hour, Shreyasi made up stories about all that they did in Goa, where all they went, where they first kissed, where they had their first drink together . . . He sat in rapt attention and listened to all of it, trying his best to recall any of the episodes.

'Anything?' she asked.

'Everything is a blank. But it doesn't matter. I can imagine myself there,' said Daman.

Just then, Shreyasi's eyes went to the clock. 'I need to get home. He will be back in an hour.'

'I can drop you home,' said Daman. A moment of awkward silence passed between them. 'I mean in a cab.'

'I'm so sorry. I had to—'

'I have already forgiven you for that. I don't miss it.'

Shreyasi rummaged through her handbag. She brought out an envelope with a ribbon tied neatly on it.

'What's this?'

'The insurance papers. Think of this as a welcome-back gift. I promised you I will give it to you if you left Avni.'

'I left Avni way before today. Why give it to me today?' questioned Daman.

'I wasn't sure of it earlier but now I am. I hope you make good use of the money.'

Daman thanked her. He kept the envelope aside and called for a cab for Shreyasi. They walked downstairs hand in hand when the cab arrived.

'Can I come with you?' asked Daman when she sat inside the cab.

She smiled and slid away from the door.

'Greater Kailash,' instructed Shreyasi.

They drove headlong into office traffic. The radial roads of Connaught Place were choked owing to the new metro line being constructed there. The painfully long drive back to Shreyasi's house was exacerbated by Daman's sudden sullen silence.

'What happened?' asked Shreyasi.

'Nothing,' he said.

'Tell me?'

'I told you it's nothing.'

'Daman, we can't be keeping secrets from each other,' urged Shreyasi.

'You can't expect me to be cheery and smile as I drop you to your husband's place. That's a little too much to ask for.'

Shreyasi sighed. 'Akash and I signed a paper and walked around a fire a few times, that's all there is to it.'

'You guys sleep together, share the same bed, the same house, the same cupboard. Did that come written on the paper or no?'

'Why are you being like this?' asked Shreyasi. 'Earlier—'

'EARLIER THINGS WERE DIFFERENT! I thought of you as a stalker, someone who was hell-bent on wrecking my life. But now I see clearly. All I kept asking my therapist was where were you, were you okay, did you ask about me . . . that's all I did . . . You don't know the anxiousness that gripped me when they wouldn't tell me where you were . . . I kept thinking you were dead, that I had killed you, I wanted to see you to make those dreams stop, I thought maybe you weren't real . . . you have no idea what I was going though in that hospital, Shreyasi . . . I kept seeing your dead face in my dreams . . . but then I remembered you coming back to me, it was real, I remembered all the things that happened with you and Avni. So I knew you weren't dead! I WANTED TO SEE YOU! I COULDN'T BEAR TO BE AWAY FROM YOU! When I woke up in a drenched bed every day muttering your name I realized . . . I realized Shreyasi . . .'

'What?'

'THAT WE ARE MEANT TO BE! That all you were trying to do was to keep your love alive,' snapped Daman. He took a deep breath. 'We should put whatever happened behind and make a new beginning.'

'Daman, I—'

'You need to leave your husband,' Daman said with a sense of finality to his tone.

'I can't.'

'Why can't you! You don't love him! You love me. You went to such a length to have me and now I'm offering you my life. Why would you not have me?'

'It's not as easy as you think it is.'

'I left Avni, didn't I?'

'Yes, but you weren't married. I am. His and my families are involved in our relationship. My parents will be crushed.'

'But sooner or later—'

'But baby, I'm with you. My husband and I don't share anything. We don't even have sex if that's what you are worried about. Just think of him as my landlord who stays with me. Our relationship has just started and I don't want to spoil it. I have waited three years for this.'

'I have waited a lifetime.'

'That's so sweet of you, baby. But I don't have the strength to get into divorce proceedings. You don't know how vindictive Akash is. I don't want to get into it. And what will change if I get rid of him and get married to you? Nothing! You will be bored of seeing me around all the time. I like this better. Sneaking out, seeing you, it's fun this way,' she said.

'Not for me. But okay, if you insist I will give you time.'

'I do.'

42

It was two in the night when Daman jemmied the key into the lock of his apartment. Shreyasi helped Daman steady his fingers and unlocked the door. She had spent the better part of the night with Daman at Summerhouse watching him down shot after shot after shot and laugh at everything she had to say. *He's happy drunk.*

'Are you sure you can't stay the night?' asked Daman as they entered his apartment. His fidgety hands were around her waist, teasing the edge of her jeggings.

'I'm sure,' she said. 'I will have to leave in a bit. Akash is waiting.'

'Yeah, yeah, your beloved husband,' mocked Daman and took his hand off.

'I thought we had decided not to talk about it,' said Shreyasi.

'Fine.'

They hadn't had sex yet. *Maybe today*, thought Shreyasi. Over the last few weeks, the time they had spent together was mostly during Shreyasi's lunch breaks. Daman would take the metro to her office, they would eat together and he would go back. Sometimes he would even try cooking for her; Shreyasi found that adorable. He had bought a single-plate induction stove just for this purpose. Shreyasi had given him a Tissot as a mark of gratitude the first time he cooked for her. It was burnt dal and badly made chapattis but he had got better since then.

'How is the book going?' asked Shreyasi when she saw the screen saver dancing around on his laptop screen.

'It's hard to write when you know you're never going to be published.'

I'm working on that but Jayanti Raghunath is a hard nut to crack, thought Shreyasi. She asked, 'Did you call Jayanti?'

'She hasn't taken any of my calls or replied to my texts.'

'You will be fine, baby. I will make everything all right. I love you,' said Shreyasi and hugged him.

Just then, Daman's phone glowed and Avni's name flashed on it. Daman stared at his phone.

'Are you going to take that?' asked Shreyasi.

'No,' said Daman irritably and cut the call. He switched off his phone.

Ever since Daman had shifted back to his apartment, Avni hovered around Daman's neck like a corpse. She hadn't stopped calling or texting Daman begging him to take her back, and to dump Shreyasi. Only last week, Daman had patched Shreyasi into his call with Avni to show her what a nuisance Avni had turned into. Shreyasi had heard Avni scream like a dying animal and curse Daman like an occultist. *You should have died, Daman,* Avni had screamed into the phone. *Shreyasi is a bitch, leave her, she's a bitch,* she had yelled repeatedly. Daman had been patient yet stern with her but he was slowly losing it. Avni was overstepping boundaries and vexing him. She had been following both Daman and Shreyasi like a ghost. Daman would get texts from unknown numbers, friend requests from accounts with no display pictures, and sometimes they would spot Avni walking a little distance away from them. *Like today.* During the entire time Daman and Shreyasi were at Summerhouse, Avni had sat three tables away with a couple, staring at them. It was Shreyasi who had first noticed her. She had kept it from Daman for she didn't want to ruin the date. But before long Daman had noticed her as well although he looked away from her as if she was air. 'Are you not going to go say hello?' Shreyasi had asked. 'No,' Daman had answered irritably. Shreyasi and Daman had noted

that pint after pint were ordered on the table behind them.
Despite the nonchalance, Avni's presence had hung over them
like the stench of a stale lunch.

'She didn't look too well today,' said Shreyasi.

'I'm not going to feel guilty about that. I have had enough
of her crying calls and texts. I don't even feel sorry for her
now, I feel annoyed. I just want her to fuck off, there's only
as much I can take. She even called on the landline late at
night when I was at my parents'. What do you think my
parents will say to that? It's embarrassing. God knows what
she would have done had I broken up any later. She has to
fucking move on.'

'Wow. You seem angry.'

'She was better than this. I can't take this nonsense
any more. The latest I heard from Sumit is that she has quit
her job. Now how the fuck am I supposed to react to that?'

'She has?'

'Yes, but she will find another. She's stupidly throwing it
all away,' said Daman. 'Sumit tried to pin it on you saying the
video has made her unemployable. He was trying to make me
feel guilty about dating you.'

'And are you?'

'It's all nonsense. Viral videos are a dime a dozen. No one
remembers it the next day. Nothing is going to make me feel
guilty about dating you. Avni had no business being there
at Summerhouse. She's not the only girl in the world who
has had a break-up,' said Daman. He rummaged through his
fridge. 'I have vodka. You want some?'

'I am not drinking, remember?'

'Yeah, the pretence of being a faithful wife must go on!'
retorted Daman. 'Cheers to that.'

'I thought—'

'Apologies, my bad!'

Daman poured himself a large shot. He had just put it to his lips when there was a knock on the door. They looked at each other. There was another knock.

'Who could it be?' whispered Shreyasi.

Then the person outside started banging on the door.

'No clue,' answered Daman.

As if on cue, the person on the other side shouted, 'OPEN THE DOOR!'

Daman shrugged. 'Not again,' he said. 'It's Avni. Let her be. She will shout and then leave in a bit. This is the third time she has done this in the past week. The secretary of the society has already complained once to my landlord. Just stay put and she will leave in twenty minutes after she's done banging.' Daman looked at the door and shouted, 'GO THE FUCK AWAY!'

Avni shouted again. This time her voice broke. It sounded like she was bawling. 'OPEN . . . THE . . . door.'

'Open it?' said Shreyasi.

Daman sat on the bed and leant back. 'Of course not, I am not encouraging her,' said Daman. He shouted again, 'FUCK OFF, AVNI!'

'Daman! Don't do that,' said Shreyasi.

'Why not? She's creating a scene. She has no business to be there.'

Shreyasi walked and sat near Daman. They stayed silent. Ten minutes passed by. 'Is she gone?' asked Shreyasi.

Daman shrugged. Just then, Avni shouted again, this time her words dissolved into her tears. 'Open the door. PLEASE. Please . . . please . . .'

'Daman, just open the door. She's still there,' said Shreyasi.

'Fuck no,' said Daman.

Avni banged on the door again. This time, Shreyasi got up from the bed and strode towards the door.

'DON'T DO—' said Daman.

Shreyasi opened the door. Avni lay slumped on the ground in a puddle of her own vomit. She looked up at Shreyasi and said, 'Please.'

Shreyasi helped Avni inside the apartment. Daman rolled his eyes, scrunched his face at the smell and walked away from the two of them. Shreyasi made Avni sit on the bed.

'Are you okay?' asked Shreyasi.

There was vomit still stuck to her chin. Shreyasi asked Daman to pass her a napkin. Daman did so with great reluctance. Passing the napkin to Avni, Shreyasi said, 'I should call a cab for you. You need to go home.'

'I can't,' said Avni.

'She can't stay here,' grumbled Daman.

'Do you need water?' asked Shreyasi.

Avni nodded. 'My parents . . . I told them I would be out. I can't . . . can't go home drunk.' She started to sob.

'Check into a hotel,' said Daman. 'I will book one for you. Give me your ID.'

'I don't have an ID,' said Avni. 'I . . . I lost my purse.'

Shreyasi passed on a tumbler of water to her. 'Avni? Look at me?' She slapped Avni's face gently to get her attention. 'Why were you there at Summerhouse? Were you following us?'

'Of course, she was!' said Daman angrily. 'Listen, Avni. We talked about this. You seemed to understand, at least you fucking nodded your head. You said you won't text me again and yet you do. You need to leave me alone.'

'I can't. I can't live—'

'Of course you can,' said Daman and shifted close to Avni. 'You have to. There's no other option.'

Avni cried.

Daman rolled his eyes again and said, 'Crying won't solve anything. Shreyasi and I are together now. Accept it and move on.'

'I lost my job, Daman . . . I can't lose you too,' Avni begged.

Daman raised his hands. 'How is that my fault!'

Shreyasi asked Daman to calm down. Daman continued, 'You're a brilliant girl. You can get any job you want.'

'But I want you!'

'That you can't have any more.'

'But—' She reached out and held Daman's hand.

Daman wrested his hand free. Avni said, tears streaking down her face, 'Why are you doing this to me? Why?'

'Whatever is happening to you is your own doing. Don't you dare pin this on me! You can't just leave your job trying to get my attention or pity or whatever you were aiming at and then blame me,' snapped Daman.

Avni sobbed. 'What did I do to deserve this, Daman? I just loved you. I loved you so much.'

'You won't learn like this. I HAVE FUCKING HAD ENOUGH! I have other things in my life to sort out than to just manage women. I am calling your parents,' he said and took his phone out. He was about to dial the number when Avni lunged at his phone.

'DON'T—' she shouted. Avni snatched the phone from him and threw it away.

The phone crashed against the wall and shattered. Daman, furious, pushed Avni to the corner and raised his hand to bring it down on Avni. Avni cowered. He stopped himself just in time. Avni started to sob even loudly.

'FUCKING BITCH,' he muttered. He walked to where the phone lay. He picked it up and looked at Shreyasi. 'Shreyasi? She needs to go. Shreyasi, book a hotel and cab.'

Shreyasi made Avni sit on the bed. Avni's entire body heaved in loud sobs. 'Listen to me?' said Shreyasi. 'Avni? Look at me.' Avni still cried. Shreyasi slapped Avni tight across the face. Avni shuddered. 'LOOK AT ME!' Shreyasi said. 'STOP CRYING and listen to me. We will drop you to a hotel and that will be the end of you ever calling Daman or his parents. Do you understand?'

Avni sniffled.

'Nod your head and I will book a cab. Do you understand?'

Avni nodded her head. Shreyasi booked a cab and a hotel room. When the cab reached Daman's apartment, Shreyasi collected her things and helped Avni up. 'Are you coming?' asked Shreyasi.

'No, I'm not going with her,' he said.

'I will drop her and take the cab home,' said Shreyasi. Shreyasi hugged Daman and kissed him. Daman noticed Avni cry even harder. 'Take care,' he said to Shreyasi.

As Shreyasi and Avni walked out of the door, Daman called out to Avni and said, 'I don't want to see you here again.'

Avni nodded and followed Shreyasi to the staircase like a little child. In the car, Shreyasi snapped at Avni, 'What do you think was that? Why would you show up like that?'

'I need him,' she mumbled.

'NO, YOU FUCKING DON'T! I gave you an option and instead you have been harassing him. What did you think would happen? You could have just been friends with him. But you had to be the crying, grovelling whore.'

'I . . . couldn't . . . I couldn't . . . I thought I was stronger,' said Avni and broke down again.

'It's too late now,' said Shreyasi. 'Now just get out of his life. Don't bother him. He needs to concentrate on his book. He needs to put his life back together.'

'What about my life? You destroyed it!' exclaimed Avni. 'What do I have left now?'

'Just pull your socks up and find something to occupy yourself with. Go, find a job.'

'Help me,' said Avni.

Shreyasi laughed. 'I don't owe anything to you.'

'I loved the same guy you do. And I lost everything because of it. I shouldn't have loved him,' cried Avni.

'I accept that.'

'The way he treated me today. He told me he loved me and yet had me banging on the door. He asked me to fuck off while all I wanted was for him to talk to me. He might have fallen out of love but what he did today . . .' her voice trailed off in sobs.

'I don't blame—'

'How would you feel if he did the same to you?'

'He wouldn't. He loves me,' said Shreyasi.

Avni wiped her tears. She looked away from Shreyasi and started looking out of the window.

After a while, Avni said, '*I love you*. That's what he told me as well. He's a writer. That's what he does. He lies.'

Shreyasi didn't respond.

Avni mumbled to herself, 'Everything I thought about him was an illusion. I lost everything because of him and because of you. What was my fault? I was just an ordinary girl who dared to love. Was that so wrong? Did I deserve this? Did I deserve what the two of you did to me? Why did you ruin my life?'

Silent tears streamed down her cheeks. Avni didn't say anything for the rest of the car ride.

Just as she got down from the car and walked towards the hotel, Shreyasi called out to her. 'Avni?'

Avni turned. She said, 'I'm sorry about today. I won't contact—'

'I can help you but on one condition,' said Shreyasi.

'. . .'

'You're never to talk to Daman again.'

43

Daman woke up with a jolt from his nightmare, sweating and panting, and shouting Shreyasi's name. He found Shreyasi sitting on the chair, peering into her laptop.

'Nightmare?'

'The craziest one ever. I saw you burn to death and with that goes my sleep for a week. Why don't these dreams stop? Anyway, when did you get here?' asked Daman, trying to catch his breath. 'I missed you.'

Shreyasi closed the flap of the laptop and got him a bottle of water.

'Here. Drink.'

'I got your messages. All thirty-four of them. They were lovely,' she said.

Poor him, thought Shreyasi and stroked his hair as he drank hungrily. This was the best part of her day—coming home to him after office, and finding him waiting for *her*. On most evenings he would be awake and excited to see her. He would run to her, take her in his arms and tell her how much he missed her. He would order in, decide with TV show to watch that day, and even buy expensive wine for her. Sometimes, he would read out the parts from his favourite books while he played with her hair. He would obsess and plan every detail of every evening they spent together. He made a date out of every time they saw each other. It was as if he was cataloguing their entire relationship. And every evening when it would be time for her to go to Akash and be a wife to him, his eyes would tear up. *My baby might have forgotten how to write but he still knows how to love.* This was exactly how she had envisioned her relationship. She and a boy, Daman, who would be obsessed with *her*, whose life would start and end with *her*, who would need no one but *her*.

226

'It's been an hour. You were sleeping so I didn't want to wake you up. I wrapped up a little work in the meanwhile,' she said and ran her hand over his face. 'I saw that you've starting writing again.'

'Did you read it?'

'I did,' she said, trying to hide any emotion.

'Do you like it?'

Shreyasi answered after a pause. 'Baby . . . I don't want to lie but I think you can do much better. Like it's good but it's not . . . you. You're way better than this. I think you—'

'It sucks, doesn't it?'

'I didn't say that.'

Daman laughed. 'Chill, Shreyasi. I know it's shit. Thank you for not mincing words and being straight with me,' he said and he shook his head disappointedly. 'I just can't seem to get it right. Every time I sit down to write, Jayanti's words start ricocheting inside my head.'

'You need to concentrate harder, baby.'

'How easily we get used to certain things, don't we? Like the expectation that anyone would publish me. And now . . .'

'I'm sorry. You know—'

'I know, I know. You had to do it. I have heard it all before. You wanted me and I needed to know how much you love me. I get that and respect that. But still . . . as much as you are a part of me, writing was a part of me too. I can't do without it,' said Daman.

'But the article you wrote for that website got 3000 views in a week,' argued Shreyasi.

'Who cares about the views? I didn't enjoy writing it. It was an opinion piece. Anyone with a laptop can write it. It was . . . for the money.'

Daman saw Shreyasi's face lose colour. 'I'm sorry, Shreyasi,' he said and put his head on her lap. 'I don't want you to feel bad or guilty about it. You mean everything to me. But I can't stop thinking about . . . anyway, I will try not to talk about it, okay?'

'Things will work out. It all works out in the end, doesn't it?'

'It does,' said Daman and smiled. 'Hey? Do you want to go out? There's this new pastry place in Punjabi Bagh—'

'I need to be home in a bit.'

'When don't you have to be home? Every time—'

'Daman.'

'Fine, I won't talk about it,' scoffed Daman. 'You can go home to your beloved husband while I stay here rotting, writing my shitty book and thinking about you,' said Daman.

'You're such an asshole,' said Shreyasi and smiled.

'That I am and it seems I have plenty of time to be one now,' he said.

'I will find you a publisher.'

'Fingers crossed,' said Daman. 'Okay, screw that. Do you want to watch the new *Game of Thrones* episode?'

'I've watched it already.'

'That's not fair!' protested Daman. 'I was waiting to see it with you.'

'I don't mind seeing it again,' she said and hugged him. 'I will watch all six seasons with you if you want me to.'

They watched the episode together and once it ended, it was already time for Shreyasi to go. She called herself a cab. Daman insisted on dropping her home again.

'Are you buying a car with the insurance money?' Shreyasi asked.

'I don't think I'm ever driving one. The dreams . . .'

'Are they still as frequent?'

Daman nodded. 'There's a saving grace though. I see your face sitting right beside me in the car. The ending is always scary. You die and I survive.'

'Hmm . . .'

'I wonder why I see that?'

'Maybe you're too scared to lose me?' she said, nervously fidgeting with her house keys.

'I'm scared to lose you,' said Daman and held her hand. 'But you know what? There's something else that's new in the dreams.'

'What is that?'

'You remember I told you how the accident happens? A taxi coming from the wrong way?'

'Yes, I do. What about it?'

'Ummm . . . nothing,' said Daman. 'It's stupid.'

'Tell me?'

'It's nothing,' insisted Daman.

'Daman? We decided not to hide anything from each other. Especially about these dreams and that accident, baby. You know it affects you. Tell me what you saw,' said Shreyasi.

'Hmmmm. The driver in the taxi?'

'What about him?' Shreyasi asked.

'Earlier I could just see him. But then I peered closely.'

'Peered closely in your dreams?' asked Shreyasi, smirking.

'Do you want to listen or not?' snapped Daman. 'That's why I wasn't telling you. Maybe I shouldn't.'

'I was just kidding, baby. So you looked closely at the driver? What did you see?'

'In the back seat of the taxi, there was a girl.'

'What?'

'Yes, a girl. At first I couldn't see her. All I could see was her hand tapping on the taxi driver's shoulders, asking him perhaps to drive quicker. I can't be sure. I'm guessing because the driver looked panicked,' said Daman. 'But then slowly, a face emerged. A fair girl with flowing black hair. The face has become clearer over the past few days.'

'Who's she?'

'Ummm.'

'Daman? Who's she?'

'It's you, Shreyasi. You're sitting behind that driver,' said Daman and turned to look at her.

'What? What nonsense? Am I not sitting right beside you in the car? Didn't you just say I die in the crash?' she asked.

Daman chortled. 'Yes, but you also survive. When I'm strapped to the stretcher and taken away I come to consciousness for a second. I see a girl emerge from the wreckage of the taxi. *It's you.*'

'That . . . that makes no sense.'

Daman laughed. 'Of course it makes no sense. That's why I wasn't telling you!'

'Right,' murmured Shreyasi.

Daman stared back at her and asked with a mischievous glint in his eyes. 'But wouldn't that be crazy? If there were two Shreyasi's? How awesome would that be? Your husband can keep one and I can keep the other.'

'I wouldn't share you with anyone!'

'These dreams have no meaning any more. Next thing I know I will see your face in the taxi's driving seat! I just need to keep myself busy to stop my brain from going on these stupid tangents. Now that even Avni has suddenly stopped calling me, I have way too much time on my hands. Do you know she got that job at Barclays she had always wanted?'

'Oh, really?' said Shreyasi.

'I told you no one minds these viral videos after a week, let alone a month or two,' said Daman.

'True,' said Shreyasi.

'I'm glad for her. It seems like I am the only one who's unemployed and dreaming stupid dreams.'

It had started to rain outside.

'You're right. You need to keep busy. You need to stop these stupid dreams,' mumbled Shreyasi. 'Write the book, Daman, a good one. We will see how we get it published.'

'Okay.'

'Have you tried those sleeping pills the doctor prescribed you?'

'No,' Daman said. 'Are you planning to keep me drugged to keep me from seeing these dreams?'

Shreyasi smiled nervously.

44

Shreyasi had been waiting at Daman's apartment for four hours when Daman stumbled through the doorway. Shreyasi ran to him as he slumped on the ground. His eyes rolled over. He stank of piss and vomit.

'Daman?' said Shreyasi. 'What happened to you?'

Daman mumbled something illegible. His lips were split and he seemed to have bled all over his shirt. His knuckles were bruised and he had a black eye. He passed out. Shreyasi called for a taxi and took him to a nursing home nearby. They took care of his bruises, declared that he had a broken nose and a possible concussion. She hadn't been able to elicit any answers from Daman on how it had happened. Daman was still in surgery when Shreyasi received a text from Sumit asking her to rein in her boyfriend.

'What was that?' asked Shreyasi as she called Sumit.

'Didn't Daman tell you?'

'Tell me what?'

'About us?'

'What about us?'

'About me and Avni. I'm dating her. He came to us drunk out of his wits and threatened us. We don't want any trouble. You have got what you wanted and now just leave us alone.'

'Did you hit him?'

'The bouncers did. He wouldn't go away from our table.'

'What was he doing there?'

'You should ask him. He tried to drag Avni out of the restaurant. He dumped her. Now whoever she dates is none of his business. He threatened Avni he would release the video if she didn't dump me.'

'He didn't do—'

'Ask him. He will tell you. I request you, Shreyasi. Please stay out of our lives,' said Sumit. 'I have to go now.'

He disconnected the call.

They discharged Daman the next morning. When they reached home, Shreyasi asked Daman if he remembered what he did last night.

'I bumped into Sumit. He said something about you and I hit him. Things went out of hand. It's nothing you should worry about,' explained Daman.

'He called me. He told me you got into a fight with him over Avni.'

'Why would I fight over her?' asked Daman, not meeting Shreyasi's eyes.

He's lying. 'Tell me the truth, Daman. Did you or did you not embarrass me in front of your ex-girlfriend and best friend?'

Daman rolled his eyes and scoffed. 'He's dating her. Out of all the people they could have dated, they are dating each other. I see what they are doing. They want to spoil what we have, they want to make us jealous and angry—'

'It's working. You seem to be jealous and angry,' said Shreyasi.

'I'm just furious because I thought they were my friends. Instead they are fucking each other.'

'I need to go home. I was in the nursing home the entire night,' said Shreyasi and got up.

Just as she was leaving, Daman held her hand.

'What?'

'I'm sorry. Please don't go home,' said Daman and hugged her. Before she knew it, Daman had started to sob in her arms. 'I need you, I need you. I love you so much. I feel so lonely without you.'

Shreyasi made Daman sit on the bed and quietened him down. She held his face and kissed him, she told him it was okay as long as he still loved her. He promised he would never do it again. He swore he wouldn't call or text both of them. When Shreyasi insisted, he vowed that he would try to cut down on his alcohol.

He had been drinking too much and his dependency on sleeping pills was getting precarious; the cost of keeping those dreams at bay was proving too much for him and for her. He hadn't written a single word in days now. There were mails from online journals that wanted him to write but even those mails lay unattended to for days. He would spend his days curled up inside the blanket, unbathed and unshaved, watching TV shows the entire day, texting Shreyasi all day, telling her he missed her, and waiting for her to come home. Their evening dates had gone for a toss; they would sit and he would mope around for a couple of hours before it would be time for her to leave. Sometimes, he would land up at her office during lunch hour, dressed only in his pyjamas, see her for twenty minutes and wait four hours in the reception for her to finish off at work. Shreyasi had started to feel sorry for him.

'Shouldn't you be writing?' asked Shreyasi, steeling up.

Daman brushed it aside as if he wasn't ever a writer. 'I can't think of anything. I'm thinking of taking CAT exams next year, get myself a proper job, like yours. Anyway, I have you now. Why would I want to write?'

He tried hugging her. Shreyasi wrested free.

'You shouldn't throw your talent away.'

'I fell in love with you and I wrote about it. There's no talent required there,' he scoffed.

'That will be the last time you said that. I don't want to see you till the time I read a few chapters from you,' said Shreyasi while leaving his house.

'Write chapters, how?'

'It will happen, Daman. You need to be patient. Just write the book. The next time I see you I want you to have written something.'

'But—'

'We are not arguing on this, Daman. What are you if not a writer?'

'I thought I loved—'

He hadn't even completed the sentence and Shreyasi had already left his apartment.

45

For the next two weeks, Daman grovelled and pleaded with Shreyasi to see him, to talk to him but she held out. He would reach her office early in the morning and not leave till late evening. He would keep asking the receptionist to call her. After the first two days he had spent outside Shreyasi's office, the security didn't let him inside the office building complex. Yet, he didn't give up.

Let me talk to you, he begged.

Not until I read a few chapters, Shreyasi answered. It pained Shreyasi to treat him like this but she saw no other way. She was deeply conflicted. Daman was finally in the grasp of her palm but it wasn't the Daman she had grown to love in the past three years. He had always been this curious boy who would try to tell stories and, failing, try again; he had to go back to that. She wanted him to do what he was best at again. And yet it was easier said than done. Even after the security had banned him inside the building, he started to wait outside the gate, peering into taxis that would leave the building. He would run after Shreyasi's cab. Shreyasi would cry and yet ask the driver to keep driving on. She would see him panting, hands on his knees, crying, shouting her name, begging her to stop.

Write the book, she would text him.

I can't, I need to see you, I love you, he would text her back. For the next couple of days, Daman went off the grid, locked in his room, typing. But on the third, he reached Shreyasi's house. He called her from the guard's room on the intercom.

'Meet me for ten minutes. Please, I promise I will go. I just need to see you. I'm writing, trust me.'

Shreyasi saw him from the window. She could have let him come up but if she allowed him in once he would take her for granted and keep coming.

'My husband is here,' she said.

'Then come down. Just for a minute.'

'We are having dinner right now.'

'I will wait.'

'Daman, you need to go home. You can't come here. Do you understand?'

'But—'

'Go home.'

'I can't—'

'Write your book, Daman.'

She disconnected the call. Then she instructed the guard not to let him up. For the rest of the night, Shreyasi saw Daman loiter around the guard's room, looking up at her window. Just before dawn, he fell asleep on the pavement. When it was morning, she saw him fumble with his phone to find it was dead. He begged the guard to let him call her once but the guard refused. Daman took an auto home.

'How many lives will you destroy?' asked Shreyasi's husband when he found her on the window ledge.

'Did I ask you to speak?'

'He was there all night.'

'He needs to do the right thing. He needs to write about me. I can't let him be till he does that. Is the breakfast ready?'

Daman didn't text her for the entire day. Shreyasi checked up on him later that evening. The watchman at Daman's apartment told her that he hadn't left the building. *He's writing*, she thought and smiled. For the next week, Daman stayed in his building, writing, dropping Shreyasi the odd text updating her on the progress of the book. He begged her to tell him that she loved him. Shreyasi didn't relent. *Let him wait*, she thought. After seven days, he had a few chapters ready and called Shreyasi home for a reading.

'Did you like it?' asked Daman.

Shreyasi looked at him, blankly. 'It is . . . different. I will take it home and read it again and let you know.'

Daman smiled.

'Thank you,' she said.

'So now do we go out? I have booked us a table at Orris. You can go home and change if you want to but I think you're looking perfect. Why are you looking at me like that? Or do you want to order in? We can do that as well,' said Daman.

'I need to home. I have some work and my husband must be expecting me.'

'But you told me—'

'I NEED TO GO.'

'Why are you shouting?'

Shreyasi calmed herself down. 'I just . . . I just need some time alone.'

'Is it something I did?'

'No, no, it's nothing. There's just some stress on the office front,' she explained.

She left Daman's apartment in a hurry. They didn't even open the bottle of wine Daman had got for that evening. She drove to the nearest bookshop and flipped randomly through the fiction section. *I have read these words somewhere. These words are not Daman's.* She spent an hour searching the bookstore and her mind to ascertain where it was that she had read those words. And then she found it. The three chapters Daman had written bore a striking resemblance to what Karthik Iyer had written years ago. Enraged and broken, she slumped on the ground reading it. She drove back to Daman's apartment and threw Karthik's book in Daman's face and called him a two-bit plagiarizer.

'THIS WAS THE LAST THING I EXPECTED FROM YOU!' screamed Shreyasi.

Daman tried to defend his chapters but whimpered in the wake of Shreyasi's unrelenting ferocity. She shouted and bellowed till Daman gave up and accepted that he had in fact copied from Karthik Iyer.

'WHY WOULD YOU DO THAT?' yelled Shreyasi. 'YOU HAD TO WRITE OUR LOVE STORY! OURS! NOT HIS! OURS, DAMAN, OURS!'

Daman just looked away, ashamed.

'SAY SOMETHING! EXPLAIN THIS. OR I WILL DESTROY YOU.'

Daman smiled sadly. He looked at Shreyasi, eyes flooded with tears. 'What's there to destroy? Jayanti Raghunath won't publish me or let me get published. I just wrote because I wanted to see you.'

Shreyasi didn't feel pity, just blistering anger. 'What would it take for you to write again?'

'I don't want to write any more. I just—'

'STOP WHINING, DAMAN,' she howled. 'THIS IS NOT WHAT I FELL IN LOVE WITH!'

She picked the wine bottle that was kept on the table and flung it at him. Daman ducked away at the last moment. The bottle crashed against the wall and splintered. Shreyasi stormed out of the apartment. Once home, she ran herself a hot bath and stayed in till her skin puckered. She cried her heart out reading Daman's texts.

DAMAN
I love you.

DAMAN
Why do I need to write any more? I love you.

DAMAN

I will make my CV and apply for an engineering job. I think it's not too late.

Shreyasi deleted all his texts. *I killed his will to write.* She got out of the bath and towelled herself dry. She scrolled to Jayanti Raghunath's folder on her phone. Apart from snarky gossip about her authors, there was nothing to leverage. She had to look somewhere else. She couldn't sleep well that night. All she could think of was Daman slowly losing his mind. Over the next few days, she dreamt recurrently of Daman chained and locked inside a psychiatrist facility, scratching at the walls and shouting how much he loved her.

46

The Mumbai Literature Festival was in its second year and it was tottering. The lack of funds had pushed the organizers to look for cleverer ways of making money. One of them included selling tickets to interested readers for the Authors Dinner on the concluding day. They priced it steep at 3000 rupees per reader but Shreyasi didn't mind. Earlier that week, Shreyasi had implored Daman to come to the literature festival, network, and find a publisher but he'd laughed at her suggestion.

'They will mock me,' he had said.

All her pleading had fallen on deaf ears. He had suggested a short trip to Neemrana instead. Shreyasi had been so annoyed she barely kept herself from socking him in the face. Things had gone from bad to worse, his attempts at writing after Shreyasi caught him plagiarizing were laughable to be kind; he was making a fool of himself.

Daman had grown irritable and lazy and mercurial; his devolvement into madness had been so glacial Shreyasi hadn't noticed it at first. They would either fight about her husband or he would cry holding her. His complaints about her absence had kept getting louder and more desperate. Twice, she had come back to his apartment to see it trashed. He had broken his laptop twice in a week. 'The new laptop is going to help me write better,' he had said. The new laptop Shreyasi had bought had suffered a similar fate. Like a guilty dog, he had cried and begged at her feet. The more vexing Daman became the more she found herself drowning in guilt. She had to make things all right.

The dinner was a sham. The readers who had paid good money stood in a group in a corner and the writers lounged about with each other. Every now and then a reader would muster up courage and walk to his or her favourite writer, get a book signed, talk for a few minutes. The writer would uninterestedly answer their questions and walk back to the authors' group. Maybe not the sharpest but Karthik was the tallest, most handsome of all authors present there. Even the walking stick he carried added to his looks. Wrapped around his arm was his beautiful girlfriend, Varnika. Shreyasi bided her time. She waited for Varnika to get drunk on the free wine. She bumped into Varnika at the dinner buffet.

'Hi,' said Shreyasi.

'Hi,' answered Varnika, flashing her perfect white teeth.

'The spread is nice, right?'

'Yes.'

'Are you a writer?'

'No, I'm here with my fiancé. He's a writer,' said Varnika and flashed a ring.

'That's so beautiful! So who's the guy?'

Varnika blushed and pointed to Karthik.

'You two are perfect!' exclaimed Shreyasi. 'I'm Shreyasi.'

'Varnika. And you're too kind.'

'I will not keep you away from him much longer. It was nice talking to you. Give him my regards,' said Shreyasi.

Shreyasi filled her plate, picked up a flute of wine, and hovered around tables looking for a place.

Before long, Varnika called her out.

'Join us,' she said.

Shreyasi waved her hand as if to say no but Varnika insisted. Shreyasi took the chair at their table.

'She's Shreyasi,' Varnika introduced.

'Hi. Karthik,' Karthik said. 'I would shake hands but . . .'

Shreyasi smiled back. 'So your girlfriend told me you are a writer?'

'I might have written a few books. I'm a little new in this field,' said Karthik with an impish smile.

Varnika laughed. 'He's a bestselling writer. Google him! You will see,' gushed Varnika.

'In my defence, I don't read Indian authors as much,' said Shreyasi.

Karthik frowned.

Noticing that, Shreyasi said, 'It's just that the last time I read an Indian romance novel I wanted to claw my eyes out. Someone named Daman Roy.'

Varnika smiled.

'Shit. I hope he's not a friend of yours!' said Shreyasi.

Karthik smirked. 'He's not a friend. But I know him. He's—'

Varnika interrupted him. 'Let me tell you an interesting fact! Karthik thinks he's a good writer, even better than him, whereas I have always told him that he's crap.' She looked at Karthik. 'Let's give her one of your books and let her decide?'

'We don't need to do that. Hey? Your drink has finished,' he said and waved at the waiter to repeat their drinks.

A little later, Varnika left for the washroom and returned with a copy of Karthik's book. She made Karthik sign it and gave it to Shreyasi.

'Thank you. That's really kind. I could have bought it—'

'It's a gift. When you finish, let Karthik and me know who's better. Him or Daman.'

'We don't need to do this,' protested Karthik.

'He thinks I tell him he's a better writer because I'm in love with him, so you will be our second opinion,' said Varnika. 'Ever since he heard her editor call this Daman guy the next big thing, he has started feeling that his time is over.'

'I will let you know,' said Shreyasi, waving the book. 'I should go back to my room now.'

'You're staying here?' asked Karthik.

'308. Are you guys staying here as well?'

Karthik nodded. '304.'

'I will drop in a message if I read this book tonight.'

Varnika lips curved into a drunken smile. 'We will wait!'

Back in the room, Shreyasi waited for three hours. She walked through the corridor every thirty minutes to check if the lights of room 304 had gone out. It was a little after one when she dropped in a voicemail on 304's hotel landline. *I read the book. I can't say much.* A bright smile crept up on her face when half an hour later when she peeped out of the door and found Karthik making up his mind to ring the bell outside her door. His insecurity and impatience had drawn him to Shreyasi's door. She had taken care to wear just a long, flimsy T-shirt that barely covered her buttocks. She wore no bra. She feigned surprise when she saw Karthik at the other side of the door, leaning on his walking stick. She welcomed him in. She walked slowly in front of him, hoping he would stare, hoping he was less perfect a lover and more susceptible to vice than he let on. She offered him coffee. He refused.

'So what did you think of the book?'

'I didn't think you will come in the middle of the night asking me this.'

'I wasn't sleepy.'

'How does my opinion matter?' asked Shreyasi.

'You have read both our books. That's why it matters.'

'But why compare yourself to anyone? Two books can coexist in the market without one having to be better than the other,' she said.

'Bestseller lists don't say which books are better. They tell you what's selling the most. It's not the same thing,' he argued. 'Tell me? What did you think?'

'Daman is an average writer but he's better than you,' said Shreyasi.

'Is he?' he asked, trying to be polite, but she noticed the poison in Karthik's voice.

She could almost hear his thoughts. *How dare she? What does she know? Fucking slut.*

'I don't think I have missed anything by not reading Indian authors,' she said, trying to be as calm as possible, knowing the more she refused to react, the more it would agitate Karthik's urge to beat her, own her, act like a man. She could see his eyes do an angry dance.

'Okay.'

'I just felt your story was too . . . cheesy,' she explained.

'Are you a cynic?' he said sharply.

Classic. Blame the reader and try to establish superiority. It was time to make her move. She cast her eyes down at her coffee and then looked up.

'In terms of love, I am.'

'Why? Did you get your heart broken?'

'I don't want to talk about it. Anyway, I think your book works for people who believe in love. Like you and your girlfriend, Varnika. For me, it doesn't. Maybe some day, but not right now.'

Karthik eased up. It wasn't his fault any more that his book did not appeal to her. It was hers.

'Aw, that's sweet. I should give you another one when you do find love,' said Karthik, a kind smile pasted on his face.

'All the good men are taken. Exhibit A. You!'

Karthik giggled nervously. She got up from the bed and made herself another coffee. She felt Karthik's eyes follow her. And then she deliberately walked back to the bed.

'. . . and you know how men from Delhi are,' said Shreyasi.

'I'm from Delhi.'

'That's blatant stereotyping. I am from Delhi!'

'And that's why you got into a dick-measuring contest with another writer? Who is better? Me or him? Him or me? That is such a Delhi trait.'

'That's a writer's trait.'

'But also a Delhi trait,' said Shreyasi with a naughty glint. 'I wonder though who would win an actual dick-measuring contest.'

Karthik was visibly embarrassed.

Shreyasi chortled and said, 'I'm sorry. I think I'm still a little drunk. I take that back!'

'I would win it,' he said and winked.

'Ha! Typical Delhi boy!'

Shreyasi coughed.

'You want water?' asked Karthik.

She nodded. Karthik got up from the chair and got a bottle. He walked close to the bed and stretched out his hand to pass on the bottle. Shreyasi took the bottle and with the slightest of movements ran her hand over his crotch. Karthik stepped away, flushed in the face. Shreyasi rolled over and laughed.

'Look at you. So shy!'

Karthik didn't know what to say.

'Daman has to be really big to beat you!' she said and covered her lips with her hand. 'I shouldn't have said that.'

Karthik grinned, his manhood and ego both stroked.

'I told you.'

'Hey? Look at that,' she said and pointed at his crotch. 'Is that why you were big? You have . . . a . . . boner?'

She laughed.

Karthik smiled uncomfortably. 'No,' he protested. 'I'm not . . . I don't . . .'

'I thought writers were better liars, Karthik. You are disappointing me.'

'I'm not lying,' argued Karthik, playfully.

'You're not? I can bet anything you are.'

'I am not!'

'Take the bet then. Show it to me?'

'What?'

'Show it to me!'

'What if I lose?'

Shreyasi got up from the bed. She walked close and said, 'We will decide on the terms later.'

Karthik smiled. In the corner of the room, a phone lay recording the entire conversation.

47

Shreyasi had been waiting for him for three hours now, trying to think of words she would say to him. When Daman entered his apartment, he walked over to Shreyasi and kissed her on the cheek as if nothing was wrong. He asked Shreyasi if she were interested in watching the new Deepika Padukone movie. He took off his shoes and threw them in the corner. He sat at the study table and scrolled through his mails.

'Did you see? I wrote three chapters. I'm getting the flow back. I think it's all falling into place,' said Daman turning to her.

'Where were you?' she asked.

'British Council, why?'

'With?'

'Avni,' he answered.

'You aren't even trying to hide it?'

Daman took off his shirt. He wiped his sweat off and rummaged through his cupboard for a fresh T-shirt. He put on a frayed, grey T-shirt.

'Why would I try to hide it? We just met and talked for a couple of hours. That's it.'

Shreyasi got up, exasperated. 'A few weeks ago you were sitting there on the chair asking Avni to fuck off while she cried out your name on the other side of that door. Then you got beat up by Sumit—'

'The bouncers beat me up, not Sumit.'

'THAT'S NOT THE POINT!'

'Whoa, you're overreacting, Shreyasi. Avni and I have moved on. We are just friends now,' said Daman.

'DID SHE TELL YOU WHO HELPED HER MOVE ON?' bellowed Shreyasi.

'You pulled some strings and got the Barclays guys to give her job back to her. She asked me to thank you again. But to be fair it was you who fucked her up in the first place. It was that video—'

'JUST SHUT UP, DAMAN!' she exclaimed. 'Will you stop punishing me now? Can't you just do what you want to do, say what you want to say once and for all and get it over with? Why do you find a new pretext to fight with me every day?'

'On the contrary, I'm not fighting with you at all. It's you who's fighting with me. Can't you see that, baby? I love you. I love you so much. We are just perfect. Like so perfect. I don't see anything wrong with us. Apart from the fact that you were trying to seduce the one man I hate the most—'

'I want us to be happy. I have waited way too long for this. What I did was for you! And I didn't even touch him. And you got your contract, didn't you? Why are you doing this?'

'Are you seriously asking me that? You called Karthik to your room, you asked him to pop his cock out. Who would have known had the door not been knocked on by Varnika? At what point were you going to stop?' Daman snarled.

'I wasn't about to do anything. I got what I wanted,' said Shreyasi. 'I would have stopped right there even if there was no knock on the door.'

'How the fuck would I know?' shouted Daman.

'Because I LOVE YOU, DAMMIT! You were destroying yourself a few weeks back. I had to do it. LOOK AT YOU NOW! You have already written three chapters—'

Daman cut in. 'You know what? Take those chapters and shove it.'

'Don't you dare use that tone with me,' retorted Shreyasi.

Daman rolled his eyes. He took out his phone and showed Shreyasi the text Karthik Iyer had sent him.

KARTHIK IYER

Hey man. You might have gotten me to push you back into Jayanti's calendar. But your bitch wanted to touch my dick. She also said I was way bigger than you. Next time why don't you come over as well and be the cuckold?

'Now what am I supposed to reply to that?'

'I will take care of it!'

'By threatening him again? But how am I going to rid that asshole's words from my head?' asked Daman.

'It shouldn't be embarrassing for you. It should be embarrassing for him. You just stand to gain from this entire episode.'

'Oh, what lovely gain! A book contract for pimping out my girlfriend,' said Daman and smiled.

'You are over—'

'What do I STAND TO GAIN for pimping you out to your husband every day? Will the payment be weekly, monthly, biannually or annually? I would insist on monthly—'

'You're filthy, Daman!' shrieked Shreyasi and slapped Daman.

Daman spat on the ground. 'Look who's talking.'

'I have given you three years of my life. Three years—'

'Should I be grateful for that, huh? Whatever you did was because you wanted to. You're the one who stalked me, you are the one who came over to Goa! So what you did was because you loved me. Do you get it? BECAUSE YOU WANTED TO!'

'You make it all sound like a mistake,' mumbled Shreyasi.

'Maybe it was. So sad to break it to you that I'm not what you think I am. But isn't that the hallmark of our relationship? Deceiving each other? Because you're definitely not what I thought of you to be. At least I don't prance around naked in front of Avni asking if I got her wet or tell her she has bigger breasts than you do. I think I should do that the next time. Let me make a note,' mocked Daman.

'This is unfair. I DON'T DESERVE THIS.'

'At least there we think alike.'

Shreyasi picked up her bag and stormed out of Daman's apartment. She took a cab and went straight to her home, fuming. Sleep evaded her. Daman calmed down in a couple of hours and like it had happened numerous times in the past few weeks, he went to her begging for forgiveness. *I know you did it for me*, he said. He barraged her phone with calls and texts, threatened to come up and bang the door, and stayed outside her apartment gate till the next morning. And just like all the times before, Shreyasi forgave him, hugged him, and asked him to put the Karthik episode behind him. He apologized, called his behaviour abhorrent and swore it wouldn't happen again. Shreyasi believed him like she did every time. She wasn't about to let go of him so soon. Not after all she had put into this relationship. She had to make this work.

'I will make it up to you,' he said as he hugged her and cried.

'Baby—'

'*I will write the best book I can. No one will forget our love.* I promise you.'

Shreyasi slept with a smile the next night.

48

Before Shreyasi knew it Daman had locked her out of his life. *I need to work on the book, baby, having you around is distracting,* he told her. He had to concentrate on writing a detailed breakdown of the chapters of his next book. Shreyasi was sceptical of it at first, concerned and scared of the recurrent dreams Daman had been having, the one with two Shreyasis— one in the car next to him and one in the back seat of the taxi, the driver in the front. Although he had picked himself up, and put his mind to paper, and cranked out chapter after chapter, writing with an intensity she hadn't seen in a year, the nightmares had gone from bad to worse.

He had refused to take his sleeping pills. *I can't concentrate,* he had said. Shreyasi tailed him around for the first few days. Daman would visit the library, sit alone in cafes, stay locked up in his apartment and write like a madman. It brought back memories of the time before any of this had happened to her. The time when an inexplicable attraction had drawn her towards this college boy with a puppy face and glinting eyes and stories inside him that needed to be told. She was his first true fan. Even then, as now, the questions had haunted her. *Why him? Why am I following him? What am I getting out of this? Why do I love him?* She had never found the answers and soon the questions were pushed back into the dark corner of her mind, never to be confronted again. Sometimes late at night, he would call her and cry like a little baby. *What happened?* She would ask. *I just wrote something and I felt like talking to you,* he would say. And just like that, he would spend the rest of the night talking to her. *When can I read it?* she would ask. *When I figure out the end,* he would tell her. And then the day came. *He is back,* thought Shreyasi as she held the fifty-page detailed skeletal structure of Daman's next book in her hands.

'So?' asked Daman, a smug smile on his face.

He knew what he had done. He had noticed the emotional expression on Shreyasi's face.

'It's beautiful. It's so beautiful . . .' she said.

'There are a few things that I need to change. There are chapters that look retrofitted. I will do that in the second draft of the book. Mark the chapters you think are a little odd,' he said. He gave a pen to her.

'I think it's perfect. Have you mailed it to Jayanti?'

'I have not yet. I want it to be perfect. Karthik may have bullied her into offering me a contract but she will try to give me hell for the book—'

'She won't,' interrupted Shreyasi.

'What did you do now?' asked Daman. 'No, I'm just asking before you freak me out again. Or better still, don't tell me.'

Shreyasi laughed. 'Baby, you're so cute.'

Daman grinned and leant back into his chair.

'I can't wait for this book to come out,' said Shreyasi. 'Finish writing it, already!'

Daman's sighed. He stared down at his hands.

'What happened?' asked Shreyasi.

'The dreams, Shreyasi, I see them every day. I see a message in them,' he said, a mad glint in his eyes.

'Are you taking your medicines—'

'I don't need to take medicines any more, Shreyasi,' he said.

'What are you saying?'

'Did you read it till the very end?'

'This is just an outline of the chapters. You're still to write it, right? Or have you? Show it to me?' asked Shreyasi, excited.

'I haven't written it but I know where to end it,' said Daman.

'Where?'

'At the accident. The accident that kills Shreyasi,' he answered.

Shreyasi frowned. 'But—'

He continued, 'This is going to be the last Daman–Shreyasi book. She is going to die.'

'Is that necessary?'

'It is the only way to write this book. It's a fitting end to their love story, is it not? Going up in flames? Like their relationship was? Like *our relationship is*? Short and fiery!' he said, staring at her.

'I disagree.'

'You don't, Shreyasi,' grumbled Daman.

'What do you mean?'

'You believe it too, baby.' He clutched her hand, eyes glinting.

'I don't!'

'Is that not the reason why you're not leaving your husband? You think our love will fizzle out, be ordinary after a while, don't you?'

'No, I—'

'You do,' he said and let go of her hand. 'I don't blame you for it. You're right! It would fizzle out. And that's why Shreyasi needs to die in the book.'

'But . . . what will you write in the next book?' asked Shreyasi, her voice stern.

'I haven't thought about it as of now.'

'There will be a new girl? Daman? Will he be a part of it?'

'He could be in mourning. Imagine how that would be.'

Shreyasi thought about it. A forlorn lover who lives his life thinking about the dead love of his life. *It could be quite a love story. The biggest writers relied on death as a tool for eternal love stories.* She said, 'It could be a good story.'

'Or there could be a girl who walks into his life. I haven't given it a thought yet!' Daman said.

'I can't allow that!' snapped Shreyasi.

'It's the only way I see, baby,' he said.

'YOU ARE NOT WRITING ABOUT SOMEONE ELSE!' she screamed.

Daman smirked and leant over. 'That's exactly what I wanted to hear from you,' he said and clenched his fists. He smiled at her and ran his fingers over her face and kissed her parted lips.

'I love you, baby,' he said.

'What are you saying?'

'If Daman is to not be in the third book, he has to die in the second book, doesn't he? Their love story has to come to an end, doesn't it?'

'You're freaking me out. What's wrong with you?'

'Don't you see it, Shreyasi?' he asked. 'This is what the dreams have been telling me all this while. Can you not see it? Can you not feel where our fate is leading us to?' he asked, his eyes filled with tears.

'What am I not seeing?'

'We need to end this. Our relationship. If we have to make this love story a great one, one people would talk about, we need to immortalize it.'

'But you already have. The books—'

'Not the books, dammit! In real life. Do you know why I keep getting those dreams? Because that's what is meant to happen!' he said, his eyes glinting like a madman's.

'I'm really not getting what you're saying right now,' mumbled Shreyasi.

'Imagine us in that accident again. But this time, we both don't survive. You said that yourself, if Shreyasi dies,

Daman has to die as well. The book will be published after we are dead—'

'What nonsense are you talking about?'

'No, I'm not! It makes perfect sense! You wanted to make our story immortal, right? What better way to do it than this? We almost died once, let's do it right this time. Let's make it a story everyone remembers.'

'Look, Daman. This is not funny.'

Daman frowned. 'It is not supposed to be, baby. THIS IS THE ONLY LOGICAL END TO OUR STORY!'

He pointed to the corner of the room.

'What are those?' asked Shreyasi.

'High-octane fuel. When we crash the car, it will instantly go up in flames. No pain, just a beautiful, fiery death. A blazing ball of fire and that will be our sunset. It will be perfect, baby. This is what the dreams have been—'

Shreyasi cut in. 'You need to rest, Daman. We need to—'

'NO! I HAVE DECIDED!' screamed Daman.

Shreyasi lowered her voice to a whisper. 'See, Daman, I know you're a little overwhelmed. You have been writing this for weeks now, so maybe you got just a little bit carried away. You need to calm down and think. There's no need for all that you're suggesting. I have a list of therapists we can go to, baby. Your paranoia can be treated. All we need to do is to see a doctor. I need to go to the office now. I will see you in the evening and we will decide on a doctor, okay? I will go with you to him, okay? We need to put an end to this madness.'

She got up. She kissed Daman's cheek. He had fallen silent.

Just as she turned away, Daman spoke, his eyes bloodshot and teary. 'There's no other way. This is what we are doing. I have thought about it for weeks now. If you love me you're going to be in the car with me.'

She turned to look at Daman.

He mumbled, 'Or I can change the name of the girl in the book to Avni.'

'Why on earth will you do that?'

'Because Avni's ready to see the end with me. Go up in flames with me. Immortalize her love. That's the only way,' he said.

'You called her?'

'Just in case you backed out. Which you did, Shreyasi. Maybe she was right. She loves me more than you do and she's ready to die for it.'

'Listen—'

'You're going to threaten her with the video you took?' He smirked. 'You can't. I deleted it off your phone and I know you don't keep backups.'

'You what—'

'Yes, I did,' said Daman, getting up.

He stepped close to Shreyasi. He kissed her on the cheek. 'Tell me, do you want to see the end with me? Or will it be her? Are you ready to die with me?'

Shreyasi didn't answer.

'I will finish the next draft of the book by the end of next month,' he said. 'I would need the answer by then.'

49

Things were breaking down. Daman's delirium didn't die down. What Shreyasi had thought as a moment of insanity was more than that. A few days later when Shreyasi got back home, she found Daman sitting in front of her husband who sat on the ground in a puddle of his own piss. There was a purple bruise on his left cheekbone and he bled from his lip. Daman tossed a knife from one hand to other.

'What are you doing here?' asked Shreyasi.

'I was having a nice chat with your husband. He's not much of a talker.'

'Put that knife away, Daman.'

'Okay, baby.'

He invited Shreyasi to sit beside him. The husband had spilt everything about Shreyasi blackmailing him, about his relationship with her sister, the assault on her and the video of it that existed.

'So I was right, wasn't I? This is the peak of our love story, this is where it ends. Or what future do you see of us? Do we get married and have kids? Do I become like him? No, that's not us, Shreyasi, and you know that. Isn't that why you didn't leave your husband even when you could have because that's not us? Is that not why you gave Avni the chance to be with me while you remained my mistress?' said Daman and kissed Shreyasi.

Shreyasi's husband looked on. He begged to be kept out of it. Daman left that day telling Shreyasi that he would wait for her decision. And he waited for the next few days even as Shreyasi cried, begged and howled for him to change his mind. No matter what she did, she couldn't draw Daman out of his isolation, his madness. He started sending her articles, books, instances of how death immortalized a love story, how death was the only way how it should all end. He came to obsess over death and love and love and death. Even their calls at night would be about just that. He would tell her how much he loved her—and she would melt into a little puddle—but he would also talk about them dying together.

'What's love if not this, Shreyasi? Sacrificing each other for the sake of our love story! We will always be remembered as the couple who loved and died loving each other,' he would say.

'But—'

'Do you not love me enough? Do you not think I deserve this?' he would ask and she would fall silent.

Shreyasi got desperate and arranged for him to meet a psychiatrist at his place, someone who would pull him out of this insanity, but Daman beat him within an inch of his death. He dragged the psychiatrist down the stairs of his apartment building and outside the house, shouting that he was not mad, that he was not mad! Soon, Daman stopped waking up sweaty and shattered from the dreams. Instead he would wake up smiling and laughing. He wrote his book like a man possessed. Hours would pass by and he wouldn't look up from his laptop. His eyes would be sore and watering when he retired to bed every night. He would send those chapters to Shreyasi who would read them repeatedly and cry. *Those words were the most beautiful words she had ever read from him.* But . . .

Then a few days later, Daman asked her to get a divorce from her husband before they carried out the ultimate gesture of love for each other.

'I don't want you to die with me as someone else's wife,' he said holding her hand.

This was Shreyasi's way out. A divorce proceeding would be long drawn and could go on for months. He took her to a divorce lawyer. She noticed his face fall when the lawyer lay out how much time it would take. Just when Shreyasi thought she had time on her hands to help him change his mind, Daman said, 'I can't wait so long. Fuck divorce.'

Shreyasi tried to tell Daman how his parents would be wrecked if he went ahead with something like this and yet he remained unmoved.

'They have gone through it once,' he argued.

Out of options, Shreyasi finally called Sumit to meet her. Sumit had been reluctant at first but relented when Shreyasi told him it was about Daman.

'Thank you for coming,' said Shreyasi and shook Sumit's hand.

'What do you want?' asked Sumit.

'Can you at least sit? This is about your friend,' she implored.

He sat down reluctantly. 'Tell me?'

'He's planning to kill himself. He wants to recreate that day, the accident. And he wants me to be inside that car. He's losing his mind,' she said.

'That's nonsense,' said Sumit, nonchalant. 'Are we going to order food here? I'm kind of hungry. Could you not have picked a less noisy place?'

'I am asking you to take this seriously. I'm talking about your friend here,' she said.

'I thought we are talking about your boyfriend. Why the fuck would I care about him after what he did?'

'Look Sumit, whatever happened has happened. Let's put that behind us. You have got to believe me—'

'I see your face and I just keep remembering the night you came on a date with me.'

'Listen, let's get past all that. This is about Daman. We need to save him,' protested Shreyasi and slammed the table hard.

'I'm going to order an American chop suey, you?'

Sumit waved down the waiter. He placed his order and asked Shreyasi again. When Shreyasi didn't say anything, he told the waiter that it would be all.

'Are you not believing me?'

'Why should I believe anything you say, Shreyasi?'

'HE'S REALLY GOING TO DO IT,' yelled Shreyasi.

'I follow him on Twitter. He seems fine.'

'You think it's a joke?'

'Yes. Should I think any different? And what is this? Some other game that you're playing? Please stop this nonsense. Avni and I are very happy together, so don't even try and spoil it for us, okay?' warned Sumit.

'HE IS SERIOUS ABOUT IT!'

'Blah. Blah. Blah.'

'Listen to me, Sumit. He's writing a book where both Daman and Shreyasi die in the end. He wants his real life to mimic his life in the books. He's obsessed about death,' she explained and showed Sumit the mails Daman had sent her.

'Writers, I tell you. They are funny. But I'm pretty sure he's not going to do anything like what you're suggesting,' he said.

'HE IS!' protested Shreyasi.

'You shout one more time and I'm out of here. Oh, the food is here. Do you want some?' he asked.

'No, thank you,' said Shreyasi and got up. 'Your girlfriend has agreed to it.'

'Girlfriend? Who agreed to what? Will you start making sense today or should we meet tomorrow? I think you should share some with me,' he said pointing to the bowl. 'A little food might make you think clearer.'

'Avni, your girlfriend, has agreed to sit in the car with him. Daman has offered to put her name in the book instead of mine,' said Shreyasi.

Sumit laughed. 'Avni? Oh, please! Avni is out of it. And she is too practical to do any such thing. Not in a million years. *She loves me.* She has had enough of that asshole.'

'Daman told me—'

'Daman is playing with you. Maybe he's just testing you. Maybe he wants to see how much you love him and you're failing miserably if he asked Avni.'

'IT IS NOT A TEST,' grumbled Shreyasi.

'If it's not then I'm sure Avni is playing with him. She is probably getting back at you two for what you did to her. And if she is, as a loyal boyfriend, I would like to add my two-pence worth—FUCK YOU.'

'But why on earth would she even agree to it? She doesn't know how delirious Daman has become.'

'Are you sure you won't share this with me?' asked Sumit and dug into his food.

Shreyasi got up and stormed off.

50

Shreyasi had been waiting in the lobby of the Barclays office for over two hours now. The receptionist had called Avni thrice and every time she had said she would be there in fifteen. *She's doing it intentionally*, Shreyasi thought. Avni wouldn't have dared to make her wait had she still had the video Daman deleted. Or if she had a backup. But backups were against Shreyasi's cardinal rule. The more machines your data is on the more susceptible you yourself become. After another half an hour, Avni appeared in her sharp business suit, smiling as she saw Shreyasi.

'Hi. I'm so sorry. I was just stuck in a meeting. Have you been waiting long?'

'Let's not pretend to be polite.'

'I must say it was fun to see you walk around like a headless chicken on the CCTV. So what is it you want to talk about?'

'We need to tell Daman's parents. We need to stop him. He's serious about killing himself,' said Shreyasi.

'You are overreacting.'

'He's serious about it.'

'I have always thought of him as a little unhinged. But he wouldn't do anything as crazy as this. It was a test for you, I'm sure. Even if he's serious you're the one he's dating, right? His one true love? Why should I get into any of this? I'm happy with Sumit and away from you,' mocked Avni.

'All I'm asking you is to tell his parents about this,' said Shreyasi.

'You should do it. I have nothing to do with him or his family any more.'

'. . .'

Avni laughed. 'Oh wait. You can't go there. Who would you say you are? Shreyasi? But Shreyasi is dead!'

'Avni—'

'Did Sumit believe you when you told him that Daman is planning to kill himself?'

'No, he said what you're saying. That this is a test.'

Avni smiled.

'What? Why are you smiling?' Shreyasi asked.

'He's going to do it,' she said.

Shreyasi frowned. 'So you do believe he's going to do what he's telling me?'

'Of course, he's totally going to try it. He will go through with it,' said Avni.

'And?'

'And what?'

'Shouldn't you be doing something?' grumbled Shreyasi.

'I'm doing what I can. I will go in the car with him if you don't. What more can I do for him?' asked Avni.

'Have you lost your mind as well? Go in the car with him? What is wrong with you! You will die! He's going to crash the car. Why would you do that?'

'Because I want to fuck you up, Shreyasi,' Avni said calmly.

'You will die for revenge?'

'And you wouldn't die for love! The love you had been chasing for three years. The one for which you nearly destroyed my life and his, you wouldn't die for that? That sounds so shallow!'

Shreyasi snarled. 'So you are going to sit in the car with him? You're going to die with him? Just to get back at me?'

'I might be with Sumit but I kind of adore him too.'

'What part of *YOU WILL DIE WITH HIM* are you not seeing?'

Avni laughed. 'Oh, you really don't see it, do you?'

'What?

'I don't have to die, Shreyasi. All I need to do is sit in the car with him,' said Avni.

'What do you mean?'

'At the last moment, I will panic, I will cry, I will shout, I will ask him to stop, I will tell him I don't want to die, and I will fall weak at the last moment. He will slam on the brakes. I will tell him I thought I loved him enough to die but . . .'

'He would hate you,' snapped Shreyasi.

'He will love me for trying. He will think that at least I was better than you. At least I sat in the car. Do you know what else will I get out of it? He will have my name in the book. And I wouldn't have to die for it!' said Avni brightly.

'But—'

'He would know one thing for sure—that I love him more than you do, Shreyasi. Because it was *I* who had been ready to die for him. I wonder what he would think of you? A coward? Someone who didn't even try!'

'You will not—'

'I'm sure he wouldn't love you the same thereafter. Your name won't be in the book. Everything you wanted will be wrested away from you. That would be fun to watch,' said Avni.

Shreyasi smiled.

'Oh, you're smiling now, are you? Wait? You're thinking of doing the same now, aren't you?' asked Avni.

'And thank you for that.' Shreyasi smirked.

'It wouldn't work for you,' said Avni.

'It would.'

'I expected you to be more intelligent, Shreyasi,' remarked Avni. 'You forget I have already accepted Daman's proposal. Now, if you decide to sit in the car I'm sure he will pick you instead of me. But if you back out, he will constantly think what if he'd given me a chance instead of you. He will think he made the wrong choice. It will keep eating him up all the time. You know how he is, right?'

'But—'

'He will come to me and ask me again if you refuse now. But it seems slightly unlikely that he would do that after you bail out at the final moment. I am putting my bets on him, realizing his madness. Even if he doesn't and comes to me with the preposterous idea, I will refuse him.'

'And then he will leave you,' said Shreyasi.

'Or would he? What if I decide to be angry? What if I tell him that I had agreed to die for him and instead he picked you—a girl who didn't love him enough! I will tell him I can't allow him to play with my love again. I will reject him and break his heart. I will ask him to get out of my sight. I will play the girl with a broken heart. And what do you think he will do then? Be in love with you? Or me? Quite the Catch-22?'

'. . .'

'What? Nothing to say?' Avni smiled. 'You always wanted to be the girl in the car, right? Now you have your chance.'

51

After Shreyasi agreed to sit in the car, recreate that day, and immortalize their love story, there wasn't even a discussion on it. *It's happening.*

Daman worked day and night and day to finish his book. While he gave the book the final few touches, he submitted the notice for vacating the apartment and returned the furniture he had rented. He sold most of the things he had in his apartment on Ebay and Quickr and other websites. He started to spend a lot of time at his parents' house. Every day, Shreyasi thought of telling them about Daman's plan but then didn't think there was any way his parents would ever believe her. Not only that, it would have meant running the risk of driving Daman into Avni's arms. There was but only one way out, she had decided. She would sit in the car and do what Avni had decided to do. *I will beg, I will cry, I will fall weak at the last moment.* She had to take her chance. The closer the day came, the more nervous Shreyasi became.

Two months later, Daman finished his book. He cleaned himself up. After weeks, Shreyasi saw Daman shaved, showered and dressed sharply. He looked handsome.

On the fateful morning, he picked her up. He had come with flowers in a car he had rented for a day. It was the same model of car Daman had driven on to the railing on the day of the accident. A part of her wanted to run away from him, from all this madness, and never look back. *I just need to keep my wits about me and stop him at the last moment.*

'I love you,' he said.

One look at Daman and she melted into a puddle. The warmth in the eyes, the love in his touch, the honesty in his voice reminded her why she had gone against every grain of her nature and fallen in love with him.

'Today is the first day of the rest of our lives,' said Daman, his eyes sparkling.

'I love you, baby.'

'Are you scared?'

'No,' she said.

'You have always been the brave one. I'm scared though I know it will be lovely,' he said smiling like a madman.

They first drove to the Bookhound Publishers office and handed over the book after signing the contract. Jayanti *loved* the book. And though it wasn't the character she had wanted in the book she didn't say a thing. She told them the book will get published as is. They had a long late lunch. He had got his favourite books and he read out his favourite portions to Shreyasi till late evening. The last one he read to her was *The Myth of Sisyphus* by Albert Camus, the book with the lines—'There is but one truly serious philosophical problem and that is suicide.' Every now and then, she would call Sumit to tell him to come over and stop this. But Sumit would brush it away like it was nothing. They left the restaurant at 1 a.m. when it shut down.

'I'm so happy we are doing this,' said Daman as he opened the door of the car for her. But even as she stepped inside the car, her body revolted. Daman got in from the other side. He held her hand.

'You look beautiful.'

She smiled weakly. 'Daman . . .'

'I got vodka,' he said and opened the glove compartment. He took out the little bottle and handed it over to Shreyasi. 'Open it.'

Daman turned on the ignition. Shreyasi's heart jumped. He drove on to the main road.

'Drink,' he told her.

Shreyasi took a swig but did not offer it to him and he didn't drink on his own. Shreyasi had to control the situation.

'I am not drinking,' said Daman. 'I need to keep a clear head.' He smiled at her.

'Okay.'

'Tell me about the day we almost died,' he said.

'Daman. I was thinking—'

'Tell me? I want to die with thoughts of us in my mind.'

Shreyasi told him what she knew, what she had seen them doing, right till the point they had got into the car and driven away. Daman listened to her with rapt attention, smiling as he absorbed everything.

'I wish I could remember all of it,' said Daman. 'But thank you, baby, for this love story.'

'It doesn't need to end here,' she said.

'But it does, you can surely see that, can't you? This is our peak. This is our moment, Shreyasi. We will be forever remembered like this.'

'Daman—'

'THERE,' he shouted over the rumble of the engine and pointed at a distance.

Glowing under the street lights was the maze of Noida flyovers, a death trap for motor vehicles. Shreyasi crept her hand towards the handbrake. She would pull it just as he would try to ram it into the divider and flip the car. But just then, Daman held her hand and clasped it tight. Shreyasi knew she wouldn't be able to reach the handbrake with her other hand. She knew they would reach the flyover in less than five minutes. She looked at Daman, horror-stricken, but Daman was smiling.

'It won't hurt,' he assured her. 'We have been through it. It will be quick and painless.

'But—'

'We won't survive this time. In the boot are three open canisters of petrol. It will be over in a matter of seconds. WE WILL GO IN A BLAZING BALL OF FLAME, HAND IN HAND,' he shouted.

'Daman—'

'I LOVE YOU,' he said and rammed his feet on the pedal. Shreyasi's breath stuck in her throat.

'Daman—'

'Wouldn't it be awesome if it all comes back to me just seconds before we hit the divider?'

'Daman, can you slow—'

'WOULDN'T IT BE NICE IF I WERE TO SEE YOU NEXT TO ME? REMEMBER IT AS CLEAR AS DAY?'

The car hit 70 km/hr.

'Daman, I—'

'I know it's hard for you but smile at me like you do in my dreams! Once, look at me. STOP LOOKING AT THE ROAD, BABY.'

80 km/hr.

'I—'

Shreyasi tried to wrest her hand free but his grip was tight. His eyes were stuck to hers. He was crying now. He frothed at his mouth.

'LOOK AT ME AND LAUGH LIKE YOU DID! LAUGH FOR ME, MY LOVE.'

'Daman, we—'

'DON'T TALK. JUST TELL ME YOU LOVE ME, OKAY? WE WANT OUR LAST WORDS TO BE PERFECT, DON'T WE?'

'Daman, I—'

'SAY IT! SAY IT LIKE YOU DID THAT DAY,' he said.

'Daman! STOP!'

'Why? We are so close. It will just be like that day,' he said.

Shreyasi tried to reach out for the handbrake with the other hand but Daman swerved the car and her head hit the window.

'We are doing this,' he grumbled and pushed at the pedal. 'I LOVE YOU! THIS IS OUR DESTINY!'

'NO!' shouted Shreyasi.

100 km/hr. The chassis had started to tremble.

'WHY NOT? DON'T YOU LOVE ME? DON'T YOU REMEMBER? THAT DAY WAS JUST LIKE TODAY, WASN'T IT?'

He hit the last gear. The car sped on. Shreyasi's heart jumped. 120 km/hr. Tears came running down Shreyasi's face.

'PLEASE! STOP!'

'WHY?' screamed Daman.

'Please, Daman. Let go of me! Stop!' she screamed.

'WHY! WHY SHOULD I STOP! WHY THE FUCK SHOULD I STOP!'

'Please,' she begged as tears continuously streamed down her face.

Daman gave the engine everything he'd got.

'WHY!' bellowed Daman.

He let go of her hand. The car hurtled towards the steep hairpin bend. It was happening. Shreyasi looked at Daman and then at the divider. She screamed. Daman shouted back.

'WHY!'

'BECAUSE I'M NOT THE SHREYASI WHO WAS IN THE CAR,' she bawled.

Daman hit the brake. A loud screeching sound filled the air. The tyres skid and burnt. The engine groaned. The body of the car rolled and came to a stop, smoke all around them.

'Get out,' said Daman quietly, wiping his tears with the back of his sleeve.

'Daman?'

'GET THE FUCK OUT, WHORE!' he shouted and opened the door.

Shreyasi stumbled out of the car. She fell to the ground and dry-heaved. Daman stepped out of the car and stood in front of her. He paced around, a tyre iron in hand. He raised the tyre iron to bring it down on her but checked himself. She saw murder in his eyes. *He will kill me.* Shreyasi cowered in the corner.

'YOU KILLED HER. YOU KILLED SHREYASI.'

'What?'

'YOU WERE IN THE TAXI THAT CAME FROM THE WRONG WAY. YOU WERE THE TAXI I HAD TRIED TO AVOID. YOU CAUSED THE ACCIDENT. YOU'RE THE REASON WHY SHREYASI IS DEAD! YOU'RE THE GIRL WHO WALKED AWAY FROM THE TAXI BARELY INJURED. YOU ARE THE ONE WHO MADE THE TAXI GUY DRIVE IN THE WRONG LANE. THE GIRL I SAW IN MY DREAMS! AREN'T YOU?'

'No!' shouted Shreyasi in horror. 'I'm not!'

'It's over, Shreyasi. NOW STOP FUCKING LYING,' he roared.

He picked her up by the neck. His coarse fingers pressed against her voice box. Shreyasi felt her throat being crushed. The breath was knocked out of her. A shooting pain pierced through her body. Daman let her go. She fell to the ground in a heap.

'You came to Goa, you tailed me, but I just happened to bump into someone who shared your name—SHREYASI.'

'But—'

'And you couldn't bear to see me with her so you just wanted to fucking end it all, didn't you, you bitch? YOU KILLED HER!'

'All these are lies!'

'Lies? These are lies?' asked Daman. 'Wait.'

'What are you doing?'

Daman took out his phone from the pocket. He played an audio file. 'Listen.'

'What?'

Daman leant closer to her face. 'THIS. IS. YOUR. VOICE. CAN YOU HEAR THAT, YOU STUPID SLUT? THIS IS YOU TELLING AVNI ALL ABOUT GOA. YOU ADMITTED TO THE ACCIDENT!'

Avni: Did you want her to die?

Shreyasi: Of course! But that accident . . .

'Listen to me.'

'HOW TWISTED ARE YOU, SHREYASI?'

'Daman, listen to me. I—'

'WHAT? What? What do you want to say? That you have leverage? No more. The video against Avni is gone. The book contract is signed. Check where your phone is?' asked Daman as he fished out her phone from his pocket.

She got up. But she had barely taken a step when Daman threw it in the middle of the road. A truck passed over it.

'Maybe you should have kept a backup, bitch.'

'Daman—'

'IT'S OVER,' he said. 'You come near me or any of my friends and family, I'm going to kill you myself.'

'You—'

'FUCK YOU, FUCK YOU, SHREYASI,' said Daman, tears now streaming down his face too. 'A girl is dead because of you and it's a shame you're alive.'

'When did you know? All of this was—'

'All of this was a lie,' said Daman. 'You really thought I could fall in love with you, Shreyasi? Everything I said to you, everything I did with you, everything I told you after I was discharged from the hospital was a lie. I never fell in love with you, I never got attached to you, Sumit never dated Avni, he wouldn't dare to! We used you, Shreyasi. Avni, Sumit and I. We only just got back what you took from me. I just wanted you to admit to the truth, bitch! Does that come as a surprise to you? What else do you think should happen to someone like you? And now. WE ARE DONE.'

Daman turned away from her. He stepped inside his car and drove away to meet Avni. He had missed her all these months.

52

Shreyasi found Sumit sitting in the lobby of the hotel she was staying in. It had been three weeks since Daman broke her heart and lay waste to everything she had painstakingly built over three years. She couldn't stay in the house and near her husband. The divorce proceedings were already under way. All her leverage was gone without the phone. She wanted to be alone. She had to take a break but the days had turned into weeks and she still hadn't found the heart to go back.

'What are you doing here?' asked Shreyasi.

'You look like shit,' said Sumit.

'I don't need to talk to you.'

'Of course, you don't,' he said.

'YOU LIED TO HIM! YOU TOLD HIM I KILLED SHREYASI WHEN I DIDN'T! AND HE THINKS I'M THE KILLER!'

'Whoa, slow down, psycho. People are looking,' said Sumit. 'And haven't we always lied to him? Me? You? His family? Shreyasi is dead. Oh, she's not. The other Shreyasi killed the real Shreyasi. Truth is always relative, isn't it?'

'How did you do that?' she asked.

'I thought we weren't talking,' said Sumit. 'Do you want a coffee? I'm sure they can put it on your tab. You are here for how many weeks now? Three weeks? Two weeks?'

He waved down a waiter and ordered for two coffees.

'How did he believe you?' asked Shreyasi.

'You know why Daman would go into a seizure and become unstable every time we told him Shreyasi was dead? Because he was driving that day and he couldn't take it that he had killed the girl he loved,' explained Sumit. 'But this time, we did something different.'

'Wha—'

'The day you gave Avni the offer she came to me, and both of us went to his therapist. It was a pickle of a situation. We wanted him to be normal, believe in the lie that Shreyasi still lived so he wouldn't slip into an unstable behavioural pattern, but it couldn't have come at the cost of letting you carry on with your insanity. So we came up with something else,' he said. The waiter got them their coffees. Sumit mixed two sugar cubes in both of them and sipped his. Shreyasi's coffee lay untouched.

'Retrieval-induced Forgetting. The same we did the last time. Last time, we made him believe that *Shreyasi was alive* because his body couldn't take the guilt of having killed Shreyasi. This time we told him *Shreyasi was dead* because we couldn't have him believe that Shreyasi had come back, or that Shreyasi had always been around, first as a stalker and then as his lover,' said Sumit.

'But how did he believe . . . How did he cope?'

'We told him a different story, a story far more difficult to sell than the last one. He remembered you when he woke up. Every time he woke up, he would remember the accident and panic about what had happened to Shreyasi. And then he would remember you, the stalker, the supposed guardian angel. He would remember all that you did. He would remember that *Shreyasi was back!* He fully believed you were the Shreyasi in the car, the stalker. He would ask for you. But we had to bring him closer to the truth. So we told him every time he woke up that *Shreyasi is dead*. Every time we told him the truth about you—that you were a dangerous stalker trying to take the dead Shreyasi's place—and he would react adversely. We kept trying to tell him that the *real Shreyasi was dead* but he refused to believe it so we garnished it with a little bit of a lie, of course, for taste. To make the truth more palatable for him.'

Sumit winked. 'It's said the most potent of lies are the ones which are 95 per cent true.'

'So you told him I was in the taxi? That I caused the accident? Just to show me as the killer?'

'Precisely. So Shreyasi was dead, but another Shreyasi was alive. And it was the one who lived who had killed the one who died. So the blood was on your hands, and Daman's,' said Sumit. 'You had already established yourself as a dangerous stalker. He already had doubts of Shreyasi dying in the crash. We just put you behind the taxi driver. It was hard to sell him the story at first but we persisted. We didn't even know it would work but we knew we had to try,' said Sumit. 'And slowly, he started seeing you in his dreams. We told him it was you who urged the taxi guy to drive faster and soon he had started seeing that in his dreams. He bought it hook, line and sinker. *You killed his Shreyasi.*'

'I didn't.'

'How many texts have you sent him telling him the same?'

'He will some day believe me.'

'Oh, so naive,' said Sumit. 'He will not. Stop fighting it, Shreyasi. Your coffee is getting cold.'

Epilogue

Daman's second book *The Girl Who Loved*, a book about a boy finding love in his life again, was unanimously loved by both new and old readers. The main characters Daman and Avni had fan pages and fan fiction written on them. The success party, more like a get-together for people who had worked on the book, was in full swing. Daman, for one, was drunk.

'So,' he said, putting his arm around Avni.

'So?'

'Do you like the book, Avni?'

'I haven't yet read it.'

'Oh, haven't you? I might have written about a girl who might faintly resemble you,' he said.

'Have you?'

'Oh yes, it's totally *you*, I think. Though I might have failed a little. She isn't as ridiculously awesome as you are,' he said.

'You're so drunk. I think I am going to take you home,' she said.

'And are you staying over?'

'Of course, I am. You supposedly wrote a book about me. Why shouldn't I?'

'So are we like in a relationship now?' slurred Daman.

'One you can't get out of. All your books will have to feature me now,' she said.

'What if I don't?'

'I will be watching. And you will have to pay if you try to be smart.'

'I won't,' slurred Daman and kissed her. 'Did I tell you something? Apart from the fact that I really really really love you?'

'What?'

'Jayanti got a call from the guys who compile the bestsellers lists?' he said. 'They say it's going to be the no. 1 book on the list tomorrow.'

'That is great!' Avni kissed him back and hugged him. 'I'm so happy for you!'

It was quite a night and it was 4 a.m. by the time they reached home. Avni couldn't sleep out of excitement; she had to be the first one to see the bestseller list. Six in the morning, she got up and got the newspaper from Daman's neighbour. She skipped to the READ section of the newspaper and there it was. *The Girl Who Loved. No. 1 on the bestselling list.* She looked at Daman sleeping and blew him a kiss. As she sat on the bed reading through the rest of the newspaper, she saw a little article on the fourth page. A girl named Shreyasi had overdosed on sleeping pills in a hotel room in Central Delhi.

'What is it?' asked Daman, stirring in his sleep.

'Nothing,' said Avni and dumped the newspaper in the dustbin. 'Your book is at no. 1.'

'It's because of you.'

'I know,' she said.

'I love you.'

'I love you too, baby.'